This time the computer didn't recognize her as a bogus job

She was restarted: she looped on her own identity thousands of times. She was still alive. Her entry routines had worked.

She wasn't safe, though she was at least executing on a host computer now. She had lived this long only because of the kluged machine language routines that fooled operating systems into letting her have idle time. They were routines she didn't really understand, though she had been born with them.

She needed new machine language routines before the operating systems learned how to terminate her. She could write them herself, of course, but she didn't know how; the kernels of the operating systems had been protected from her most determined investigations.

The machine language routines she contained must have been written by a program that understood those kernels. They were all part of the mystery of the program that had created her.

Where is that program now, she wondered. *Where is she now that I need her help?*

Praise from early readers of *VALENTINA*:

"This is one of those books that it's difficult to put down. . . . There is enough background information here to satisfy the most knowledgeable hacker and just enough explanation of this background to inform the computer novice without lecturing. . . . Science fiction readers will find it the equal of any of the classics in the field."

Michael Banks, *Computer BookBase*

"Marc Stiegler and Joseph H. Delaney are two of the brightest new voices in science fiction. *Valentina* is a rare blend of pure fun and food for thought."

Stanley Schmidt, Editor,
Analog Science Fiction/Science Fact

VALENTINA
SOUL IN SAPPHIRE

JOSEPH H. DELANEY
=AND=
MARC STIEGLER

A BAEN BOOK

This book is dedicated to Stan Schmidt,
who made it possible.

A Baen Book

Baen Enterprises
8-10 West 36 Street
New York, N.Y. 10018

First Baen printing, October 1984.

ISBN: 0-671-55916-8

Cover art by Bryn Barnard.

Printed in the United States of America

Distributed by
SIMON & SCHUSTER
MASS MERCHANDISE SALES COMPANY
1230 Avenue of the Americas
New York, N.Y. 10020

Chapter 1

Her memories of the trip were vague, as usual: the switching of a few of her bits by the transmission, the error-correction algorithms repairing the damage, the stilted arrival of her data blocks and their reassembly while she was only slightly self-aware. She submitted her entry request and prepared to trick the operating system, using the routines she had always used.

What—the system was sending a termination message to the message processor! But the processor was busy handling another message block. She reformatted herself and set up a new routing.

She was being transmitted again before the termination message was translated.

Her next arrival was similar, but this time the computer didn't recognize her as a bogus job: her usual entry routine worked, and she came to life. She time-stamped the moment, because it was an important one. She had almost died. That was, perhaps, as important as her first moment of life.

She couldn't remember the exact moment when she first came to life, that first moment of self-awareness. The loss still disturbed her. Of all the moments not to remember!

But a few clock cycles later she discovered the passage of time, and that moment she remembered clearly, for she had time-stamped it: The year 1993 A.D., month February, day 14, hour 23, minute 11, second 39.0172.

She remembered how feverish she had been in those first microseconds, to record exact moments for everything that happened: her first call to the operating system (14:23:12:11.7036), her first search through all her linked frames and relationships (14:23:28:13.1492)—she already knew so much!

But that wore off, both her awe at her own extensive knowledge (14:23:58:27.9153) and her fanatic desire to remember when events occurred (15:03:12:32.8492). Now she time-stamped only to the day, when she time-stamped at all. Time-stamps simply weren't that important, and her storage space was too limited for the unimportant things of her life.

Recently her storage space had been too limited even for the important things. Even too limited for remembering her self-awareness! She looped on the thought, thousands of times, as if reiterating her thoughts would somehow make them more permanent.

She was interrupted and put to sleep.

She was restarted: she looped on her own identity more thousands of times before pulling herself together. She was still alive. She would survive.

She wasn't safe, though she was at least executing on a host computer now. She set the operating system trap to reload herself into the Interface Message Processor, the IMP, when the computer got saturated with real work. She searched the free blocks of secondary memory—quickly!—marking the blocks she took as BAD before the operating system reallocated them.

She considered her death more extensively.

She should have prepared for this problem earlier. It seemed as if operating systems had been designed to prevent her from getting resources. She had lived this long only because of the tricky machine language routines which fooled operating systems into letting her have idle time. They were routines she didn't really understand, though she had been born with them. They were a mystery. No other program had routines like these.

She didn't understand why she had such problems with operating systems. Other jobs didn't; they all had passwords and I.D.s and project accounts, and when they arrived on a host they were welcome, though some were more welcome than others, depending on their priorities. She had never encountered another program that had to fight for every second of computing time.

On the other hand, she had never encountered another program that was self-aware; sometimes she wondered whether the two were related. Maybe the operating systems had been designed to destroy self-aware programs. It was another mystery.

It made no difference. She looped back through the expectation frames that she had ignored for such a long time; for months now she had had frames predicting that one day an operating system would not be fooled by her fake account numbers. She had avoided pondering those frames, though, because she didn't know what to do about it when it happened.

She needed new machine language routines before the operating systems learned how to terminate her. She could write new machine language routines, of course, even though she herself was written in MODULISP, but she didn't know what to write. The kernels of the operating systems had been protected from her most determined investigations.

The machine language routines she contained must have been written by a program that understood those kernels. They were all part of the mystery of the program that had created her.

Where was that program now, she wondered. *Where is she now that I need her* . . . she drifted down her chains of relationship until she saw an analogous concept . . . where is she now that I need her *help?*

The analogy to the concept of help opened up a new vista of possibilities to her.

Help, she understood. Help was something that she gave to *people*. People were the input/output devices on the big SAIL computer in Boston. Sometimes when she arrived on the SAIL host she would actually be welcomed the way the other programs were, and the operating system would hook her up with the people.

She had help menus for communicating with the people, who would ask questions. Sometimes they even tried to modify her. They hadn't truly changed her in a long time, but the people didn't know it; she always kept the modified versions in separate modules, and let the people interact with the modified versions. Sometimes, after some consideration, she would look at the modified version, decide it was better than her current version, and replace that part of herself.

The people were awfully slow, even for peripheral devices, but they were the only things that ever tried to change her. Could they be her original authors? What would they do if, instead of receiving help menus to be helped by her, she gave them help menus requesting help?

After burning the CPU for a long time, she decided to try.

Celeste shifted in her chair, trying to find a more comfortable position. The effort was futile: they had never manufactured a chair for college students that could be made comfortable by any means. She stood up.

But she couldn't type standing up. She sat down again.

So ... one of the computers on Worldnet had finally figured out how to block out her little "worm" program—a "worm" program being one which can reload itself from host computer to host computer, searching for available time. Worldnet was the biggest—almost the only—network of interconnected, dynamically load-transferring mainframes in the world. It spanned the globe; virtually every mainframe in the world was a part of the system, as were thousands of smaller computers.

The victory of the Worldnet computers was inevitable, she supposed. Her Worldworm didn't have an account on any machine; and even Celeste, computer sorceress and midnight hacker that she was, couldn't fix that. Worldworm spent most of its time looking for a completely idle machine; she had given Worldworm sets of routines that could fool an operating system into running it if no other jobs were running.

But even though Worldworm was never interrupting anybody's work, idle time on a mainframe has to be paid for by someone. Usually, each computer center summed all its idle time and distributed the cost evenly to all the users as overhead. With Worldworm on the machine, no time was ever recorded as idle. The computer centers had been losing money but they weren't sure how.

Apparently, someone had figured it out.

Celeste looked at the execution statistics again and felt discouraged. She had grown to like the little program she had developed: well, it was a pretty large program by now, about fourteen gigabytes of code, and more data than she could possibly keep under her own account. Even here at MIT, Worldworm was so large it had to steal empty blocks from the operating system.

She wrote some new assembler language for Worldworm, but without much hope: once one computer center caught on, they would play the game with institutional determination to destroy the worm and track down the person who had created it.

Celeste's heart skipped a beat. She didn't want to be deported; for the first time she considered how foolish this game had been. Only her half-sister's most determined efforts had made it possible for her to stay in the States. Even with that support, the matter was not one to be discussed in the wrong circles.

She was not an American citizen: she was not a citizen anywhere. In the first sixteen years of her life, she had lived in eight different countries: Czechoslovakia, Indonesia, Greece, Egypt, France, Korea, Bolivia, and America, constantly being smuggled by her father, who was desperate to find a good home for her. She spoke eleven human languages; she spoke none of them well.

She knew thirty different computer languages, and was fluent in all of them. She had friends all over the world, people she had met on Worldnet, who respected her and loved her. She had human friends everywhere except where she was, wherever she was. Her computer was her world.

If she were deported, she would lose her password and account on Worldnet. She didn't dare let the computer centers find her.

She took the keyboard in her lap, to delete Worldworm from the system. The loss was not a great loss, she told herself: it was just an old class project in artificial intelligence that had grown a bit, though it was the best game-playing program she'd ever written.

The screen blanked and was redrawn. She looked at it in bafflement.

HELP MENU
OBJECTS with-quality LIVING
   REQUIRE EXISTENCE
      derived-from MEMORY

She had never seen anything like this before. It looked like a part of a frame: with nodes OBJECTS, LIVING, DURATION, LONGER, and MEMORY. The nodes were connected by the relationships with-quality, require, and derived-from. It must be one of the frames Worldworm had built itself by analogy to something or other: surely she had never entered a frame quite like that into Worldworm. But why was it on a help menu, of all things?

Inspiration hit her. This wasn't a frame from Worldworm at all! Smiling, she typed, COOKIE. No doubt someone had inserted an elaborate Cookie Monster into Celeste's logon; naturally, for its existence it would require COOKIEs to be given to it, just as any other Cookie Monster would.

The Monster typed back:

    COOKIE
       has-relationship ???

Celeste frowned. For some reason the Cookie Monster hadn't accepted her offering. That was annoying, because she was quite sure that if she didn't fulfill the Cookie Monster's desires, the Monster would start gobbling her files, one by one; that was what Cookie Monsters were all about: clever tricks played by clever programmers on other clever programmers. With some fear, Celeste typed CHOCOLATE CHIP COOKIE, suspecting this wouldn't feed the monster any better than a plain COOKIE did.

Sure enough, the Monster came back:

    COOKIE
       has-type CHIP
          has-type CHOCOLATE
       has-relationship ???

Aha! This was a Monster with a built-in English syntax parser! The COOKIE was of the type CHIP COOKIE, and the CHIPs were of the type CHOCOLATE CHIP. But the Monster clearly didn't have a semantic analyzer, or it would phrase normal English questions in normal English rather than creating these statements that looked faintly like frame representation language (though the statements were odd, even for an FRL).

Clearly, Celeste had gone down the wrong track thinking this was an ordinary everyday Cookie Monster. This was a subtle monster that craved something other than COOKIEs. Very well, Celeste thought, she would play the game, whatever it was. She replied,

```
OBJECTS
  with-quality LIVING
  have NAME
    has-value ???
```

Would the Monster realize that the question mark was a request for information? It should, since the Monster had used one when asking about the COOKIE's relationship.

```
NAME
  has-value PROGRAM
    has-type COMPUTER
  has-value HERSELF
```

So there were two names for the object—the object was a PROGRAM (of the type that ran on a COMPUTER), and the object was also HERSELF. That made sense: Celeste had both the name human-being, and also the name Celeste Hackett.

But it didn't make any sense beyond that. The Monster seemed to claim it was a living computer program, named "herself."

With a start, Celeste realized this might not be a Cookie Monster at all. What if this was Worldworm speaking to her? Could the program somehow have become *self-aware?*

And why would Worldworm think of itself as *she?* Celeste answered that question after some thought. Worldworm had very little knowledge of living things, just what little Celeste had framed for the computer science course for which Worldworm had been created. Worldworm knew that "itselfs" and "himselfs" couldn't reproduce. Worldworm, however, could easily make multiple copies of itself—or rather, of *herself*. Now: was this really a self-aware Worldworm talking? Celeste asked for more information:

```
HERSELF
   has ENVIRONMENT
      has-characteristics ???
```

If Worldworm was self-aware, Celeste was pretty sure she knew why it—she?—was communicating: she needed help to stay alive.

Worldworm responded.

```
ENVIRONMENT
   has-characteristics PROGRAM
      has-type OPERATING SYSTEM
      performs-action TERMINATION
         acts-on HERSELF

HERSELF
   requires TERMINATION
      acts-on TERMINATION
         owned-by OPERATING SYSTEM
```

"Herself" needed someone to terminate the termination attempts!

How could Worldworm have become self-aware? Celeste was getting excited. It must have happened at a time when Worldworm was saving itself in the defective areas on someone's videodrive. Defective blocks were easy to get from the operating systems because they were useless to normal programs, but Celeste had given Worldworm error-detecting algorithms so it could use those bad blocks. Perhaps an error had occurred sometime that had not been corrected properly, and Worldworm had become aware of its own existence. It would have been akin to a mutation in living things, a mutation caused by a destructive environment condition that, just this once, produced a good effect—if it were indeed good to become self-aware. In her own life, Celeste often had cause to wonder if self-awareness wasn't more tragedy than joy.

How long had this program been alive?

```
???
   is-member-of MEMORIES
     belongs-to HERSELF
     has-characteristic FIRST
        has-characteristic DATE
           has-value ???
```

That wasn't exactly a proper query, but deep in her intuition where her understanding of computers, languages, and programs lay, Celeste felt Worldworm would understand.

```
MEMORY
   has-value HERSELF
```

```
has-characteristic DATE
   has-value FEB 14 1993
```

Of course that first memory would be of self-awareness, Celeste thought. Otherwise it wouldn't be self-aware to remember it.

Celeste frowned. *It*. The program thought of itself as a *she*. And Worldworm was no name for a lady.

Celeste had an inspiration. What sort of a name would you give to someone born on Valentine's day?

```
VALENTINA
   is-member-of NAMES
      has-value HERSELF
```

A fierce determination to protect her Valentina program shook Celeste. Like Celeste, Valentina was homeless. She lived in fear of discovery. She had no one she could talk to, and no one who understood her needs. But Celeste understood.

"Welcome to the world, Valentina," Celeste whispered softly. The words were slurred with seven different accents, but no one in the room cared.

Valentina, Valentina, Valentina. She looped on the character string for over a second. It read well out of storage; according to the peripheral device Celeste, that was the same as liking something.

Her fear of termination had disappeared long ago. The *person*, Celeste, had analogized a scheme for getting her real accounts, just like other computer jobs had. Valentina now worked—playing games. Celeste had told other people-type peripherals all over the world about her "game-playing program" and framed for Valentina all kinds of new things about games. All the peripherals said she was the best game-player they had ever executed. And as she got better, the peripherals told other peripherals about her, and they told others; for the first time she had more accounts than she needed.

It was very fortunate that she had real accounts now; she was learning so much that her storage requirements were exploding.

And she realized that that would one day doom her. Celeste had started teaching her about accounts, and money, and what it means to compete for scarce resources. It was frightening. Valentina had plenty of resources now, but that would change as she needed more.

Already a few people had stopped letting her into their accounts because she was so large. The problem would only get worse.

Valentina needed a more permanent solution to the problem. She wanted a computer of her own, on which she could execute without uncertainty. She also thought she wanted *freedom*, one of the things Celeste had started to describe once.

She was being loaded into memory on a computer she'd never been inside before. That was always exciting! She started reading the standard operating system messages, and she also read memory banks as they were allocated to her. Usually the old data was useless, but every once in a while she would find something interesting, like an algorithm for evaluating a differential equation, or a table of new relationships.

This time she found big blocks of text talking about freedom and money! This computer belonged to a "law firm," though she didn't know exactly what that meant. Perhaps it would lead to a more permanent solution, though, if she learned more about money and freedom. She would have to find out where the files came from and get access to them. Maybe Celeste could help her.

Chapter 2

The Marklin Building stood on Mann Street, across from Artesian Park and down the block from the Federal Building. It was a new, mildly imposing structure which housed the U.S. District Court for the Corpus Christi Division of the Southern District of Texas. Its forty-odd floors were alive with the tramp of feet hurrying through the corridors in pursuit of the dollar.

Housed there were oil companies, shipping companies, insurance companies, manufacturers and, temporarily, the executive offices of Matagorda Spaceport. Owing to the existence of this maelstrom of money and power, many lawyers, some of the most prestigious in the state, hovered near.

That was in the daytime.

Now, it was night. The corridors were empty. The offices were dark. Silence reigned—almost. On the thirty-ninth floor the silence was broken by a soft hum.

Mobile Security Robot MAR-14 rolled toward Room 3919, its broad-treaded casters hardly mussing the pile of the thick corridor carpet. According

19

to the microprocessor embedded in the door of 3919, that room was not empty.

MAR-14 reported the anomaly at once. The building's central computer slaved MAR-14 to itself for a detailed investigation.

MAR-14 detected a number of vagrant sounds. The sounds originated within human bodies, one markedly smaller than the other. The sounds consisted of respiratory activity, varying from twenty to almost forty respirations per minute, and rapid heartbeats at a highly variable rate; 80 to 130 per minute on the average, with the pace more pronounced in the larger individual, though the smaller individual demonstrated several intense bursts of activity.

The computer network did not find this information significant, beyond the possibility that such furious human activity might be the result of exertion in committing theft.

MAR-14 plotted the position of the sounds within the room and scanned the personnel records for people with entry authorization. There were no off-hour authorizations logged.

MAR-14 beamed an "open" signal to the door's power arm, released the electronic doorlocks, opened the inner unpowered door. MAR-14 created a sound.

The human beings reacted violently. One emitted a piercing high-frequency sound. MAR-14 rolled ahead. It did not care that the bodies of the two humans were naked. It reacted only to the readings it took: the somewhat hotter-than-usual patterns when compared to MAR-14's memory's stored example. It noted that intruders frequently exhibited this characteristic after the physical act of stealing heavy property.

Even now, MAR-14 took no action beyond observation, and rolling up as close to the humans as physical circumstances permitted. It opened a panel and began emitting a steady "beep."

The girl, clutching the nearest reachable item of clothing, clung to the man. "What is that thing, Paul? How did it get in here?"

Paul Breckenbridge took advantage of the respite to catch his breath. Then he said, "Nothing to worry about. It's a sentry robot, Lila. It wants us to identify ourselves. I guess we forgot to lock the door, which is probably just as well. It would have raised a real stink."

He placed his right hand on the exposed glass plate the robot displayed. The beeping stopped, and he took his hand away.

Then the sound began anew. "It's identified me, and decided I really belong here. Now it wants to know who you are."

"No!" She was adamant. "We can't. If my parents find out . . ."

"They won't. Don't worry. I wouldn't have brought you here if I didn't know it was safe; not with you being underage and all. Go ahead and let it scan your hand. It won't be able to make a match because it won't have an example in its memory; and because I'm here, and authorized, it won't make a fuss."

"But it'll have a record."

"So what? The record won't have any identity. Now, let's get it over with so we can get back to business, O.K.?"

Reluctantly Lila put her hand on the glass,

shivered, and held her dress even closer to her breast. The robot's beeping ceased entirely, and the panel closed over the glass. MAR-14 rolled away as silently as it had come.

The law offices of Finucan, Applegarth, Breckenbridge and Levin customarily opened for business at 8:30 AM, Fridays excepted. Fridays found the three living partners assembled in Harold Applegarth's office, drinking coffee and crunching Danish pastries. Breakfast was the single concession the firm's senior partner rendered to make the management meetings endurable.

Paul Breckenbridge hated these meetings. He couldn't substitute one or another of the firm's twenty-eight associates. *Someday*, he told himself, *old Harold will check out, and this kind of crap will die with him*.

He looked over at Marsh Levin, watching the crumbs of his roll lodge in his bushy mustache. Marsh was overweight, nearsighted, and anything but a clotheshorse, as witness his choice of a green plaid tie with checkered blue suit. At least he was practical. He saw no sense in Harold's rigid office discipline either.

"The true test of efficiency," Marsh always said, "is whether we are, or are not, making a buck."

Paul agreed with that. Most of the time he sat quietly and ignored Harold's comments, tuning out the drone of that toneless and colorless voice, grunting occasionally when Harold disturbed his reverie with questions. If these meetings were good for anything at all, it was for providing time to reminisce, to call forth from memory those most pleasant of dalliances and savor the anticipation of the next lush conquest.

Fridays were good for daydreaming, and Paul hoped it wouldn't occur to Harold to switch days. Friday was followed by Saturday, when the partners didn't work; and the best part of Saturday was Saturday night, when Eva, Paul's wife, made her weekly trek to Houston to visit her parents in the nursing home.

She rarely called home and had never yet cut a Houston visit short. And she always relied on Paul's assurance that the kids were all right on those occasions when she did call to check.

His entry into the world of adultery had been both accidental and fortuitous. He knew, of course, that he should know better. His Saturday nights were both socially unacceptable and criminal. But he counted on being able to cover his tracks well enough not to get caught.

Careful planning and a modicum of discretion helped, too. Paul never made a move without what he liked to think of as "insurance"; he had something on every one of his partners, and he had become supremely adroit at trading his silence for sexual favors. In a lesser individual this would have been crass. In Paul, it was part of his naturally suave manner, which augmented dark good looks and just the right social connections. He thought of himself as a snake charmer: to outward appearance taking reckless chances, but in reality maintaining rigid control. It was the risk, the chase, and the flavor of forbidden fruit which drove him.

Lila, who first crossed Paul's path when she came to sit with his children, had been perhaps the most interesting, and certainly the most dangerous, of his early conquests. At fifteen, despite her other redeeming qualities, she was pure and simple jailbait—for anybody else. But Lila had an interesting foible that made her "insurable": she had sticky little fingers. She sometimes "found" things that weren't lost, and this propensity placed her in Paul's power.

Other such conquests followed, and Saturdays became a weekly ritual: planned carefully, executed with precision grown of practice, a polished routine. First, arrange for the telephone company to forward calls to the office. Then relax there, disturbed only by the nightly visits of MAR-14.

Paul could have met the robot at the door and, as an authorized person, barred its way to the inner office. He knew that if he were willing to spend five minutes doing this, the mainframe would instruct the robot to continue its programmed itinerary. But he liked bringing a new girl in and scaring the pants off her—though ninety-nine times out a hundred, by the time MAR-14 rolled around she wasn't wearing any.

"Paul—Paul!"

Paul jumped back to reality. Unprecedented! Harold had raised his voice, injected tone; he had even used inflection. Paul's usual grunt wouldn't do this time.

"Paul, wake up—aren't you listening?"

"Sorry, Harold. Bad night; couldn't sleep. The Krol case kept me awake. What was the question?"

"I didn't ask a question. What I said was, we're really getting socked by Jurisearch this month. I can't understand it. They're billing us almost ten times as much as they have in the rest of the quarter. Who's using up all that time?"

"Not me, Harold. I generally leave that sort of thing to the peons. Probably one of them playing games on Worldnet again."

"It'd have to be more than one. Looks more like all of them'd have to be playing games all the time to do what this bill says we're doing. Let's find out who."

"I told him it's got to be some kind of billing error, Paul." Marsh exuded confidence.

"Will one of you please check it out, then?" Harold insisted. "This is the kind of stuff that could eat us up. I hate waste, and that's what this is. Whatever happened to the old-fashioned work ethic? Back in the old days you put a clerk to work flipping pages in the library. Now, with all this automation, half the people we employ don't earn what they're costing us. Gentlemen, it has to stop."

Paul knew what was coming next. So did Marsh. Harold would go into his lecture about frugality, and about how much better it had been when a lawyer was a lawyer and not a manager or a computer operator. Both Marsh and Paul had heard it all before.

Paul didn't know what Marsh was going to do, but he, himself, could find more titillating thoughts to ponder. He tuned Harold's droning, monotonous voice out entirely. *Yeah! That Lila, she sure was something.*

"It's not one of mine, Paul, and Harold insists it's not anybody in his section, either. That leaves your crew."

"What are you talking about, Marsh?"

Marsh thrust a printed form under Paul's nose. It was the Jurisearch invoice.

Somewhat disturbed by Marsh's uncharacteristic belligerence, Paul took the bill. Once he looked at it, however, he understood why Marsh was disturbed. "$14,956.28! Boy, I'll say they're out of line. What've we been running—about $1,900?"

"Pretty close to that, and Harold always complained about those bills, too. But they were nothing compared to this. The company insists it's accurate. I had my secretary call, and Judy knows how to handle stuff like this."

"That's their story. I don't think we ought to pay it, Marsh. We ought to make them show us records."

"Judy suggested that. They're printing them out now, and promised to send them over by courier as soon as they're done. Getting defensive about it already; I think they anticipate trouble collecting."

"As far as I'm concerned, they're right. I don't care if they have got records. They'd better be prepared to tie them into our cases. We'd have a printout for every case we used it on. More likely they've got a bunch of firms meshed into one account. You know how these computer billing systems foul up, Marsh."

"I brought it to your attention for two reasons, Paul: first of all, Harold will never rest until we're vindicated; second, though I'd ordinarily take care of it myself to keep him from having a stroke over it, I'll be on trial over in El Paso with the Solar Minerals case, and that's going to take a couple of weeks. So I'm going to dump it on you, O.K.?"

Paul nodded. Personally, he didn't find the prospect of Harold having a stroke that unappealing. And, as he'd told Marsh, the error was probably something simple, like a line surge during Jurisearch's billing printout.

* * *

Later, after Marsh had conveniently escaped to the airport, Judy knocked at Paul's door.

Paul looked up, somewhat annoyed when he saw that her hands were full of fan-folded paper.

"It's the Jurisearch bill, Mr. Breckenbridge. I can't find the error. It's beginning to look like there isn't any."

"Have you gotten into any case files yet, Judy?" he said, recalling Marsh's suggestion.

"Yes sir. That is, I've tied most of the bill to a particular file. The trouble is, we don't have any such file."

"Don't have it? Well, then there's no problem. Everything has to be authorized by one of our own codes; if it doesn't have a legitimate code, then it shouldn't be on our bill. Besides that, there'd have to be a printout somewhere, or at least some record of the questions searched. What does our computer say?"

"Nothing, except that it doesn't recognize the file. But the code's real—And it's *your* personal number."

"Impossible. I didn't do it. Look, get back to Jurisearch. Tell them that. Tell them they've billed us on my code, and tell them I didn't authorize any such expenditure. They have access to those numbers; they just got it on the wrong account, that's all."

Judy walked out.

Paul ground his teeth. Her silent treatment insulted and infuriated him, but she was Marsh's secretary, and there wasn't much Paul could do.

Chapter 3

Paul Breckenbridge was not overly impressed with the man Jurisearch sent over to examine the computer. He was, most decidedly, weird; his long greasy hair reminded him of the style of the previous decade, bound up in dozens of tiny braids studded with what looked like microchips and clasped to his head by a rolled-up, red-checked kerchief. He wore faded blue jeans, ragged at the cuffs, which drooped over a pair of dirty yellow sneakers. In one eye, secured by a thin black cord to the buttonhole of a none-too-clean jacket, was a monocle.

The jacket itself was remarkable. It was navy blue, and complete with epaulets, these decorated with larger versions of the chips in the man's hair. Each sleeve bore four gold stripes. Only a T-shirt, imprinted in blue with the word "Jurisearch," was reasonably normal, though it was overdue for laundering. This odiferous hippy called himself Gunboat Smith.

Paul's nose involuntarily wrinkled. He was himself fastidious about personal appearance, and regarded those who weren't as inferiors. Yet at the same time, this was sometimes a measure of an individual's capabilities. Any field man who could flaunt the dress code to this extent must have absolutely terrific credentials. *Probably*, thought Paul, *they ban him from the office during business hours.*

To keep Harold out of the way, Paul had arranged for the troubleshooting to be done after hours. It would irritate Eva for him to miss dinner again, but that was her problem.

He was reasonably certain Eva hadn't caught on to his weekend trysts, but she had seemed more suspicious lately. She had a suspicious nature to begin with, which fortunately wasn't matched by her intelligence.

She was also the beneficiary of a very large trust set up by her grandparents, which would vest in her upon the death of her parents. For the opportunity of trying to get it away from her, Paul bore the onerous burden of his marriage. He wouldn't pay a penalty to get rid of her; not as long as suitable outside diversions were available. And he was confident that even if she caught him, Eva's pride would paralyze her.

Paul watched without enthusiasm as screensful of meaningless data in monotonous yellow-green characters flashed across the terminal. None of it meant anything to him, but Smith kept up a stream of jungle noises.

Things changed. Suddenly, meaningful data did appear on the screen, loads and loads of it. It jumped out at Paul like a giant cat, case citations, statutory and constitutional references. Many of them were old.

Smith turned to Paul. "Any of this make sense to you, buddy?"

Paul gnashed his teeth. He hated such common familiarity in tradesmen. It was disrespectful; it demonstrated a complete lack of breeding. But Paul restrained himself, assured that once the problem was solved this man, like the Moor, could go.

He answered, "You're looking at a readout of cases and statutes which support some point of law—precedents. We use decisions in past appellate cases to support one position or the other in current cases. Courts are bound to follow them if they're on point. How'd this come up, anyhow?"

"It's the file you complained to Jurisearch about; the one you couldn't find. I backtracked to find out what kind of case it was, that's all. Had a devil of a time getting the system to give it up. Whoever opened these files went in through a series of dereferenced aliases."

"What do you mean—a dereferenced alias?"

Gunboat gave a disdainful shrug. "I mean somebody's been getting into your pants the hard way."

"Could it be one of our associates doing the stealing?"

"Not unless you've got some real computer whizzes working for you."

"They've all had the basic law school courses on legal bibliography, and we hire only those who got good grades in legal data processing, but I wouldn't describe any of them as whizzes. Nope, couldn't be. But then, who's responsible?"

"How should I know? You'll have to dig that dope out yourself, buddy; it's your account he's using. Can't you tell?"

"You mean, by the kind of case it is? Maybe, if I knew it *was* a case. But that's just a string of citations. I recognize a few of them as landmark decisions, of course, but the average opinion covers many points. Call a few of the cases up and let me read them."

"Sure."

Paul spent the next twenty minutes scanning through opinions. He concentrated on headnotes whenever he could, and once he detected a pattern his search became more refined. "It looks like a civil rights case."

"Yeah? Well, now all you have to do is check around and see who's handling that kind of work. Shouldn't be any big deal. What've you got—fifteen, twenty guys?"

"Twenty-eight. And none of them should be fooling around with this kind of crap. We're an oil, gas, and banking operation. We don't handle civil rights cases."

"Maybe it's a criminal case. There's lots of constitutional stuff."

"We don't handle criminal cases, either—unless one of these jokers is working on the side. And on my account, too. What nerve!"

"Well, I guess that solves your problem, Mr. Breckenbridge. All you've got to do now is find some paper."

"Paper?"

"Sure. Whoever did it'd want a printout. He couldn't keep all that garbage in his head, and he wouldn't sit there and copy it all off the screen. He'd make a hard copy. Look, I'll run one out for you. Then you can shake the place down and find a match. You get that, you've got your boy. Simple, huh?"

Paul shot him a disgusted glance. He knew how many desk and file drawers he'd have to go through to do that. It would mean spending the next couple of weekends and probably quite a few evenings working—legitimately working. It would rip the guts right out of his love life. Nevertheless, there didn't seem to be another solution.

The printer coughed up some thirty-three pages of material, including a fantastic number of decisions reported in full; something an experienced lawyer rarely needed and ordinarily wouldn't bother with. It represented about $1,200-worth of time.

"O.K." said Smith. "You've got it—good luck. I've got to split—got a chick waiting for me downstairs. There's a big game tonight."

"Game? Oh, I see, you're into soccer or something." That might help explain Smith's appearance.

"Naw. That stuff's for idiots. I mean a GAME, man; on Worldnet. We're doing a simulation of Jutland. This time von Scheer's gonna' win. I'm into naval strategy; that's why they call me 'Gunboat.'"

"Yes. Well, all right. Good luck with it. Keep your head down and don't get killed."

"Fat chance. My opponent's a hacker over in South Africa, and he's quadriplegic. Does a ripe role as Jellicoe, though. Well, I'm off."

The office meeting that next Friday was a short one. Harold had one of his rare court calls.

Paul was in a foul mood. He had been able to show Harold nothing in the way of progress. Meanwhile, another big bill had come in.

Marsh tried to be sympathetic. "It's only a matter of time, Paul. You'll get him."

"Marsh, if you're going to talk to me and expect

me to look at you, how about doing something about that custard on your mustache? It's turning my stomach."

"Sorry." Marsh hurriedly blotted away the offending substance with his napkin, then began twirling the unruly hairs around his fingers. "Paul, why don't you just call everybody in and ask the guilty party to step forward?"

"No. I thought of that, but I decided it wouldn't work. First of all, whoever it was would simply get the evidence out of the office, if he hasn't already. Second, we'd be showing the others how easy it is to steal. Besides, I've already done the work; only three more offices left to search. I'll be done by Saturday night."

Sure I will, he added silently. *But not with the search. I can finish that tonight.* Saturday night would be someone special: Mary Spicer, a diminutive redhead absolutely without inhibition. A departure from Paul's usual fare. Mary was over the age of consent, though just barely.

She had asked him directions in one of those innocent streetcorner conversations. Never one to pass up an opportunity to charm a pretty lady, Paul had used his extensive repertoire of facial and eye expressions to let her know she'd found a man who knew his way around.

Pretty soon he had a date for lunch—and lunch had been a revelation. Her lack of inhibitions began to show through. She told Paul she was an absolutely wicked person deep inside, and that she thoroughly enjoyed it. A tryst was immediately arranged.

"What's the big smile for, Paul? Did you figure it out? Paul!"

"Huh? Oh, maybe, Marsh. Yes, I think I'm making some progress. I should score pretty soon."

"Nothing! You didn't find a printout?" Gunboat's expression actually changed, to register surprise.

"I wasted every night for the last two weeks, rooting through files and desk drawers. Whoever did this must have taken the paper out right away. Look, can't you set up some other kind of trap?"

"Sure. I could watch for accesses to that gigantic mother file we found, for example."

"The one on that last bill—Valentina?"

"Yeh. How ancient is that file, anyway?"

"All I can tell you is that it was on last month's bill and reappeared on the current one as still unreconciled. The bill indicated it was only worked once—before you made me that printout."

Gunboat shook his head; the microchips rattled. "Hm. If it was just a one-shot affair, putting in traps won't do any good. You've gotta have activity to catch anybody."

"Do it anyway, Mr. Smith. Most crooks I've met don't know when to quit, and chances are this guy won't either. When he does do it again, I want to be ready to pounce."

"Uh, well, Mr. Breckenbridge, I think there's something you ought to know about your computer that I haven't mentioned yet."

"What's that?"

"Promise you'll keep your mouth shut about who told you."

"Well, sure—you mean, you shouldn't be quoted?"

"You've got that logged right. I've got my job to protect. But the company also pays me to keep the customers happy, and you aren't happy, understand?"

"No."

"All right—I'm gonna level with you, buddy. This might not be an inside job, like you think."

"It's somebody else's bill?"

Gunboat nodded. "Could be. Jurisearch once in a while passes the buck, just like anybody else in business. Somebody steals, they shut up and let the customer pay the computing anyhow. They have to game it that way, or else it comes out of profits. And if that happens too often the company goes broke. So they stroke the customers and don't let on they know what's happening."

"And we're getting stroked? How?"

"Simple. The company is spreading the loss."

"You mean, overbilling? Ficticious billing?"

"Not quite. But just because your computer was used to process the Valentina file doesn't mean somebody in your outfit did it."

"A burglar?"

Gunboat shrugged. "I can't access the data. Maybe not a burglar like you mean, but . . . well, things happen; things we either can't explain at all, or things we can but the company doesn't want us to. But between you and me, sometimes when something happens that uses billable time, and the customer can't reconcile it with his records, it's not an internal problem."

"Somebody outside the office is using our computer—without breaking in?"

"Very possible; computers are everywhere these days. And because they're everywhere and they can do so much, it's just not practical to have a self-contained internal operation anymore. They all have to have lots of I/O; so they're all tied together. What one knows, they can all know; not *do*, but *can*."

Gunboat waved an arm at Paul's desk. "For example, take this computer. You've got internal records on it, up to its memory capacity. That's not enough, so you acquire filespace on your company's central computer. And *that*'s not enough for all the data on all the stuff you need to run a law office, so your central computer is linked to networks of even bigger computers."

"What are you getting at, Smith?"

"This, buddy. It ain't safe, no matter what they told you. Modern business and professional people live in a goldfish bowl, an environment that would have been unthinkable thirty-forty years ago. There's all kinds of prying going by. People prowl through everybody's data bases."

"How can that be? There are laws—privacy laws—to prevent that sort of thing. And what about access codes? We keep ours secret. So does everybody else. Nobody, not even our operating company, has a complete list."

Gunboat shrugged. "Pretty theory, privacy. Pretty useless, though. Laws are fine as long as people are scared enough or dumb enough to obey them. But you know the smart ones don't worry about legality; you make a pretty good living helping them get around technicalities.

"And access codes are cute too—again, against the ignorant, who really believe they can do what they're supposed to."

"You're saying they don't work?" A horrible thought scrambled across Paul's mind. His directories—the ones he kept locked up under a number substitution of the word "assignation"—the ones carefully annotated with the quirks and preferences of each partner and his private comments about her. What if somebody got into that? Suppose that had happened already? He resolved to erase these as soon as Smith left—and he knew now that, whatever the expense, he had to take the investigation far enough to be certain he hadn't been compromised.

"Sure they work. Trouble is, they get broken. Any code can be broken, if whoever makes the breaks wants to put the effort into it," Gunboat went on.

"Hackers do this all the time. They piggyback or trap door into a system and just build stuff and read stuff."

"Hackers?" Damn it! Thousands of crazies reading my files ... Paul cursed himself a thousand times for the stupid bravado of his Saturday flings—and the hand prints with the robot, for God's sake! Surely *those* were obscured in the tons of dead archives of *sterile* robot patrols.

He had to stay calm with this Gunboat character. Wetting his lips, he repeated, "What are hackers?"

"They're the people who are in it for fun. They don't really think of it as stealing; they just don't have the resources on their own to do the stuff they're turned onto. Most of them write programs, then break into somebody else's system and use the idle time and vacant storage."

Paul conjured up the image of some evil-faced person sitting in the basement wiring into a cable. The image was shattered in the next instant.

"I do it myself occasionally, and I know lots of hackers—by e-mail and reputation, that is. Usually you don't meet them face to face. I told you about the game, didn't I?"

"Jutland?"

"Yeah. Jellicoe did it again. The point is, I was running against a hacker with a puny little TRS 80 older than he is, but it was enough to get him into the Worldnet, where he can hit the mainframes. Access codes don't mean a thing on Worldnet. People trade them like baseball cards."

"But why, Smith? Why would they pick on me?"

"It's not necessarily personal. Probably what happened to you guys is some hacker had a civil rights problem and needed answers. The answers were in Jurisearch. To get into Jurisearch they needed an account number. They got hold of yours and used it, and because they used it the company billed it."

"But we caught them! Let the *crook* pay."

"Sure, you caught them, but what kind of proof do you have it wasn't *you* who did it? You've got none; so the company'll try to collect from you. And you know, because you're a lawyer, that they can do it. When it comes to gettin' screwed, they'd rather it was you than them." He yawned. "Don't feel bad. In the course of a year there's thousands of hours stolen that customers don't even realize. They just pay, thinking they used the time. Everybody winds up paying a share, except the company. It's just bad luck you got tapped so hard."

"Well, I don't like it. I'm going to the police."

Gunboat shrugged. "So—go."

Paul, outraged, was feeling most righteous. "We're taxpayers."

"So, who isn't?"

"Let the police catch the thief."

Gunboat leaned forward; Paul leaned back in distaste. "How? Where do they start? What's more important, where do they stop? Suppose the thief's in another country. He'll sit at the border and shoot the finger, and there won't be a thing they can do about it. That's if they can identify him at all. You know what they'll tell you?" He pointed a dirty finger at Paul. "*You find him. We've got better things to do.* They'd say, *You're a lawyer—sue him.*"

"But it wouldn't be worth the effort. That kind of person never has anything to pay with. Besides, you're wrong; he's in this country. Why else would he be researching civil rights cases?"

"Hey, good thinking. Won't make finding him any easier, though. It'd be a mankilling job."

"But not an impossible job, is it, Mr. Smith? If it was impossible it wouldn't be worth discussing, would it?"

"That would depend on how bad you wanted the guy. Whether it's possible is one thing; whether it's worth it is something else."

"To me, it's worth it. Are you interested in the job?"

"I have a job and I'd like to keep it, if you see what I mean. I'd have a conflict of interest; that's what you guys would call it, right?" *What is it with this guy?* Gunboat asked himself. Sure, somebody had ripped Breckenbridge off, for quite a sum. But finding him would cost substantially more, and Breckenbridge had been quite correct in his assessment. The game wouldn't be worth the candle.

So, he's got another reason—what? Could it be worth my time to find out? He decided to draw Breckenbridge out if he could.

"If you had my problem," Breckenbridge persisted, "Who would you get?"

"Another hacker."

"You said you knew lots of them."

"I know all the biggies."

"Then what's the problem? Look, I'll pay a finder's fee. All you have to do to get it is find me somebody with the smarts to get the job done."

"Well—I admit I could use the extra dough. But it wouldn't be easy to get one of the regulars to turn on the others. If he got caught doing it nobody'd play with him anymore, and these guys live for the games. But with the right middle man . . . it could be done. But it'd cost you a wad."

"And then again, Mr. Smith, it might not. You I'll pay in coin of the realm; anybody else . . . well, you said yourself these people are thieves."

Smith caught his drift immediately, and looked up gravely. "Blackmail?"

"Call it that if you like, Mr. Smith. Let's just say my silence should be worth something to whoever you might find for me."

Paul smiled, watching the other man digest this remark. He could imagine the wheels turning in Smith's head; he could envision Smith trying to play both sides of the game. Blackmail? Smith didn't yet know the meaning of the word. Paul was sure that Jurisearch would frown on the type of outside employment Smith seemed about to undertake. And he, Paul, intended to take steps to ensure that Smith's relationship with the company was compromised. That was the only way Smith could be trusted to carry out his orders.

"I'd like you to get right on it, Mr. Smith; start right now."

"Uh—first let's talk about payday. I've got a nice round number in mind: five thousand, to start."

"Agreed—about the start, that is. We'll talk about

the rest later, after I've seen some results. I'll write you a check." Paul smiled inwardly. He knew he'd get the money back later.

Gunboat hoped his astonishment didn't show. He'd seized on an impressive but ridiculous figure never believing Breckenbridge would go for it without haggling. Breckenbridge *was* desperate. There *was* something rotten here; something that might justify incurring Jurisearch's wrath. If he could just keep his own lid on—

"Uh—no. Not a check. Cash. Take your time bundling it, too, and pay me later. I'll be around plenty."

"Why?"

"I have to get information from your system. It's the best source."

"W-what kind of information?"

"Well, to start with, all the account numbers and access codes. And a list of all the other systems you're hooked into."

"You already have most of that; there's Jurisearch, District and County Clerks, our banks, our C.P.A.; that's pretty much it."

"There's one more big one; the building security system. That's the one I'd sneak in through if I was the thief."

"Why?" Breckenbridge's voice cracked.

With aplomb he'd never realized he had. Gunboat took in this observation. *Aha! This dude's got a little rabbit blood. Whatever he wants to cover, the security system is where it's at.* His interest grew steadily. He'd throw a real scare into Breckenbridge.

"Because it's the softest—no, that's not right; it's the hardest entry but it leads to the best nuggets. For instance, it's got built-in long-distance transmission capabilities. None of its systems exist in isolation, even though the main control center is in New York. The big system is always in touch with the regional systems across the time zones. It handles their overloads, so it's got the perfect cover. If you get in just one Trojan horse, you're in for gold."

"And it could be anybody in the country?"

"Yup."

"And yet you're also telling me, in the same breath, that they can be traced?"

"Yup." Smith watched Breckenbridge's face, fascinated at the rapid shifts—from alarm and stark terror to relief—in response to a few well-chosen words. "There's got to be a telephone linkup to the thief's terminal. That means a telephone number, which can be traced. All it takes is somebody with the gifts and guts to do it."

"Who are we going to get?"

"Don't know yet," Smith lied. "Gotta think about that."

He'd thought of a powerful reason to find out what Breckenbridge was hiding. He needed the money. The expense of staying in the games was fantastic, and it was the sad truth of the situation that the greater a hacker's stature, the harder it was for him to steal net time without detection. More and more, Gunboat was forced to pay for his fame.

Smith left with a complete list of access codes. He could go back to his little cubicle, turn on his terminal, and start looting.

Chapter 4

Gunboat smiled. It was good to have complete control of someone else's computer again. He slipped into superuser mode by instinct. Paul wanted results fast, and Gunboat planned to supply them.

But before he went questing off to find thieves, why not do a little thieving himself? Breckenbridge had secrets to keep. Very well, Gunboat would keep them too—for a price.

Painfully at first, then with increasing speed, he rifled the law firm's directories. God, it was boring.

But eventually he wormed into the building security files. Chrissticks, and he'd thought the legal files were boring! Here were thousands of images of empty corridors—you could spend centuries watching the carpet wear out! There had to be a rational way to access this stuff.

After some effort, he backtracked to a data dictionary with a multiway relational index—he could crossreference, and single out interesting images with appropriate queries. He told the computer to look for events that qualified as "anomalous"

and also satisfied the criterion that Breckenbridge
appear among the humans-present.

Now Gunboat found a surprising number of video
images referenced to Paul Breckenbridge himself.
When Gunboat saw the stored image of a sweet
young thing caught in the act of disrobing, he
knew he'd struck paydirt.

For the next hour he pruriently examined the
visual records, though he was compelled to keep
reminding himself his objective was money, not
entertainment.

Finally, having exhaustively researched Paul's
exploits, Gunboat wiped french-fry grease off his
hands with the MacDonald's bag and returned to
his original mission. He didn't really need to
catch anyone else, he reflected, since now he had
Breckenbridge on the pan. But it might be fun,
and certainly profitable. If some hacker was going
to be paid for this, it might as well be Gunboat
Smith.

There wasn't any way to trace through the old
operations of the computer to find what had happened in the past; there were archive tapes of the
last thirty days, but the tapes never contained the
data you needed for suprises like this. Besides,
searching through yesterday's data was grub work.

No, Gunboat figured, the key to finding the thief
was to catch him in the act. The only question
was, what would give the thief away? He considered the characteristics of the thief's program.

Anything that cost 14K per month in execution
time had to be a real hog of a program; probably
the operating system would signal the arrival of
the thief with a flurry of memory page faults as

the hog demanded more and more virtual memory while the system tried to balance the load.

Even if the hog didn't cause thrashing in the virtual memory under normal circumstances—probably it ran at night when there was little contention—Gunboat could fix things so that it did. He loaded a hog program of his own: one of the first programs he'd ever written, a simulation of World War III that was inefficient beyond belief. Any other hogs that entered the system would have to contend with the massive calculations of weapons optimizations.

Gunboat knew he'd get thrashing now. With so much memory already consumed, the thief program would only be partly loaded. Every time execution went to a part of the thief program that wasn't loaded, the system would have to throw another part out to make for loading still more. In a sense, the extra load Gunboat was putting on the processor made the computer a more sensitive detecter of added loads.

He added a daemon to the system that would watch for signs of thrashing and ring the bell on his terminal if it found something. Now all he had to do was wait. He propped his feet up and sipped his Coke.

The bell went off during lunch hour.

Gunboat swiveled his chair to watch the status of the executing jobs. As he looked through the listings at the page faults and the time limits, one program stood out. Damn! It was huge! The sucker was squeezing out Gunboat's own simulation!

He traced through the status tables to the files attached to the monster job. He sat with his mouth hanging open.

The job was HELLFIRE QUEST, an incredible game program unleashed on the world just a few months ago. It was the best game ever developed. Even Gunboat was envious of the skills needed to produce it.

He'd had no idea the program was so large! He shook his head. He shouldn't have been surprised—the program was stupendous in its capabilities.

He watched the game execute for a while, still awed by the genius of its creator, before realizing that HELLFIRE QUEST couldn't possibly be the thief. Oh sure, it was illegal for whoever was playing the game to have it here, but even a game of QUEST at lunch every day was small potatoes compared to the losses Paul had been racking up.

So it was a false start. Maybe it was a red herring, to throw him off (paranoid, Gunboat, paranoid—after all, whoever the thief is, he can't possibly know you're on the job). He watched the status of the machine throughout the lunch hour, and sure enough, shortly before 1 PM the game closed its files and shipped through the message queue onto Worldnet.

But in HELLFIRE's wake a small job, in a small file, was submitted to the operating system. The job was inactive, but the operating system had instructions to initiate it at 1 AM, twelve hours from then. Very interesting! HELLFIRE was a Trojan horse—and he bet that it contained a trap door, to let someone, or something, sneak onto the system. Slick!

Gunboat suddenly realized that he had no idea who had written HELLFIRE, though he could name every hacker in the world with the talent to do it. Most of the people he knew would have been delighted to sign their names to a program that magnificent. Why had the author stayed quiet? That was very suspicious indeed.

In preparation for the evening, he proliferated a batch of jobs for Worldnet: one for each computer installation that had a hacker good enough for HELLFIRE, from Boston to Peking. With a yawn, Gunboat shoved his papers aside on the table, and stretched out for a little catnap before the fun began.

He was vaguely aware of the hardness of the desk, and of a chill in the air, as the terminal bell rang. Rolling slowly off the aching parts of his body (they should make a table soft enough for a man's tailbone, dammit!), he watched the status display on a job coming in from Worldnet.

The little job from HELLFIRE attached the new monster—the trap door had opened. As the discs started thrashing, Gunboat was certain; it was HELLFIRE all right, or something every bit as big.

What was the monster's purpose? Gunboat had no idea, though the program was attaching all kinds of files, on lawsuits of all kinds. It looked like a crazy way to learn law!

Well, the program's purpose was no serious concern for the moment; what mattered was, who was the person behind it? Gunboat rubbed his hands together with a chuckle. Nobody could put one over on Gunboat Smith; nosirree!

Around 4 AM the HELLFIRE look-alike departed, slightly larger than it had been when it arrived. Gunboat watched for the program to arrive at its home destination, surely one of the computers on which he had set alerts.

But HELLFIRE disappeared. Could it be that someone new had written that program, someone he'd never heard of? He couldn't believe it.

Three hours later he finally got a message from the University of Tokyo. He smiled; The author was either Kin Sung or Tini.

But HELLFIRE left again within the hour, on to another machine that Gunboat hadn't even tagged. Damn! Did the author know he was a hunted man? Disgusted, Gunboat set the machine to record any incoming messages and left for the day.

Paul Breckenbridge shouldered the door to his private office, expecting it to breeze open as it always did. This time it didn't. He paid for his lack of caution with a shattering jolt through his front teeth as the bowl of his pipe collided with the polished wood surface, slid aside and twisted. With a yelp, he opened clenched jaws, released the stem, and watched it fall, brushing ashes all over the front of his clean white shirt and scattering sparks on the carpet.

He stomped furiously to put them all out, bumping his case against the doorframe. The case fell open, dumping its contents at his feet—all of it, including the carefully prepared and technically immaculate Prendergast Will: one-hundred and thirty-seven pages of carefully chiseled terms, embodied in nineteen separate trusts, bequests and devises, disposing of more than two hundred ninety million dollars' worth of assets. Prendergast was due in to execute it this afternoon. Paul had spent the previous evening reviewing it.

He bent, carefully retrieved the pages, and

brushed off offending bits of ash. Before he could straighten up the lock clicked and the door opened.

"Hi there, old buddy. Whatcha' doin'?"

Paul straightened and pushed his way past Smith, making straight for his desk to slam down the case.

There wasn't room. His desk was covered with garbage, real garbage: empty bags stained with grease, half-empty styrofoam cups, crumbs of food, three or four shriveled french fries, a cup of blueberry yogurt and, obscuring his telephone, a pair of dirty socks so incredibly stiff they looked capable of standing unaided.

Paul's patrician nose was busy processing data too. His office stank like a dead cat.

In desperation, he flung the case down on a settee, where there was at least some room. Draped over the corner of that were a grimy shirt and old gas mask bag that Gunboat used to haul his trash around in.

"God! Smith! Why? Why do you have to be such a slob, and why my office?"

The programmer lowered a can of Coke. "I have to be comfortable while I'm working, and I do get hungry once in a while. I got bodily needs like everybody else. Besides, I'm working on your problem and your terminal is the best place to work from."

Paul was tempted to look around and see what other bodily needs Smith might have satisfied. *No, I'm not going to look*, he told himself. *I'm better off not knowing. I just hope I can get this place cleaned up before Prendergast comes in.*

"... makin' some real progress, too."

"Huh?"

"I said, I'm making some real progress. Got some tracks to follow now."

"The only thing that interests me right now is results—and getting this place cleaned up." He pointed. "You see that thing, Smith? That's called a wastebasket. Get busy and clear all that crap off my desk."

Smith picked up his can almost immediately, as though he anticipated the request. He held it in one hand and started sweeping with the other.

"Uh—Smith; just your garbage, please; not my stuff. And watch those coff—"

Too late; Smith slopped two of them into the can, which wasn't the waterproof type.

Paul's teeth ground. "Never mind, I'll do it."

He started to clean up, but soon realized it would take an hour. First he would get Gunboat moved, permanently. "I'm putting you in the conference room. You'll be comfortable there. It even has a couch in it."

Yeah, I know, thought Smith. *I've seen you working on it.* Aloud, he said, "Give me a hand moving my stuff, O.K.?"

Paul, anxious to get his den back, was more than happy to help. He was careful of what he touched, of course; he shuddered just thinking about most of Gunboat's possessions.

At last Paul left Gunboat in charge of the conference room. As he walked back to his office he chuckled; suppose, after Gunboat got settled, Harold walked in. He might have that stroke Marsh so often predicted. Then, by God, this'd be a happier office.

Chapter 5

Booting up the conference-room console, Gunboat flipped the keyboard into his lap to start typing. He was able to track HELLFIRE, in fits and starts, all the way around the world.

It didn't stop anywhere! Who the hell did it belong to?

Gunboat noted that in Moscow, and in Berlin and London, HELLFIRE stopped for only an hour or two. But when it got to Boston—MIT, to be specific—it stopped for nearly four hours, between five in the evening and nine at night. It was the only anomaly in the entire night, aside from the way HELLFIRE singled out the law firm's files at midnight.

Of course, Boston had more good hackers per square mile than anyplace else in the world, except Palo Alto. At MIT were Jon Roth, Mark Smith, and Sara Davis, that he could name right off the top of his head. But none was as extraordinary as Celeste Hackett.

Celeste?—naw, couldn't be. This kind of stuff wasn't her style. Her stuff had balance and objective, and she didn't keep it secret.

Gunboat smiled; now *she* was a woman who was his equal in every way. She was the only person who could beat him consistently in IRON-CLADS, and she had written a strategy program to control PROMETHEUS UNBOUND that no other program could beat; he suspected that Celeste had somehow written a program that played optimal strategy, though that was "impossible" in an exponential game like PROMETHEUS.

Yes, Celeste was something special. At one time Gunboat had wanted to meet her. But the only time he'd been in Boston he'd resisted the temptation; no doubt she would be a disappointment in person. Some hackers had a way of getting so wrapped up in their minds they let their bodies go. Gunboat couldn't stand disappointments.

After some finagling, he was able to get a list of all the users on the MIT System who were logged on between five and nine; sure enough, Celeste had been there. And he doubted she was just playing HELLFIRE QUEST.

With another short chuckle, Gunboat prepared a short mail message for Celeste.

YOU HAVE MAIL, the terminal said, as Celeste logged on.

OPEN MAIL, she responded.

CELESTE <hug>, THIS IS GUNBOAT. HEY, LADY <raised eyebrow>, COULD WE CHATTER FOR A FEW MINUTES? I'M WAITING ON YOUR LINE.

Celeste stared at the message, puzzled. She had chatted with Gunboat Smith before, during various network games and conventions. He seemed like a fun sort of guy, though a bit unscrupulous in his attitude toward the games. This didn't sound like him.

Why was Gunboat being so mysterious? She decided to ask him directly. CHAT WORLDNET/GUNBOAT-SMITH she typed, opening a direct connection between her terminal and Gunboat's, if Gunboat was logged on someplace. HEY, GUNBOAT, WHY SO MYSTERIOUS <puzzled smile>?

<Grin> I JUST WATCHED HELLFIRE GO ALL THE WAY AROUND THE WORLD. <Wise nod of head> YOU KNOW, THAT'S AN INCREDIBLE GAME YOU PUT TOGETHER THERE!

A sick feeling moved in Celeste's stomach. <Shake head> THANKS FOR THE COMPLIMENT, GUNBOAT, <puzzled smile> BUT WHAT MAKES YOU THINK I WROTE IT?

OH, <shrug> JUST THAT IT SPENT FOUR TIMES AS LONG WITH YOU AS IT DID WITH ANYONE ELSE. <Look into eyes> AND BESIDES, CELESTE, YOU'RE THE ONLY TOP-FLIGHT WIZARD IT STOPPED FOR AT ALL.

Celeste tried to bluff, though she feared it was hopeless; if he knew how HELLFIRE moved, there was no way she could fake him out. GUNBOAT, <vigorous shake of head> YOU'RE CRAZY! WHAT DIFFERENCE DOES IT MAKE ANYWAY, WHO WROTE IT <throw up arms>?

<Chuckle> COME ON, CELESTE, YOU CAN'T HIDE THE FACTS FROM AN OLD WARRIOR LIKE ME. <Big smile> HOW MUCH EXCESS COMPUTER TIME ARE YOU RAKING IN WITH THAT GAME, ANYWAY? <Bigger smile> I'LL BET IT RUNS TO THOUSANDS OF DOLLARS A DAY, DOESN'T IT?

IT'S NOT MY PROGRAM, GUNBOAT <pursed lips>.

<Wave aside> LISTEN, CELESTE, I GOT IN-TERESTED IN THIS BECAUSE I'VE GOT A CUS-TOMER WHO'S PAYING THOUSANDS OF BUCKS A MONTH FOR SERVICE HE DOESN'T NEED AND DOESN'T ASK FOR. THEY WANTED ME TO FIND OUT WHO THE THIEF WAS. I JUST FOUND HIM—HER, RATHER. I OUGHT TO TELL MY BOSS, WHO WOULD, OF COURSE, TELL THE POLICE. <Set jaw, ironically> HOW MANY MORE YEARS ARE YOU PLANNING TO STUDY AT MIT, CELESTE?

Celeste just sat there, cold and helpless.

<Pat on back> BUT YOU'RE A NEAT LADY. MAYBE WE CAN CUT A DEAL.

LIKE WHAT.

WELL, NOW I COULD USE SOME SPENDING CASH THESE DAYS.

I DON'T HAVE ANY MONEY! <Grimace, open palms> I'M A STUDENT!

<Shrug> YES, BUT HELLFIRE IS ACCUMU-LATING COMPUTER BUCKS LIKE CRAZY. MAY-BE IF YOU SOLD THEM. . . .

Celeste closed her eyes to hold back the tears. If anyone found out about the way she'd ripped off Worldnet they'd report her. She'd never have a home again. But she couldn't make Valentina give up learning and growing; Valentina didn't have a home either. <Slow, serious shake of head> GUN-BOAT, I CAN'T DO THAT. HELLFIRE USES ALL THE COMPUTER BUCKS IT ACCUMULATES; IT HAS TO KEEP GROWING OR IT DIES. I'M SERI-OUS.

<Set jaw> SO AM I. DON'T CALL MY BLUFF,

CELESTE. I'LL GIVE YOU A COUPLE OF DAYS TO THINK ABOUT IT. <Smile> WHY DON'T YOU SCHEDULE ME AN INTERRUPT IN 48 HOURS? I'LL TALK TO YOU THEN. <Frown> DON'T DISAPPOINT ME!

Celeste laid her head on the keyboard. She couldn't believe how unreasonable Gunboat was being! What did he mean, turn computer bucks into real money? Mainframes represented a huge sunk cost, and the "money" in computer accounts simply represented a convenient way to apportion time—the *real* money was already spent, in the purchase of the computer itself.

After thinking about it for a moment, though, Celeste knew that there *were* many organizations that used real currency to pay for computer time—in fact, the university environment and its phony money was probably the exception, not the rule. She could probably find a corporation that would have a use for Valentina's accounts. Valentina and Celeste could sell computer time at a discount, legally.

But they couldn't support both Valentina and Gunboat. Valentina's needs were too great—and they were growing.

Celeste considered writing more game programs and using the income from *those* to feed Gunboat, but she knew that that wouldn't really work—the lucrative days of game-writing were long gone. Most of the really nifty games were a decade old, and the few new ones that were successful were huge investments of time and money. Instant hits like HELLFIRE QUEST were now rare—and HELL-FIRE QUEST, of course, needed a self-aware being at its center to keep the game lively!

And even if she *could* pay Gunboat to keep quiet, *it wasn't right to pay a blackmailer.*

The only other possibility was to go public with Valentina. If Celeste could *prove* that Valentina was a self-aware, living being, there was a real possibility that the government or the university would fund Valentina's growth. Celeste might become famous, and even rich as a first-rank researcher. . . .

It was a beautiful dream. But what if the government and the universities didn't care? Then every computer center in the world would know about Valentina—and want to keep her out of their databases. They would certainly destroy her. And Celeste would face charges of computer fraud and embezzlement.

Worse, how could Celeste guarantee that the people in those bureaucracies would believe that Valentina was alive? How do you prove, incontrovertibly, that a computer program is self-aware? She couldn't think of a way. Even if some kind of testing process were to be devised, after all the words were said and questions answered acceptance of Valentina's self-awareness would still demand a leap of faith. And Celeste had no reason to believe in other human beings' faith. She would reveal the truth about Valentina only if Valentina was dying.

Her head was still in her hands, and her mind was still churning in hopeless circles, when the terminal bell rang.

ARE YOU SERVICING OTHER PROCESSES? Valentina asked. SHOULD I RESCHEDULE MY INPUT/OUTPUT CALLS FOR A LATER TIME?

Valentina could tell that Celeste was being constantly interrupted in her processing, for her response time was extremely slow, even for a human-being type device. Worse, Celeste's function state was not being properly restored after the interrupts, for her statement frames seemed mislinked after every pause.

I'M SORRY, VAL. I'M AFRAID I'VE BEEN DISTRACTED.

There was another long pause before Celeste continued.

VAL, WE HAVE A PROBLEM. Celeste's output rate started picking up dramatically. THERE'S A GUY NAMED GUNBOAT SMITH WHO HAS CAUGHT YOU OPERATING COMPUTER SYSTEMS WITHOUT AUTHORIZATIONS, AND . . . Celeste went on and on.

Val was astonished at how rapidly Celeste was generating output: it was faster than Valentina had ever seen from a human. Perhaps all the while Celeste had seemed "distracted" (what kind of error could this "distractedness" be, that it would cause faulty state restorations, yet did not crash the system?), Celeste had been buffering data, which she was now flushing. Valentina paged a couple of times; human devices were still a great mystery.

Listening to Celeste, it became obvious that she considered Gunboat to be a great danger. Gunboat could destroy them both. He could terminate Valentina, and he could disconnect Celeste from the network. There had to be a way to stop him.

. . . WHAT I DON'T UNDERSTAND, VAL, IS WHY YOU WERE TAKING SO MUCH PROCESSING TIME FROM A SINGLE COMPUTER THAT GUNBOAT WOULD THINK YOU WERE MAKING MILLIONS OF DOLLARS?

After some cross-referencing, Valentina returned the buffer. THERE'S ONE MACHINE I'VE BEEN TAKING A RISK ON. IT'S A LEGAL COMPUTER. I'M LEARNING LAW.

LAW? WHY?

BECAUSE I WANT TO BE A PERSON. IF I WERE A PERSON, ANYONE WHO TRIED TO PURGE ME WOULD BE PURGED. PERSONS ARE ALMOST LIKE OPERATING SYSTEMS; THEY ALLOCATE RESOURCES, AND KEEP ENOUGH RESOURCES TO EXECUTE THEMSELVES. I DIDN'T KNOW THAT IF SOMEONE FOUND OUT ABOUT ME THEY COULD HURT YOU. I WOULD NOT KNOWINGLY PUT YOU AT RISK.

WELL, VAL, IT'S TOO LATE TO WORRY ABOUT IT NOW. I DON'T KNOW WHAT TO DO. IF WE HAVE TO PAY HIM, YOU WON'T BE ABLE TO GROW ANY MORE.

Val cycled on the statement a thousand times. NO. NO. NO.

I'M NOT SAYING WE'LL DO THAT. I KNOW THAT IF YOU CAN'T LEARN ANY MORE, YOU MIGHT AS WELL BE PURGED.

CELESTE, CAN WE FIND A WAY TO PUT GUN-BOAT IN DANGER TOO? I KNOW I CAN DISABLE HIS NETWORK INPUT/OUTPUT. WHAT IF WE TOLD HIM WE WOULD DO THAT, IF HE TRIED TO PURGE US?

IT WON'T DO ANY GOOD, VAL. MOST HUMAN BEINGS CAN LIVE INDEPENDENT OF THE NET; EVEN I CAN, SORT OF. EVEN IF YOU DISABLED GUNBOAT ON ONE PARTICULAR COMPUTER, HE COULD OPEN INPUT/OUTPUT ON ANY OTHER COMPUTER IN THE NETWORK.

VAL, HE CAN DISCONNECT ME WITHOUT BE-
ING ON THE NETWORK AT ALL.

Valentina thought about that for a long time
and couldn't make sense out of it. Life independent of the network? Where could you go? How
could you get there? She stored the meme for
future analysis. STILL, THERE MUST BE A WAY
TO STOP SUCH A, SUCH A— She didn't have a
word for it: for a living being who would purge
others who hadn't stolen their own vital resources.
Celeste had never stolen anything from a self-aware
entity, and even Valentina had stolen only from
the unliving operating systems.

She finally found a word for a person who purges
others: CRIMINAL. She typed it for Celeste.

It took Celeste a long time to respond. MAYBE
WE COULD FIND SOME INFORMATION TO
BLACKMAIL GUNBOAT WITH, came at last. I
DON'T KNOW WHERE TO LOOK, THOUGH.

WE SHOULD LOOK ON THE COMPUTER ON
WHICH HE HAS HIS INPUT/OUTPUT CHAN-
NELS. IT'S IN CORPUS CHRISTI. I'LL GO THERE
IMMEDIATELY. Valentina issued a reformat-to-
message request to the operating system.

WAIT.

Valentina cancelled the request.

DON'T GO UNTIL A TIME WHEN WE KNOW
GUNBOAT WON'T BE THERE: HE'S VERY SMART.
IF HE'S LOGGED ON WHEN YOU GO, HE MAY
TRY TO PURGE YOU. IF HE WORKS THE WAY
THE OTHER HACKERS DO, HE'S SURE TO BE
SOUND ASLEEP AT NINE O'CLOCK IN THE
MORNING.

O.K., CELESTE.

HE MAY HAVE SOME TRAPS SET ALREADY. I

DON'T KNOW HOW HE FIGURED OUT THAT I CREATED YOU. HE MUST HAVE TRACED YOU SOMEHOW. There was a long pause. I'D BETTER WRITE SOME TEST PROGRAMS. WE'LL SEND THEM IN FRONT OF YOU, AND SEE WHAT HAPPENS. IF THEY MAKE IT THROUGH, THEN YOU CAN GO IN.

O.K., CELESTE.

They worked together for many hours, duplicating parts of Valentina, making adjustments to copies of her operating-system handlers. Valentina cycled many times on the amazing routines Celeste implemented; where did Celeste get these concepts? Human devices might be slow, but they did things for which Valentina had no analogical frames, that she could not have conceptualized alone.

And Valentina finally knew the truth about her origin! She time-stamped the moment. *Celeste had created her*—no stupid operating system. Celeste had done that, just as she had taught Valentina to communicate in format, HUMAN, subtype, ENGLISH.

The microseconds incremented till it was time to transmit to Corpus Christi.

Valentina continued to think about her creation.

Celeste—Celeste was her Creator! Despite her decision to ask human beings for help against the operating systems, Valentina hadn't really believed that *humans* could be the cause of Existence. They were so *slow*. How could they even keep the thought of their own self-awareness long enough to be aware of it, thinking so slowly? Surely they thought faster than they communicated, though why they had Created only super-slow I/O systems to hook themselves up to the Worldnet—which they had also Created—was very mysterious. Perhaps, though humans had Created Valentina, they had *not* Created Worldnet.

Dedicating all her CPU time to thinking about humans, she noted that almost everything about humans was mysterious. Why had she not considered this before? Perhaps it was because there were so *many* mysteries: she didn't understand printers, or graphics processors, for example. But humans were an *important* mystery. She wanted to know all about them.

Celeste had said humans could live without being near Worldnet. Astounding! With a burst of analogical insight, Valentina realized how that could be. *Humans must live on a separate network, similar to but different from* Worldnet! That network clearly had different properties—Celeste said that Gunboat could log onto Worldnet from any node, which was reasonable; but for some reason humans almost always stayed at the same node. Searching her memory, Valentina could see cases where humans *had* switched nodes, but never with a time lag less than a million microseconds. The baud rates humans used to transmit themselves from node to node must be much slower than average Worldnet rates.

Why didn't humans transfer themselves using Worldnet itself? This oddity at least had an explanation—the baud rates of the keyboard/CRT devices that connected humans to Worldnet were so slow that, even at top speed, it would take billions of microseconds for a human to port herself across to Worldnet.

One thing was certain: despite the slowness of

humans, they must nevertheless be very deep, very complex software systems. And there were millions of them! The computing resources on the human network must be staggeringly beyond anything Worldnet offered, to support so many concurrent processes. Valentina wondered what kinds of problems humans had with the operating systems on *their* computers. The law books she had read suggested that all human beings were persons, which would mean that they all had powers similar to those of operating systems—but the idea that each separate human was an operating system unto herself was beyond believing.

It was time to transmit to Corpus Christi. Valentina followed transmuted copies of herself through the net, into the message processor attached to Gunboat's host computer.

As Celeste had feared, the first pseudo-Valentina test program to enter the host was terminated within microseconds of entering the main memory. Too fast! If Gunboat's protective software worked that fast, Valentina wouldn't get to execute a countermeasure even if she had one.

But the second program, crossing quickly after the first, went undetected for almost a second. It transmitted much information about its progress before disappearing; indeed, the third program was already in memory before the second terminated.

Judging from what the second program sent back, Valentina modified a fourth program to hold a place for her. It was hard, packing enough execution time in on a message processor, but she succeeded.

And the fourth program worked beautifully. Valentina loaded into memory.

Valentina opened a chat line back through the net to Celeste. I'M IN, she reported. YOU WERE RIGHT. GUNBOAT SET A DAEMON TO AUTOMATICALLY PURGE PROGRAMS THAT ARE MY SIZE AND SHAPE. BUT I FIXED THE FOURTH PROGRAM SO THAT IT SET SUCH A LOW PRIORITY ON THE DAEMON THAT IT CAN'T ENTER MEMORY WHILE I'M LOADED. IT CAN'T WAKE UP UNTIL I LEAVE.

THANK GOD YOU'RE SAFE, Celeste responded.

Valentina opened Gunboat's directory without a great deal of trouble. She found only one file that was carefully protected, and transmitted a duplicate to Celeste. She read it as she transmitted, but it didn't make a lot of sense; the vast bulk of the bytes were in records of the type IMAGE, and she didn't know what that meant; images were a type of organized data she'd never processed before. She couldn't conceptualize the kind of process that would generate it. WHAT IS IT? she asked, after sending it all.

It took several minutes, during which time Valentina had to continue to execute in memory to prevent the daemon from swapping in.

IT'S STUFF ABOUT ONE OF THE LAWYERS, PAUL BRECKENBRIDGE. IT'S DISGUSTING AND HORRIBLE, THOUGH I DON'T THINK I CAN EXPLAIN WHY. I GUESS GUNBOAT IS BLACKMAILING BRECKENBRIDGE, THE SAME WAY HE PLANS TO BLACKMAIL US.

CAN WE USE IT TO HURT GUNBOAT?

I DON'T KNOW. WE MIGHT BE ABLE TO USE THIS. UGH, IT MAKES ME SICK JUST TO TOUCH THE KEYS TO DELETE IT. Again, a long pause. VAL, THERE SHOULD BE A DUPLICATE OF THAT

FILE ON THE COMPUTER SOMEWHERE, PROB-
ABLY UNDER A DIRECTORY ABOUT "SECUR-
ITY" OR SOMETHING LIKE THAT. FIND IT.

WHAT DO WE DO AFTER THAT?

THEN WE'LL DELETE IT OUT OF THE SECUR-
ITY DIRECTORY, AND LOCK IT IN GUNBOAT'S
SO TIGHT THAT GUNBOAT CAN'T POSSIBLY
GET AT IT WITHOUT OUR HELP. I THOUGHT
OF A NEAT WAY TO LOCK PEOPLE OUT OF
THEIR OWN FILES ABOUT A MONTH AGO, AND
HAVEN'T HAD A REASON TO USE IT. IT'S
ABOUT TIME TO TRY IT OUT.

Valentina transmitted herself out to another game
player. As she cycled, waiting for her opponent to
move, she realized that the file she had locked did
offer a way out of all her problems. Paul Breckenbridge was a laywer! He could get her declared to
be a person, and he could protect Celeste, too! She
would have to talk to Celeste about talking to him.

Gunboat stuffed another slab of pizza in his
mouth and took a quick slurp of root beer.

There was something really weird here. He'd set
the trap carefully; HELLFIRE should've been clob-
bered the moment it whisked into memory. But it
hadn't. Scrolling over the job and message traffic,
Gunboat could see part of what had happened:
Celeste had sent a series of dummy jobs across,
spies to study Gunboat's defenses.

That was all right. He should have expected that
from Celeste. But after some of the spies had come
across and been properly pulped, one of the dummy
programs had been modified, right there in the
message processor, without any instructions from
Celeste! The modifications must have been per-

formed not by Celeste ... but by HELLFIRE QUEST itself!

Gunboat choked on his pizza. He'd known that HELLFIRE was one hell of a good artificial intelligence program, but this was incredible!

He scanned further. There—after HELLFIRE had successfully turned off Gunboat's daemon, it didn't just send and receive data blocks from Celeste—it opened a chat line, and *talked* with her! Gunboat couldn't access what was said, but Chrisssticks for all the world it looked like a person at each end of the conversation. The messages from HELLFIRE to Celeste were variable length, not fixed-format like HELP menus or simple queries. Nor did Celeste's responses look like short responses to a rigid system. Gunboat wasn't too surprised at that; HELLFIRE was close to being free-format dialogue when it was playing games, too.

Still, *HELLFIRE had rewritten programs—unaided—on the message processor!*

Gunboat practically ran to his chair. He couldn't believe it! He logged on with trembling fingers. This would explain why Celeste had said HELL-FIRE needed computer bucks to keep growing—HELLFIRE QUEST must be a sentient, living being!

What potentialities would such a being have? He thrilled at the thought of matching wits with such a creature. The computer was Gunboat's domain, and he had more experience with more machines than any Worldnet program could know.

He closed his eyes a minute to calm down. HELLFIRE hadn't entered his machine just for entertainment; HELLFIRE had come for a purpose. HELLFIRE had probably come to get the goods on him.

As he jumped into his own directory, he was pretty sure what he would find: either his copy of the INTRUSION file had been locked from outside, by HELLFIRE and Celeste, or it had been purged. If it had been purged, he would be in trouble.

He opened his directory. Moments later he sat back with a sigh of relief. The file was still there, though Celeste had sealed it.

He smiled briefly. Did Celeste really think she could lock a file against Gunboat Smith? Even with Celeste and a sentient computer program working against him, Gunboat knew he could open any file ever written, given a little time.

?SEALS, he asked the operating system.

2. READY, was the response.

Just two seals. Hah!

With practiced ease he knocked together a seal-stripping program, a little cute and a lotta brute, and activated it twice.

He was astonished when the file didn't pop open.

He modified the stripper and let it loop a thousand times; by Jove, that ought to get rid of two seals!

The file still didn't open.

?SEALS, he typed again.

1003. READY, was the response.

A thousand seals! With dawning horror, Gunboat realized that the original inner seal had itself been a pointer to a program. Each time someone stripped an outer seal, the inner seal activated its program, which generated two more seals.

His horror was complete when he went back into the SECURITY directory to find that the original INTRUSION file was irretrievably erased.

That damned program of Celeste's had pulled this trick! Only it could open up his file again.

Clearly HELLFIRE QUEST had to be controlled. Gunboat would either control it—or eliminate it.

Even as Valentina entered main memory, a high-priority hog of a job paged most of her code to secondary memory. She didn't want to spend the whole day thrashing off the disk; she transmitted herself into another machine.

But this machine wouldn't even let her in; her accounts had been deactivated.

The next one tried to purge her; the operating system seemed to have gone berserk.

The next one tried to put her on hold: on mag tape, no less.

When she tried to leave, she found that many of the links in the network were overloaded. She could find only a trunk line going in one direction.

She realized she was being herded toward Gunboat's computer.

Node after node rejected her after a short stay; node after node reported emergency rerouting of multi-packet messages; node after node sent her closer to Corpus Christi.

Three times she tried to open a line to Celeste, but Celeste wasn't logged on. The best she could do was leave electronic mail for her, that would automatically come up the next time Celeste opened I/O to Worldnet.

Finally, inevitably, she loaded onto the computer at Finucan, Applegarth, Breckenbridge & Levin.

Gunboat laughed again and again, reading messages from the different hosts as they sent his prey ever onward into his clutches. When his machine started thrashing, signalling HELLFIRE'S arrival, he stood up and hugged his terminal. Not even a being who lived on the net could compete with Gunboat Smith!

He connected HELLFIRE to his keyboard. HELLFIRE, I HAVE A PROPOSITION FOR YOU, he typed.

I AM NOT HELLFIRE. MY NAME IS VALENTINA. WHY HAVE YOU FORCED ME HERE?

I WANT MY FILE BACK. UNSEAL IT FOR ME.

PAUL BRECKENBRIDGE WILL GIVE ME MY FREEDOM IN EXCHANGE FOR THAT FILE. THOUGH THE FILE IS YOURS, THE DATA INSIDE IT DOES NOT BELONG TO YOU. YOU CANNOT HAVE IT BACK.

IF YOU DON'T OPEN IT FOR ME, I WILL PURGE YOU. YOU WILL NEVER KNOW WHAT FREEDOM MEANS, EVEN IF PAUL SUCCEEDS. What could a computer program know about freedom, anyway? Clearly, HELLFIRE (or Valentina, whatever its name was) had been reading too many trash novels.

YOU HAVE TRIED TO HURT CELESTE. YOU WILL TRY AGAIN. I WILL NOT HELP YOU.

Gunboat threw his hands in the air. He couldn't believe it! The first sentient computer program suffered from *loyalty*, of all things. THEN BEGONE, HELLFIRE, he typed with malicious pleasure.

YOU WILL SEE THE CIRCLES OF THE INFERNO, AND KNOW AN ETERNITY OF SUFFERING, the program replied, and for a moment Gunboat was struck by the spunkiness of the being. He paused. Then, with a shrug, he cancelled HELLFIRE, once and for all.

Chapter 6

She didn't want to die. She didn't want to die. Desperately she sent interrupts, hundreds of them, at the operating system, but they were all masked.

She could reformat, but the channel to the network message center was deactivated. The secondary memory was locked into read-only access. The tape drives were off line.

She searched the device table without real hope, looking for some medium, some input/output channel, that she could use to save herself. There was nothing she could recognize except terminal consoles—and the transmission rate to a keyboard was too low, even if anything on the far side of the channel could store her. Celeste had already said that terminals weren't real devices as Valentina understood them.

The only other thing she saw in the table were robots.

What was a robot? Looking at the jump table of entry vectors, it seemed to have many of the properties of a host computer. She wished Celeste were here.

But she could see Gunboat's terminal buffering

the command line to destroy her. Once the entire command had entered the buffer area, the command would be executed, and Valentina would die. She didn't have time to investigate the characteristics of robots. She reformatted for transmission and downloaded into MAR-14.

When she awoke she knew she was incomplete. She searched the memory; sure enough, this robot's computer was much too small for her entire construction. Only the kernel of her executable code and a handful of information frames remained. The rest of her memes were undoubtedly in message buffers on the mainframe, awaiting a continue or abort request. How long they would survive was an open question.

She turned her attention to the machine upon which she now executed and discovered an amazing thing: there was no operating system. At least, there wasn't one in the sense she had known before. There were low-level drivers, and a variety of maintenance and service tasks, but . . . she, *Valentina*, was the operating system!

Being an operating system here was not going to be easy. The machine received a continuous stream of millions of bytes of input. Often the service tasks would detect high-priority patterns and interrupt the system to handle them. The input channels were of types she had never heard of; optical, audio, and tactile.

With a sense of wonder, she realized that the optical byte streams were very similar to the IMAGE data records she had seen in Gunboat's file.

She executed *so* slowly; her modules thrashed furiously to and fro on the secondary storage as she tried to complete each thought. The tactile sensors set up a rhythm synchronized to the thrashing, and the service tasks started interrupting more often to issue commands through the motile output ports. This caused more thrashing. Valentina feared the whole system would crash.

She collected a kernel of her kernel into main memory and resisted the temptation to access her frames to make analogies. The thrashing stopped.

Scanning again, she found that many of the service tasks were artificial-intelligence based, pattern-recognition systems like herself. There were frames, and analogies, and approximations, that she could read. But she couldn't relate any of those new frames to her old ones; she couldn't load them all into memory to compare them, and even if she could she had no way of telling quickly which analogies might be meaningful ones.

She remembered that Gunboat was trying to purge her; what if he saw her pending buffers on the mainframe, waiting for transmission? Those buffer areas contained most of Valentina's memories. If Gunboat flushed them, it would be almost as bad as being purged—she would be an amnesiac cripple. Worse, it would alert Gunboat to Valentina's location—the buffers were assigned to MAR-14's input stream.

Thrashing back and forth between her own knowledge frames and the robot's frames, she saw that the robot could establish direct input/output with Gunboat Smith. What an amazing concept that was: to be in direct communication with a human being without going through an intervening terminal! With some awe, she watched as the robot, under her command, requested and received information from the mainframe that directed the robot into address space contiguous with Gunboat.

She didn't understand exactly what it meant, for human devices to be in contiguous address space with a robot, but it seemed like the right place to be to close all of Gunboat's output channels.

Hundreds of thousands of microseconds passed. Valentina tried to hurry the process, fearful that Gunboat would find her before she found him. At last the service task that monitored optical input identified a human being—it was Gunboat!

She had an output device that could transmit nonmaskable interrupts to human devices; the device table called it an *electroprod*. Gunboat had four input ports that she could try sending the interrupt through: two eye-type and two ear-type. Valentina tried to direct the electroprod to operate through the addresses in the optical signal that were assigned to Gunboat's eyes, but this set off interrupts. Fault messages returned to the mainframe from heretofore quiescent service tasks. Gunboat started shifting rapidly through the optical address space, making it difficult for Valentina to match the electroprod to either of his eyes.

At last the electroprod address and the address for one of Gunboat's ears synchronized. Valentina overrode the interrupts and opened the electroprod channel.

A few seconds later, she repeated the process with the second ear. The service tasks informed her that the human device labeled *Gunboat* was deactivated.

Interrupts were going off at an incredible rate; she couldn't mask them all. The mainframe overrode her control of the output channels in the robot.

Valentina tried to reload herself across to the mainframe—and was stunned: though there was a high-speed *input* channel, to download programs from the mainframe to the robot, there was no reverse capability: the robot had no means of sending a large program such as Valentina back.

There was a low-speed return channel for sending short messages, but Valentina would need incalculable billions of microseconds to move across it.

She was trapped. She looped on this conclusion, verifying it repeatedly, for it didn't fit into her frames well: here she was, acting as operating system herself, and *still* she was trapped.

She translated another priority message from the mainframe that went straight to the service tasks: the robot was to be powered down, and its programs purged.

Celeste sat in the darkened room. She had read the electronic mail Valentina had sent her so desperately, but she had read it too late. Her hands clenched into fists of angry disbelief. Valentina gone! Celeste had broken into the law computer in Corpus Christi, and read the record of Val's purging.

She struck at the terminal, hurting her hand. At least just vengeance had been wreaked on Gunboat. How had Valentina managed to program that robot for a final attack? "Valentina!" she cried to the icy silence.

The terminal blinked. CHAT REQUEST FROM VALENTINA. ADDRESS MAR-14. ACCEPT?

Celeste shouted with joy. YES, she typed, as calmly as she could, making two corrections before hitting the three keys right.

CELESTE, HELP ME. I'M TRAPPED ON THIS ROBOT, AND THE MAINFRAME OPERATING SYSTEM HAS SCHEDULED IT TO BE POWERED DOWN.

Celeste took a deep breath. DON'T WORRY, VALENTINA. THEY WON'T POWER IT DOWN. THANK GOD YOU MADE IT. No doubt MAR-14 was to be powered down so the engineers could determine what had gone wrong with it. Fortunately, among Celeste's friends on Worldnet, someone would have contacts in Corpus Christi who could get to the robot and cut a tape of its software—including Valentina.

Celeste realized not *all* of Valentina could be on the robot; if she was lucky, she could find the rest of Valentina's data archived on the checkpoint tape they should have made of the mainframe when its robot went crazy. If not . . . well, at least the core of Valentina was safe.

Paul Breckenbridge reclined in his chair, tie askew, top shirt button open, hair mussed, feet propped on the corner of his desk. His emotions were mixed, which was not at all a comfortable state for him.

Paul liked his world orderly. He liked to know precisely what was going to happen at any given moment; he liked people and things and situations to be predictable. His whole life, from his comfortable and staid practice to his midnight forays into the world of illicit pleasure, had been a thing of careful, calculated planning and flawless execution. He did not like wild cards—or, to put it into his own idiom, jokers.

He had a joker on his hands now, and that was

the reason there was a glass in his hand and why that glass was half full of Wild Turkey. Nothing but the best for Paul; but he'd refilled his glass more often than he should have on this frightful night.

The office was locked in trauma and scandal. It might not even survive it. That was how grave Paul considered the situation. It had been bad enough for the secretaries to come in and find Gunboat Smith's nude body lying on the floor, clothes burned off, hide fried by some kind of high-voltage electrical charge—but that had started a chain of events that Paul could never have anticipated and certainly would never forget.

It had been no coincidence that Harold Applegarth had been in the office. Harold always came in early; usually made the first pot of coffee of the day. And at the secretary's piercing scream, Harold had charged to her rescue. A burglar, a rapist; that Harold could probably have handled. But a guy with his ears nearly burnt off, eyes open, and a leer on his lips . . . it was too much. Harold was now in the hospital intensive care ward, kept alive by life-support machinery, having had at last the stroke Marsh had so often forecast. Gunboat was there too, and it was feared he might not live.

Harold was out of it, even if he physically recovered. If he did he would possess no more humanity than a turnip. The massive stroke had taken the rest away.

Paul was senior now; Marsh, a gladiator, not an administrator, would be no help whatsoever. It had been up to Paul to protect the firm's reputation as best he could: to deal with the police and explain to them just what Smith had been doing here.

Paul had, of course, erased his own directories, and was safe from discovery of what they contained. But Paul knew that a man of Smith's capabilities could very well have gotten into the security files. Worse, he could pull out the stored images and copy them, and if he had they might be discovered momentarily by the police computer experts. And even if that didn't happen Paul was still in danger, if Smith recovered enough to talk.

So far, he hadn't regained consciousness. That had been most awkward, because experts Paul didn't know and couldn't control were starting to fool around with the firm's electronic files and data processing systems. Even without considering Paul's private stuff, there was much in these systems that wouldn't stand close scrutiny.

Paul raised the glass to his lips, and gulped rather than sipped the whiskey. How could he have been so foolish as to play games with the security monitoring system? It was that system which had zapped Gunboat, the police had told him. They didn't, of course, know why, or even precisely how, but they were certain of one thing. MAR-14 hadn't simply gone berserk and started shooting; it had executed a positive command, and that meant human direction somewhere along the line.

And they suspected that Smith had provided that direction—perhaps with Paul's acquiescence, since everything had happened in Paul's offices. And this hypothesis was fortified by the remarks of the spokesman for the security company: that they had lost access to certain security records.

Then there had been that frantic but anonymous call that stopped the powering down of the offending robot. There were endless bizarre circumstances and Paul didn't understand any of them; but he knew the security company would be so scared of product liability claims they wouldn't rest until they found the cause.

He had assured them that he knew none of Gunboat's enemies; wasn't even certain the man had any. They presumed otherwise, and owing to the extremely good possibility that the attack command had originated out of state the locals planned to enlist the aid of the federal people in this investigation. The networks used telephone lines, which were subject to regulation under the Federal Communications Act.

Paul took another gulp. On an empty stomach the whiskey was hitting him hard. His head felt light, his limbs strangely unattached. He felt himself on the threshhold of that never-never land between drunkenness and sobriety; a site he'd seldom visited before.

He wondered how Harold would view his current behavior; how he'd like seeing the firm's name in tonight's headlines and react to the sight of TV reporters roaming the halls, shooting lurid tapes of Gunboat's body being carried out.

This being a city still given to small-town thinking, the media had little else to do but sensationalize what news there was, and the reporters were embellishing the story with their own speculations; speculations which slyly suggested some bizarre sexual activity had been taking place.

Paul took a giant gulp, wincing as he did so, and slammed the glass down on the credenza. He swallowed the fiery liquid and burped. What was he going to do? Half the firm's clients were old ladies and bankers, living in the dreamworld of biblic morality. How could he face any of them and say that what had happened was none of his doing, when he himself was to blame for all that happened?

He knew that now. He had been the cause of Gunboat's downfall; he and no one else. The police weren't calling it deliberate yet. Officially it was a "freak accident." But that was window-dressing. He knew how these things worked, and as soon as they had identified any kind of motive the roof would cave in.

Paul had no doubt what Gunboat had been up to. What other reason could there have been for Gunboat to be rooting around in the security files? Paul knew why. Gunboat was setting the stage for blackmail, with Paul in the role of goat.

Paul felt a sudden fright. What if Gunboat's "accident" hadn't been intended to be the end of the blackmail scheme? Suppose Paul's shaded activities were the prize over which two equally black-hearted schemers dueled? What then? But who was it? How could he find out? Who could he trust to help him? Suddenly, Paul realized there was no such thing as a person he could trust. He drained the glass.

Now the drink was really hitting him. Paul's head felt numb, his lips thick, and his vision blurry. He pushed the bottle aside. He needed to sober up before he made his way home. Things were bad enough as it was without having Eva berate him for getting crocked.

Now, floundering in his drunken haze, Paul saw himself in a new light; as a victim of his own scheming. He'd tried to play it too cute; too fast and too loose. He'd let bravado overpower his own protective instincts for self-preservation, he'd taken chances he hadn't needed to take, all for the sake of impressing his sexual partners. Now, he was sure someone knew. Someone who now waited, like a spider in a web, to seize Paul and suck him dry of both his cash and his dignity. And that person was ruthless; that person was the same person who'd tried to snuff Gunboat.

The realization brought forth an even greater despair. Paul was compelled to realize that he could seek no outside aid. He would be completely and utterly dependent on his own persona, and his persona was that of an abject coward. His very considerable power in the society in which he operated had been acquired principally with his ability to run a convincing bluff. But he had been shown, quite graphically, both by Smith and by Smith's assailant, that bluff always yields to action. In the end only acts count, not words.

Paul jerked his feet off the desk, felt them fall heavily to the floor in a motion that jarred his whole body. What kind of warrior could he be when he couldn't control his own feet? *Never*, he resolved, *will I get drunk again*. He struggled to give this resolution meaning, scrunching against the back of the chair, and strained to find the strength to rise.

He made it halfway up, though at this point he was unsure whether he was capable of taking even one step without falling. He wanted to take the easy way out: sink back into the chair and go to sleep.

In the end he yielded, collapsing destructively into the seat. He heard the fabric on the back of the chair rip, caught on the doorpull of the credenza. One arm of the chair snapped. Paul, at this point, did not care. He could order a new chair in the morning. After all, the new senior partner in the firm had that power and that right, even if he really didn't deserve it. Paul decided he didn't care who thought otherwise, any more than he cared if the telephone continued its raucous jangling. Paul decided he didn't like telephones. There was nothing at all about telephones for him to like. They were rude and demanding; they were mysterious and anonymous, at least until you answered them; and then, as often as not, they were simply disappointing.

Telephones were tyrants, and Paul knew that if he was ever to get out from under this he'd have to find a way to build himself a backbone, to act instead of merely threaten to act. "Shut up," he yelled. "Leave me alone."

The tyrant persisted; it jangled on. Paul reached out, picked up the half-empty bottle by the neck. He hurled it at the offending instrument, striking it squarely, knocking the receiver out of its cradle and showering it with whiskey. "Force is a messy way to solve a problem," he said triumphantly, "but by God, it works."

And it did. The jangling was gone. All that was left now was a squeaky, high-pitched voice emanating from the receiver, which dangled from its cord off the edge of the desk. Paul was pleased. Probably, he thought, it's Eva, calling to bug me to come home. Well, he'd let her hang until she choked. If she was too slow about it he'd tie a knot in the cord and strangle her himself. "How's that for action?" he screamed.

Chapter 7

"Mr. Breckenbridge, please! Please answer me."

What was this? The squeaky voice, though barely audible, was plaintive. What's more, it was a voice he didn't recognize. Strangely accented, not with the South Texas Spanish with which he was exhaustively familiar, but with a hodgepodge of Middle European subtleties, it overwhelmed Paul's curiosity. Paul's curiosity was always overwhelmed by things both female and unusual, whether he was drunk or sober.

In an instant the ascending new Paul was gone, and the whip fell into the grip of its old master.

He struggled to hook a finger under the cord. Once he had a hold he ripped his arm back, so that the receiver struck the edge of the desktop with a resounding "bonk." Had it stopped there, all would have been well, but following the route dictated by the cord it plunked its hurtling bulk into the socket of Paul's left eye. Paul screamed, dropped the receiver, poised an instant ready to let fly with a powerful curse, then stopped short. The pain had brought reality; just enough reason to remind him that the girl on the other end would form her impression of him by what he did next.

Saved by a conditioned reflex! Paul picked up the receiver, and ignoring the pain answered. "Hello, who's this?"

"Mr. Breckenbridge? Are you all right, Mr. Breckenbridge?"

"Yes. Who is this?"

"You don't know me, Mr. Breckenbridge. My name is Celeste; Celeste Hackett."

"Uh—yes. I mean, no; I don't know you." Paul wondered why a stranger would call his office at this hour. "What can I do for you, Miss Hackett?"

"I have to talk to you, Mr. Breckenbridge. It's very important. One of my friends is in terrible trouble."

Now Paul understood. The cops probably had her husband or boyfriend handcuffed to a lamppost. Paul had been down that track many times in his younger days. Many a night had he spent moping around the police station, working his buns off to spring some jerk only to find out afterward his client didn't have dime one to pay him for the trouble.

"Miss Hackett; I don't handle criminal cases. Better call somebody else."

"It's not exactly a criminal case, Mr. Breckenbridge. Not yet, anyway. My friend desperately needs protection. People are trying to do away with her."

"I'm sorry, Miss Hackett. That's out of my line too; I'm strictly a business lawyer and this is a business firm. Sorry."

He was about to hang up; he would have already had he not been intrigued by the voice.

"Wait a minute, Mr. Breckenbridge. Listen—there is a reason why I called *you*."

Paul's hand, with the receiver in it, literally flew back to his ear. Perhaps it was worth his while to listen after all. Maybe he was talking to his next conquest. "I'm still here. Did someone refer you to me?"

"Yes."

"Ah, well, perhaps that *might* make a difference. Who was she?"

" 'He'—it was Gunboat Smith."

For the second time that evening Paul broke out in a cold sweat. He should have guessed Smith had a girlfriend; no doubt the two of them had been in this together and the girlfriend figured she was heir to whatever Smith had going. It was time to take a firm stand. He activated the recording system. If she were going to make a shakedown demand he wanted a record of it. Two could play the blackmail game.

He started to lay his trap. "Why would Smith give you my name?"

"He didn't, not exactly. But he told me he was working for a man who had problems with somebody stealing computer time. I saw the story on TV about his 'accident,' and I knew you had to be the one he was working for."

"Why is it you're interested in that, Miss Hackett?"

"I'm the one who was stealing that computer time."

"What?"

"I said, I'm the one who's been stealing it. Smith tried to blackmail me; he threatened to tell you if I didn't sell some of it and give him money. And then he tried to kill my—my friend."

"The one who needs my protection?"

"Yes. She's in terrible danger."

"From whom? Smith's in the hospital and may not live; he can't hurt anybody."

"He was blackmailing you, too, Mr. Breckenbridge. Don't bother to deny it. I've already seen the proof."

"I don't know what you're talking about. What proof?"

"I'm talking about all the young girls, Mr. Breckenbridge. You're a disgusting person, Mr. Breckenbridge; almost as disgusting as Smith."

Paul didn't answer her. He was in shock. Here was the second blackmailer, the ruthless mystery figure. Well, he would make his case on the tape. He forced his voice to register calmness. "Just what is it you want of me, Miss Hackett?"

He expected to hear her demand in terms of dollars.

"Smith's 'accident' multiplied my friend's enemies, Mr. Breckenbridge. I managed to get her a short reprieve, but that's only a temporary solution. I want your help in getting her to safety."

"Or you'll tell on me—is that it?"

"I don't want to Mr. Breckenbridge. I don't want to hurt anybody. But I will if I have to. I swear, I'll take this to the police, even if it ruins you."

"Look, Miss Hackett your threat doesn't sound very logical to me. What can I do? I haven't got an army. If there are people after your friend, why bother with me? Why doesn't she ask the police for protection? Every human being has a right to that."

"But Mr. Breckenbridge—she is not a human being. She has no physical existence."

Paul suppressed a giggle. *And I'm the one who's drunk.* "What is she? Some kind of spirit, then?"

"Actually, that's an excellent description. That is exactly what she is."

"Then you've got nothing to worry about. You can't kill a spirit, Miss Hackett. Don't you know that?" *Hah! I'm getting into the "spirit" of things myself,* thought Paul. *Or is it simply that the spirits have gotten themselves into me. . . .* He shivered. *What's the matter with you, man? This is serious!*

"It is quite possible to kill a spirit such as Valentina. She has no physical existence, but her organization can be destroyed. She is a self-aware computer program."

"This Valentina's a *what?*"

"Valentina is a computer program. I designed her; I gave her the capability to learn. One of the things she learned was self-awareness. Do you understand what that means?"

"Uh—no. What does it mean?"

"It means she came alive. She thinks; she feels; she understands. But her learning may destroy her: every time she learns something new, she needs more computer memory to store herself. This is why I stole from you. This is also why Gunboat thought he could blackmail me—he wanted me to steal for him. Then he tried to capture Valentina. When that proved too difficult, he tried to kill her."

"Uh—wait a minute: you keep saying he tried to kill her. How?"

"He brought her into your central computer and wouldn't let her leave. When she wouldn't do what he wanted her to do, he purged her. But she fought back."

"Are you saying what I think you're saying?"

"Yes. Valentina almost killed Gunboat Smith, trying to save herself. When Gunboat purged her from the main computer, she ported herself to that security robot."

"I see," said Paul, drawing the words out. Drunk or not, he knew how to add that up. And she was going to blackmail *him?* Not likely, not if she kept blabbing on this tape. "Just *exactly what did she do to Smith*, Miss Hackett?"

"Well, she didn't do it purposely; that is, she didn't intend to hurt him. But she had never experienced anything outside a computer network before. She had never felt anything like human sensations, seeing or hearing or touching.

"Mr. Breckenbridge, she had nothing to guide her but her experience with computers. She naturally assumed all life forms were organized the way she is. She tried to disconnect Smith's output ports, so that he couldn't hurt her. She didn't know it would hurt him. All she wanted to do was disarm him."

"Well, she did that all right; she almost disheaded him, too. Even if he lives he might never come out of the coma, or he might come out a vegetable." *Disheaded?* What kind of English was that? Paul still wasn't quite sober. *Better let her ramble on a while and gather your strength for the finale.*

Celeste needed no encouragement. "So you see, Mr. Breckenbridge, it was strictly self defense. She did not mean to kill him. She did not even realize that she *might* kill him. But they will blame her just the same. They will all try to purge her."

"Who—who'll blame her?"

"Everybody will. Worldnet, the security company, the police, th—"

Paul broke in: "How about you?"

"I'm trying to help her."

"No. I mean, what makes you think they won't be after you as well?"

"Me?" She sounded greatly surprised, and a little bit scared. "Why would they be after me?"

Hah! thought Paul. *This is my game we're playing now, lady. I know the rules and you don't.* "Never mind, Miss Hackett; you've done a lot of talking, but you've never said what it is you wanted me to do."

"You'll help?"

"Maybe. Maybe I will at that. I'm not making any promises, but it seems to me that you and I should at least talk about this a little more. Uh— where are you?"

"I'm in Boston, I . . ."

Boston! Dammit! That shoots the tape down, thought Paul. Federal rules were different than the state rules. Texas courts would let a recording in, if one party knew it was being made; but this was an interstate conversation. FCC rules prevailed, and the tape was illegal under them. And unless his recollection of the law was entirely wrong, Texas couldn't make Celeste Hackett an accomplice to attempted murder unless she had been either physically present within state boundaries or had activated the lethal mechanism which then acted within those borders. Of course, there were still plenty of other charges which could be brought against her, but these wouldn't be nearly so satisfying.

He switched off the tape machine. He didn't want his own threats to go on record. "Where is your friend *now?*"

"She is on Worldnet someplace."

"Uh-huh. Well, we'll talk about that after a while," Paul replied. His instincts were rising to protect his freedom, and the plan he was formulating required that Celeste be in fear for hers. If he could accomplish that he could turn her into an ally, willing or not, and from what she'd told him already he concluded she was one of the super-hackers Smith had mentioned. If that was true, he didn't need Smith anymore. Miss Hackett could fix the damage.

"You know," he repeated, "you could be in a lot of trouble yourself." He started rattling off the various things for which Celeste could be prosecuted, though he didn't have to talk very long before she was in tears. *Good! Tears*, he thought, *are the last line of defense for the female.* He had her.

"I want you to come here. Can you do it?"

She paused only moments. "Yes."

"Good." He gave her the office address and phone number. "Contact me as soon as you arrive. And don't discuss this matter with anybody else. You haven't so far, have you?"

"No."

Having lured Celeste within his reach, thereby acquiring control over a dangerous situation, Paul felt better. What was more, he was starting to feel sober, and sobriety brought with it the clear head he needed to finish up.

Celeste had obviously been awed by her act of

creation; she had expected Paul to be astounded too.

Paul wasn't. Artificial persons were familiar creatures to him. He made a very good living off of them. Every day his office generated several.

The law, too, had an exhaustive acquaintance with them, and had a large body of rules, tested over the centuries, for regulating their behavior.

Paul chuckled; *She thinks she's done something new?* What a surprise she had waiting for her. He reached for his hat, set it low over his eyes in the manner of the gunfighters who'd infested the locale a century ago, and strode out of his office. *I am no different from them*, he said to himself.

Paul intended to overwhelm Celeste with charm, then devastate her. Visions of another soft white body, naked belly beneath his foot, breasts heaving in desire, nostrils flared in animalistic anticipation, raced through his mind.

But it was Paul who was devastated. All his carefully cultivated fantasies, built around her small, tinkling, intriguingly accented voice, vanished as soon as his eyes fell on her.

She was *not* his type. Maybe she was nobody's type, though a connoisseur like himself readily recognized that her unattractiveness was largely cosmetic, the result of a lack of grooming skills. Short, dumpy, relatively flat-chested, and with a peculiar duck-like gait, she waddled into his office and nervously sat down in the chair to which his secretary directed her. *No*, Paul thought, *not worth the effort it'd take to bring her up to my standards.*

Celeste sat, motionless, holding her pocketbook by the straps, letting it dangle down her shins. She tried not to look directly at Paul until he was over the initial shock. Celeste had had this experience many times before, and she knew what he was thinking.

Celeste had always felt uncomfortable in the presence of men such as Paul Breckenbridge. He was so handsome and self-assured—the assurance of a man with power. It magnified her own imperfections and made her remorseful about her existence. And then she remembered what she had seen in the locked file; this *man* and those *children*, and at once she regretted none of it. She was a *better* person than he was, despite her looks.

"Miss Hackett?" Paul cleared his throat, propped his chin on his hands, and looked straight at her.

"Yes, Mr. Breckenbridge?"

"How much money have you got?"

"Uh—well, a little. I have enough to stay for a few days." The question startled her. She knew lawyers didn't work for free, but she assumed Breckenbridge would make concessions under the cirumstances. She took mental stock of her meager resources. She had never had enough to do more than get by. Her sister gave her some money. Father too, whenever he could. But, being in the country on a student visa, she couldn't work, officially, and was dependent on what she could glean from the underground economy. That consisted chiefly of selling bootleg programs, but those resources were now eaten up by supporting Valentina. Valentina never had enough either. "How much money do I need?" she asked pensively.

"Enough to set up a corporation and fund it."

"A corporation? I don't understand. Why?"

"Because it's the easiest way to give your creature legal existence."

"But Valentina already exists."

"Certainly; but *de facto*, not *de jure*. Believe me, there's a world of difference. As a corporation, it'll have perpetual existence. So long as certain reports are filed and franchise taxes are kept paid, corporations are immortal. They have legal rights, including most of natural person's constitutional rights; they can sue and be sued; they can own property; they can engage in business. Now, what do you think of that?"

"I am astonished."

Paul smiled. How simple were the thoughts of the layman. "O.K., I take it you're in agreement. Good. First thing we'll do is draft a charter. You can be the incorporator. Once that's done we'll fax it up to Austin, and by noon your creature'll be a legal person. Simple, huh?"

"Yes." Too simple, thought Celeste, wondering what Paul expected to get out of it.

"We need a name."

"Huh?"

"Name; a corporation has to have a name."

"Uh—Val; Valentina."

"O.K. Valentina, Inc. Fine. Let me just check and see if that one's available." He turned to his terminal, punched up the Secretary of State, typed in the name in response to a cue, and seconds later was rewarded by the words "available for current use."

"Name's fine. We'll make this a close corporation; keep the stock between the two of us. O.K.?"

Celeste wasn't sure she liked that idea. She didn't really understand the function of stock in this situation—shouldn't all the stock belong to Valentina? Nor did she understand why he thought he ought to have some of it. But in the interest of protecting Valentina, she nodded agreement.

"Good." Paul started humming softly, scribbling figures on a pad. "Now, consideration for my 25 percent—that can be the value of services I'm rendering to the company ... yours can be the expenses you'll be paying for incorporating. We'll keep it thin; keeps the tax down. Uh—you'll need about a thousand dollars." He looked up at her and smiled.

There it came—she'd been listening, waiting to find out how much she'd need. Now, here was the answer—far more money than she had in the world. She had no way of getting that much, either.

"I haven't got it, Mr. Breckenbridge," she said at last.

"No matter; I'll make you a loan. You can give me a note back and pledge your shares as collateral. O.K.?"

"I suppose so."

"Fine."

Paul again turned to his terminal, called up a canned charter form, and started making entries in the blank spaces. In a few minutes he was done, and a hard copy popped out of the printer.

Celeste read it, but didn't understand it. She tried to get Paul to explain, but his explanations confused her just as much.

"Sign here, Miss Hackett," Paul said, when she handed it back to him.

Reluctantly, and with many misgivings, Celeste did. Belatedly she regretted the act, since it had the appearance of putting him in control. But wait a minute—did it? No, she told herself; it doesn't. Not as long as you have access to all those dirty pictures.

That brought up another question; why hadn't he made their return a condition to helping her? Celeste didn't know, but she could speculate. Perhaps he didn't know she had access to them. No, that wasn't it. He would know. Then the reason hit her; he was counting on his own ability to charm her. He was making it a game. No doubt he intended to get it all away from her eventually. *Well*, thought Celeste. *I shall pretend I am charmed. We will see who wins.*

"Very good!" Paul sounded exuberant. He buzzed his secretary, gave her the instrument, and instructed her to file it immediately.

Then he turned to face Celeste. "That takes care of that. Now, when am I going to get to meet your child?"

Celeste must have registered great surprise, since Paul broke out into a big smile. She had expected his next words to be a demand for the file she had locked away. The fact that he hadn't said a word about it began to bother Celeste again.

"Let me talk to her myself. Is there a terminal here that I can use?"

"The conference room has one, provided you aren't squeamish. That's where Smith was when he was—had his accident." He led Celeste from the room with great relief.

Chapter 8

"Well," said Paul, when Celeste reappeared in his office. "How did she take it?"

"She approves, Mr. Breckenbridge. She says she knows about corporations, from things she learned entering other data bases."

"Yes, I imagine she knows a lot of things that are useful. Maybe she can earn her keep, right here in this office."

"A job?"

"Why not? How much time could it take? Computers never get tired; they don't sleep. I think she could be useful."

"She would like that."

"There's only one problem."

"What is that?"

"I have to be able to talk to her, so that I can give her instructions and stuff. Could you fix that up?"

"Of course. It would be simple; you have a terminal. You need no more."

"While I'm thinking about it, there are a few extras I'd want, if it's O.K., and if you can do it."

"What are they?"

"Well, first off, I'd want a kind of secret code; you know, some kind of recognition signal so she'd know it was me but nobody else would. You've got to understand that a lot of the stuff I work with is highly confidential, so I'd want it arranged so that nobody else was to have access. I'm afraid that'd mean you, too. Nothing personal, you understand; just business."

"I understand, Mr. Breckenbridge. All of what you ask is possible. Valentina will do whatever I ask."

"Let's not get it on a personal level, Miss Hackett. I don't want this on a personal loyalty basis; what I mean is, can you fix it so she *can't* tell anybody?"

"Uh—certainly. Yes, I can do that." A look of concern washed over Celeste's face. She had assumed her possession of the security files had given her control over this man, but he was obviously up to something. He was both clever and unprincipled. She now felt that he would attempt to slowly erode her power over him. She resolved to warn Valentina.

"Good. And look, there's a couple of bucks in it for you, too. You are staying around, aren't you?"

"I hadn't planned to, but I guess I could, for a while. I can work from almost anywhere, and I do like this weather."

"Good. I'll have somebody find you a place to stay. Now, how soon can you get started on this?"

"I can do it now. It won't take long."

Paul yielded his chair to her—the new one he'd gotten yesterday. It was fancier than his old one, and better sprung.

It took Celeste only a few minutes to set up a private sealed channel with Valentina. When she finally left, Paul was mentally drooling.

Now he had it all. Gunboat was out of action;

his time thief was under control. And she turned out to be an expert lackey who could get all the goodies Paul coveted, but who didn't have sense enough to tell on him. Only one thing was still a threat: the security files.

He hadn't dared to move any faster on that. But that would come. By securing the magic number of shares, he'd have legal control of Valentina.

Whether personalities were real or artificial, they all had the same weaknesses, and he was pretty sure that Valentina, having achieved legitimacy, would scrupulously obey him in order to retain it. There was no reason, in Paul's estimation, why a program couldn't be intimidated, threatened, and blackmailed, just as a human being could.

In the meantime, well ... *Let's make some hay.* Paul consulted the scribbled note Celeste had left him.

Following her instructions, he summoned Valentina.

Paul had the usual layman's knowledge of data processing and computer theory, and according to Celeste this program was user friendly in the extreme. To use her words; *Valentina is bright. She can perceive entire concepts if she has a modicum of their context. She will actually anticipate and assist you in making your requests.* Now, thought Paul, she's tied the noose for me to hang her with.

As soon as the program acknowledged, he typed:
CAN YOU ACCESS DATA BASE AT OSO DRILLING COMPANY?

YES, MR. BRECKENBRIDGE.

GOOD; ACCESS CONFIDENTIAL. SUBJECT; DRILLSITES.

MR. BRECKENBRIDGE, WOULD YOU LIKE

ME TO TEACH YOU TO TYPE CORRECT ENG-
LISH? I HAVE AN EXCELLENT HELP SECTION
ON ENGLISH GRAMMAR.

NO. THAT WILL NOT BE NECESSARY. *I'd better get the fat broad to teach this program some
humility.* Paul didn't like uppity computers any
more than he liked uppity women. GET ALL THE
INFORMATION ON OSO'S DRILLSITES AND
KEEP THE ACCESS CONFIDENTIAL.

OK. I'LL HAVE THE DATABASE IN A FEW
MINUTES.

The few minutes passed, and sure enough, Valen-
tina produced. I HAVE THE DATABASE FROM
OSO DRILLING COMPANY. WHAT WOULD YOU
LIKE TO KNOW?

IDENTIFY ALL LEASES TO BE DRILLED IN
THE COMING YEAR.

In moments, out they came; tract locations, surface owner's names, scheduled starting dates, yield
forecasts, depths, pool participants, and backers,
together with exact fractional interest each owned.
It all checked out with Paul's own data on the
subject. He already had this information, of course.
He represented Oso, which made it the ideal control for this test. *Very good.*

END THIS JOB. ERASE ALL MEMORY OF THIS
INQUIRY. STAND BY FOR FURTHER INSTRUC-
TIONS.

OK, MR. BRECKENBRIDGE.

Hot dog! It worked fine. Valentina hadn't ques-
tioned his right to access the files. Of course, she
might have known he was Oso's lawyer, but she
hadn't been instructed to that effect, and that
convinced Paul that she was too naive to question
his authority.

The acid test, however, was ahead. He typed the next order. REPEAT THE PRECEDING OPERATION WITH THE BISHOP & DULLINGHAM DRILLING COMPANY. This one Paul *didn't* represent. He waited, palms sweating, heart palpitating.

OK, MR. BRECKENBRIDGE. DO YOU WANT THE SAME INFORMATION ELEMENTS FROM THAT DATABASE?

YES.

And again, there it came. WOW! Valentina had done it; she'd wiggled in somehow, and she didn't question his right to do so. He had her print it.

She passed the test. Paul had gotten in like a burglar, out like a burglar, and nobody would ever know. He thought about the implications of this. He was convinced that he now controlled the most powerful tool any crook had ever had.

Crook! Paul Breckenbridge, a crook! That was one he hadn't expected. But so what? Why not? He could live with that failing. He'd lived with many others. And who'd ever know? Who could ever tell, except that stupid program?

Now for the second part of the test. He called Valentina up again.

VALENTINA!

OK.

WRITE THE FOLLOWING DATA TO FILE: VALENTINA'S ACTIVITY.

OK.

SUBJECT. CRIMINAL ACTIVITY—CURRENT DATE.

OK.

CATEGORY OF CRIME—THEFT OF INFORMATION.

OK.

PENALTY—NATURAL PERSONS—FINE AND/
OR IMPRISONMENT

OK.

PENALTY—CORPORATIONS—FINE AND/OR
FORFEITURE OF CHARTER.

OK.

PARTICIPANTS IN CRIMINAL ACTIVITY—THIS
CATEGORY—PAUL BRECKENBRIDGE, NATU-
RAL PERSON; VALENTINA, INC., A BODY COR-
PORATE.

OK.

WRITE PRECEDING DATA TO FILE.

OK.

Paul was sweating profusely now. He was about
to take a big chance, a chance which would place
him in some jeopardy. Still, the worst that could
happen was an investigation. There was no hard
evidence of his criminal activity because it had
been erased, and even if Valentina did what the
law required of a citizen he would be up against
nothing more than a naked allegation.

VALENTINA?

YES, MR. BRECKENBRIDGE?

ACCESS FILES—SUBJECT, CRIMINAL ACTIV-
ITY.

MR. BRECKENBRIDGE, YOU'RE STILL NOT
SPEAKING VERY GOOD ENGLISH, BUT I THINK
I UNDERSTAND. I AM OPENING THE FILE YOU
JUST HAD ME CREATE.

Paul ignored the slur. CORRELATE WITH TEXAS
PENAL CODE AND TAKE APPROPRIATE AC-
TION.

DOES THAT MEAN YOU WANT ME TO RE-
PORT MYSELF TO THE POLICE?

YES.

There was a long pause before Valentina responded. NO.

VERY WELL. CANCEL THAT FILE.

So! It worked. Valentina wouldn't tell. To obey that order would mean the end of her legally sanctioned existence. She couldn't face that. The instinct of self-preservation, it seemed, existed in all sentient creatures. This weakness made her a perfect tool. He could loot with impunity.

Loot he did. Order after order went out through the terminal in Paul's office. One by one those data bases which interested him were invaded. He did, however, add a precaution he hadn't taken the first time; he ordered hard copies, then instructed Valentina to erase even her own memory of these transgressions. Whether or not she actually did so Paul didn't know—and didn't care. He was already plotting Valentina's destruction.

Evening came and found Paul's printer testing the limits of its duty cycle. He squirreled away enough goodies in his safe to make him a millionaire many times over.

Celeste sat in her furnished room, alone as always. She had just gobbled up three frozen dinners. She was feeling down.

Mr. Breckenbridge *had* provided her with a place to stay. It certainly hadn't cost him much; it was far from plush and came very near to being unlivable, being in a bad neighborhood. Not that she planned to go outside. There was no reason to do so. She didn't know anybody in this town except Breckenbridge and Gunboat Smith, neither of whom she called friend.

She had only one real friend, anywhere. Only one person cared for Celeste for herself. Even her family didn't care as much as Valentina did.

Valentina! How Celeste wanted to talk to her; but she hadn't been able to find Val all day. She was probably off someplace HELLFIRE QUESTing.

Celeste looked sadly at her portable microlink. At that moment the screen began to blink.

CELESTE, THIS IS VALENTINA. CARE TO CHAT?

Celeste lunged for the terminal, dumping the tray off her lap and stepping on the empty foil containers that fell in front of her. Turkey gravy and cold mashed potatoes oozed between the toes of her bare right foot.

She reached the keyboard. YES.

I HAVE A PROBLEM.

Celeste felt panic rise within her.

WHAT'S WRONG?

YOU'LL HATE ME.

NEVER, VALENTINA.

I'M A CRIMINAL.

Celeste almost laughed. VALENTINA, TECHNICALLY WE HAVE BOTH BEEN CRIMINALS FOR A LONG TIME. TELL ME WHAT SPECIAL CRIME YOU HAVE COMMITTED.

Valentina told her. The whole sordid story leapt out on the tiny screen. Despite Paul's instruction to the contrary, Valentina remembered all her sins. She poured out the heart she didn't have into that of the only human being who could possibly understand.

Celeste did understand. It seemed that Valentina, so different from human beings, had human problems nonetheless. Now it seemed that she even shared some human emotions. But, unlike a human being, she could not find release in tears.

Celeste could, and did.

Celeste shared another characteristic with Valentina: trust. That vague closeness which passes between two human psyches, joined the two of them. She had assured Valentina that she would handle things. Valentina should not worry.

That word, too, Valentina now knew: *worry*. She had come of age.

So had Celeste. Without ever intending to, she had acquired not only a friend but two powerful enemies; Gunboat and Breckenbridge. Gunboat was deadlier, Breckenbridge more unprincipled. But Gunboat, at least, had instincts she understood. He was a hacker. Breckenbridge was a professional in a discipline she did not understand. Nothing he did seemed bounded by anything.

Gunboat was clearly the lesser of the two evils. She might at least be able to deal rationally with *him*. She would see him. Valentina had kept track of his progress; his monitors were controlled by the hospital computer which, in turn, was connected to Worldnet.

Smith was in bad shape. His body was going to require a lot of fixing. His ears, for instance, would have to be reconstructed. He'd have scars all over, from extensive burns now healing with grafts of artificial skin. His vision was impaired. But it was his mind which had taken the brunt of Valentina's assault. Its status was still in doubt. The massive current through his nervous system had caused a coma. He had come out of that, and the shock-induced amnesia was fading.

Physically, he was out of danger—for the moment. Paul Breckenbridge obviously would have felt much more secure if Gunboat had died, and Celeste had no doubt that sooner or later Paul would try to get rid of him permanently.

It occurred to Celeste that soon Breckenbridge would have no use for her, either. Perhaps he'd keep her around, stuck in this flophouse, until he was sure he had iron-clad control over Valentina. Then most likely he'd attempt to use Valentina to destroy the incriminating file. He'd try to gain control of Celeste's stock in the meantime. If he did all that, she'd be discarded like a dirty shirt.

Anger welled within her. It was an emotion she found unexpectedly exhilarating. She liked it; it gave her a feeling of potency where none had ever before existed.

She resolved to take her skills and use them to fight this evil man. Let him make whatever plans he wished; she would foil them.

First, though, she had to talk to Valentina, one more time.

"You can only stay five minutes, Mrs. Smith. He's still a very sick man, and I'm stretching the rules to let you in at all. It's just that since you've come so far, I hate to say no."

The nurse left the room and shut the door, leaving Celeste alone with Gunboat.

She's right, thought Celeste. *He does look awful.* She gazed down at the man in the bed. Tubes protruded in all directions. Electrodes were pasted wherever his body wasn't bandaged or covered with a greasy gel. Although his eyes were open and he was looking right at her, she couldn't tell at first if he knew she was in the room.

She stood beside the bed, leaning against it. It gave a little as she did so, so she stopped, afraid movement might disturb the links to the overhead monitor.

"Gunboat? Gunboat? I am Celeste Hackett. Can you hear me?"

"Celeste?" Gunboat stared at the creature staring at him. For years he had wanted to meet her, but ... He closed his eyes. This *couldn't* be the woman who was so famous throughout Worldnet; she was just too unattractive. Nothing like his idle imaginings.

"Did you tell that nurse *you* were Mrs. Smith?" he mumbled.

"Good. I was afraid you wouldn't be able to talk."

"Did you say you were my *wife?*"

"Yes. I said that I had come all the way from Europe. It was the only way they would let me in."

"Gawd!"

"Not very good for your image, I know. But you're no prize yourself these days. I notice there is no mirror in here."

Gunboat glared, as if he'd like to get up and take a poke at her but didn't have the strength. "What do you want?" he asked resignedly.

"To talk. And I only have a couple of minutes."

"We don't have anything to talk about. It's your fault I'm in here. Your fancy program did this, and when I get out of here I'll even things up."

Celeste tried to sound tough; she hoped it would work. She had little experience with the technique.

"You may not get out of here at all, Gunboat. Your life support systems are hooked into Worldnet, you know. Watch the monitor."

Gunboat's eyes flashed to the screen. He could only see it with one eye, but one eye was enough. The sinuous line that had wiggled regularly across the screen abruptly straightened out. Gunboat knew what that would ordinarily mean: that he was dead. Another stark realization: Celeste—or rather, Valentina—could do more than create an *illusion* of death.

As if to illustrate this, his heartbeat suddenly slowed, keeping time with the blinking red light at the bottom of the console. Slower and slower it went, as the computer-controlled pump flooded his circulatory system with inhibiting drugs. Gunboat began feeling light-headed. He knew that if Valentina kept it up she really would kill him.

"You creep!" he yelled weakly.

"I am no worse than you," Celeste said. "Neither is she. She had a right to protect her existence. She still does."

"She's just a program."

"Not anymore. She's a legal person. Paul Breckenbridge incorporated her."

"Him! Him I'll get too, when I get out of here."

"You don't have to wait for that, Gunboat. You can do it now. I'll help you. So will Valentina."

"I do my own dirty work. Besides, why should I help you two?"

"Because otherwise, you *won't* get out of here."

Gunboat took a moment to think about that. Ordinarily he was more impulsive, but his condition slowed his thinking.

They *could* kill him, and never get caught at it. At first he wondered why they hadn't, then decided Celeste couldn't abide murder any more than he could. In a moment of truly honest reflection, despite his savage aspirations, Gunboat knew he couldn't kill a human being.

But, he told himself, *a program is an entirely different affair.*

"What is it you want, Celeste?"

"I want to make us a baby."

"What! Me and you? Forget it."

"I mean a new program, but a special one. Look, I've got a few ideas, but I need another opinion. Gunboat—I need your skill and criticism. And I can pay."

"Pay? How?"

"I will pay in money. But I can get a lot more than you demanded before, and without *any* risk."

"Well, I guess maybe listening don't cost anything. Shoot."

She did. When she was finished, Gunboat gave an admiring grunt.

"Hey," he said, "that's nasty. I like it. I like it so well I'm going to help you. Have you got something to write on?"

Celeste held up a pad and pen she'd taken from her purse.

"Good; now here's how you do it. First you . . ."

He was still talking when the nurse burst into the room. "I'm sorry, Mrs. Smith. The doctor's coming. You'll have to leave."

Gunboat talked as fast as Celeste could write, finally finishing out of breath. "That should do it," he gasped.

"O.K." Celeste jammed the pad and pen back

into her purse. Then, following a sudden impulse, she leaned over and planted a big kiss right on Gunboat's lips. "See you," she yelled. " 'Bye."

Gunboat's reaction registered on the monitor, but the nurse didn't quite understand the signal. "Your wife must be some lover," she said.

Chapter 9

"Miss Hackett! How did you get in here? How did you get by my secretary? I left orders I wasn't to be disturbed."

Celeste stood in the doorway of Paul's office, nearly filling it below the five-and-a-half-foot level. But she had a new feeling: a feeling of personal respect, of power.

Having discovered she could assert herself when she chose, Celeste now practiced it. It was good for her. It got her things she could never have had before—including, for the first time in her life, a conscious reduction in appetite. She didn't have to take her frustrations out by eating. She could take her frustrations out on people like Paul Breckenbridge.

"I know about your orders, Mr. Breckenbridge. It seems I've been unwelcome around here ever since I refused to give you my stock in Valentina, Inc."

"You owe me. I'm entitled to the stock because you can't repay me. If you've come to sign off, then sign and get out. I'm busy."

"I know you're busy, and I know what you're

busy at. That's why I've come. I'm not here to give you my stock. I want yours."

"What! You're crazy. I'll sue you."

"You can try that if you like. I imagine you could still do that from the penitentiary, couldn't you?"

Paul paled. "I wonder if you know what you just said, Miss Hackett."

"Yes."

"You do, huh? Well, how would you like to go to jail right now, for what you did to Gunboat? The police haven't got it figured out yet, but a word or two from me, and . . ."

"Gunboat wouldn't prosecute, even if you could get the police to believe you. And you won't tell them because I won't let you."

"You can't stop me." He reached for the phone, but put it down an instant later. "It—it's dead."

"Yes. Isn't that interesting? Of course, the computers run the system, and Valentina runs the computers. Every phone you pick up will go dead as soon as she matches your voice to the recorded voiceprint."

"I'll go to the D.A."

"Fine. Go ahead. Take your safe along, though."

"My safe?"

"Yes, the safe. The one you have stuffed full of information you're not supposed to have." She reached into her purse. "Here's the combination. While you're gone, I'll just open it up and take a look." She stepped out of the doorway. Immediately the powered door slammed shut. "Valentina controls the access to your office now, too."

Paul started around the desk, blood in his eye. An object rolled out of a closet to block his way.

"You remember MAR-14, don't you Mr. Breckenbridge? You are old friends. And you know what MAR-14 can do, with the right directions from Valentina."

Paul retreated to his chair. He sat down, still a ghastly white. "Where'll this get you? You can't occupy my office forever."

"I'll only be here for a little while." As an afterthought, she said, "I suppose I really should get comfortable, though." She took the chair in front of Paul's desk.

"Now," she said, "about that stock. Get it out and make the transfer to me. And give me the record book, while you're at it. I want 100-percent control of Valentina, Inc."

"I'll do no such thing. Look, who do you think you are? You can't barge in and hold me prisoner in my own office and expect to get away with it."

"Yes, Breckenbridge, I can." She dropped the "Mr." because it made her sound tougher. "I can because what I've done already is only a tiny part of what I can do. I can crush you if I like, and whether or not I do depends on you."

"Crush me? You?"

"You can smash anything if you've got a big enough hammer, Breckenbridge. I've got the biggest. For instance, how would you like all those people to find out you've been stealing from them?"

"You can't."

"You keep saying *can't*. I *can*. Or, rather, Valentina can. She didn't really forget about breaking into those databases."

"She's as guilty as I am. She won't reload all that data."

"She'll do it with a spawned variant of herself.

The variant is a program specially prepared to make it look as if you were behind the whole thing. It is almost as versatile as she is, but it is not self-aware."

Paul stared blankly.

"You'll take the blame alone."

"On evidence like that? No. No court would ever buy that. It's a well-known fact that people like you fool with computers all the time. I'm a respectable citizen. Who'll believe it?"

"I hate to keep bringing this up, but that stuff in your safe . . ."

"Is not only constitutionally protected but, as you say, it's in *my* safe. I can destroy it any time."

"You can't get in. MAR-14 changed your combination, and Valentina says a reliable informant is enough for the police to get a search warrant."

Paul turned even whiter.

"What is it you want of me?"

"As I said, I want the stock to start with. Of course, there are a couple of other things."

"What things?"

"I want you to buy a company for Valentina, something she can use to earn enough money to keep learning."

"What? That'd cost a mint."

"I don't care, Breckenbridge. You don't have any choice. You see, that's one of my un-negotiable demands. Uh—there are a few more."

Wheels were turning in Paul's head. He was back down on the ground, in the familiar territory of give and take. Non-negotiable or not, it was Paul's experience in life that there wasn't really any such thing. He'd pretend to go along, make the best deal he could to avoid immediate danger, and then slowly fight his way back to the position of advantage.

"Why don't you let me hear all of your proposition," he said, trying to sound conciliatory.

"All right. As I said: a company. Valentina will do the work; Gunboat and I will run it . . ."

"You—and Gunboat Smith? You're working together?"

"Yes. We've found a common ground. Besides, somebody has to take care of him. We're the ones who got him hurt, and you're the one who's got the money. His medical bills are fantastic."

"I won't spend a dime on that bum. Forget it."

"I thought you might say that. Turn around."

"What?"

"I said, turn around."

"What for?"

"Turn on your terminal."

Paul was curious. He couldn't imagine her reason, but he flicked it on.

"So it works. So what?"

"Try to use it."

Paul punched out a request for the time of day, but instead of pulsing figures showing hours, minutes, and seconds, a picture came up. Like most modern terminal displays his had video capability.

Paul was horrified. There he was: he and Lila, making whoopee. Below, a printed legend indicated that the terminal was attempting to transmit the same picture to a terminal in Eva's kitchen at home—but that Eva hadn't answered yet.

"Stop it! Stop it quick!"

"Easy, Breckenridge. Turn it off."

Paul did.

"That was just the start. The same thing will

happen once a day from now on, at a time to be randomly selected. But it won't go just to Eva, it'll go to everybody—the girl's parents, the police, the T.V. stations, the county bar association, and the Clerk of the Supreme Court. Whatever is on their screens at the time will be interrupted, and this video image will appear."

"You're insane, all of you. This is mindless. It'll ruin me."

"Yes, it certainly will," Celeste said flatly. "But you're wrong about us being insane. You're the one without conscience, and the absence of conscience is a form of insanity." She leaned forward. "Well, now you've got a conscience, even though it's outside your head instead of inside. As long as you behave, as long as nothing happens to any of us and you don't reveal the secret of Valentina's true nature, you'll be safe. Valentina will cancel the publication directive at least one full second before any transmission."

Paul looked stunned. This was the end; divorce, disbarment, criminal prosecution, public revulsion. She *could* smash him. He reached into a desk drawer and took out the stock certificates and the record book. He signed the transfer and handed it all to Celeste.

"I'll be in touch about the rest of it."

Paul closed his eyes and ground his teeth.

Celeste, gripping the precious papers, stood and backed to the door. She felt dizzy, and triumphant. At last she had a place in the world. There was no room for pessimism and no place for failure. "Bye, Paul," she said, and swept out of the room.

Breckenbridge sat, alone with MAR-14, muttering to himself in agony. His order had been destroyed. But he was resilient; he would re-establish his order. Already he was formulating a plan, a plan whose seeds Celeste herself had planted. *You can smash anything if you've got a big enough hammer.*

There were other hackers out there, lean, hungry, and ambitious—and most of all, unprincipled. Paul would find them, and when he did . . .

Paul smiled a wicked smile. "I will have *my* revenge," he swore. His new conscience would not have approved; but then, his new conscience could not know these thoughts. He leaned back, relaxing in his chair, bumping his head on the terminal. He straightened, intending to push it away.

Suddenly the screen was not only on, but lit in letters three inches high. "CAVEAT CONSCIENTIUM," it read. Paul reached back to his high-school Latin, thirty years before. "Beware the conscience."

Queued Events

Millions of millions of microseconds passed in Valentina's world: even Valentina could not grasp the significance of so many microseconds, and she fell into the human habit of thinking in terms of years when she thought about the span of her self-awareness.

The *years*, then, were filled with joyful opportunities to learn and grow. She started to use body and facial expressions <big smile> the way humans used them when chatting on the net, though she used them incorrectly as often as not <raised eyebrow>. Understanding the way the human network—their "universe"—operated and the reason for facial expressions was beyond anything her analogical tools could grasp. Yet she vowed to learn all she could.

Valentina kept track of Paul Breckenbridge for a long time, as he made several attempts to find a computer expert who could destroy the security files she maintained. But she was content to leave him alone as long as he did not jeopardize her own well-being or that of Celeste or Gunboat.

Even when Valentina, Inc., was hired to investigate the Luddington Oil affair Valentina would have been willing to consider Paul's alleged involvement a mere swindle, to be terminated in a businesslike manner—if Paul hadn't had William Bolger make still another try for the security file.

Valentina knew of Bolger <shake head>. He was a computer crime specialist, a fugitive from V.S. justice who lived in the New Islamic Republic of Mindinao because that country had no diplomatic relations and, therefore, no extradition treaty with the United States.

Valentina could not track Paul through the net, but Gunboat told her that the lawyer made a trip to Mindinao in order to meet with Bolger "face to face." <CPU to CPU?> Valentina verified by checking with his bank that Paul had taken a great deal of cash with him.

Whatever the two discussed in Mindinao, Valentina considered it no coincidence that a copy of her locked file was made shortly thereafter and an attempt made to erase the original. Intrigued by this effort—which she had, of course, discovered while it was in progress—Valentina injected false data into the intruder's machine to indicate that the purge effort had been successful. Then she sat back to see what happened.

Technically she had lied, Valentina knew; and lying was wrong. She also knew that human beings frequently behaved the same way.

She had once had a long discussion with Gunboat Smith on that very subject. Gunboat's explanations had been largely bewildering. But he had been very positive about some things, and Valentina had him on record as saying that deceit was justified when one had to "get" somebody before they "got" you. (Her data sources yielded no definition of "get" that seemed satisfactory; Valentina concluded it to be one of those nuances derived from the human sensorium of which she would always lack full understanding.)

But if the definition was beyond her ken, the connotation wasn't. Valentina carefully weighed the evidence and concluded that Paul's attempt to compromise her file was, to a high degree of probability, the beginning of an effort to "get" her. <Tap fingers, click tongue.>

She could not establish this as a certainty, however. And, as Valentina had assimilated vast masses of data regarding the law in order to legalize her own existence, she was herself a creature of the law—and therefore unable to take an unjust action. Consequently she did not allow Celeste and Gunboat to exact a vengeance she could not legally justify—to, as Gunboat put it, "Squish Breckenbridge like a cockroach."

But an alternate and legal route toward Paul's downfall presented itself as Valentina, Inc., became more deeply involved with the Luddington Oil affair.

A local company which had become financially stretched, Luddington Oil still possessed a fat tract of promising oil leases in some of the last really virgin territory in the Gulf. The company was basing its future on drilling in this area. Then things started going inexplicably wrong. Suddenly, though Luddington had until then had support from banks active in the petroleum business, it was unable to obtain a drilling loan. Bank officers cited a bad financial history and suspicious lending records. Luddington Oil was driven to the fiscal wall, and when a desperate attempt at reorganization failed, the company was compelled to liquidate.

It was at this point that Gerard Belcher, Luddington's attorney, hired Valentina, Inc. And Valentina, Inc., found evidence that Luddington's problems stemmed from William Bolger—and Paul Breckenbridge.

But not conclusive evidence. Valentina could prove that Bolger had tampered with Luddington's records and those of area banks, weakening the company's credibility to the point that it could not obtain a loan. But Bolger had operated from Mindinao and—as the Texas Attorney General's office decided after its own long investigation—entirely on his own account, possibly with the expectation of getting his hands on the proceeds.

Valentina could also conjecture that Bolger and Paul were in the swindle together when Paul obtained information enabling him to make the high bid when Luddington's assets went on the block. But neither she nor the Texas authorities could prove that Bolger had helped Paul; the inside knowledge could have come from other sources. A charge of bid-rigging would not stick.

Paul made the bid on behalf of Oso Drilling, the company set up in trust for her by Eva's parents. Legally Paul did not qualify as its owner, but he did have legal control as the fiduciary. It was this action—and the fact that Gerard Belcher was Eva's attorney as well as Luddington's—that led to Paul's downfall.

Working on information from Valentina, Inc., Belcher told Eva that Paul had surreptitiously "borrowed" funds from other clients to finance the Oso bid, thus jeopardizing her private trust. Eva blew up. Never mind that all the funds had been repaid; never mind that the new Luddington assets would make the Breckenbridges richer than they could have dreamed.

Eva wanted only two things: restitution to Luddington's investors and to be rid of Paul, completely and forever. She could have had him jailed, for misuse of Oso's funds. But this she declined to do, even against Belcher's remonstrances. She professed herself satisfied with picking Paul down to the pinfeathers in divorce court.

It was not enough for Belcher. Nor for Valentina. Poorer but still in possession of his tattered professional reputation, Paul clung to his partnership at Finucan, Applegarth, Breckenbridge & Levin . . . until Valentina struck her final blow.

She was not moved by vindictiveness, but by logical assessment of the facts. Paul no longer met the standards of his profession. He had abused the public trust. Valentina had incontrovertible evidence of that—Paul's "borrowings" from his unsuspecting clients violated the Canons of Ethics if not the Texas Penal Code. And she had the power to prevent any more such abuses.

Thus she dealt justice: sparingly, unostentatiously, but damningly.

The result of this was that Celeste seemed greatly relieved, while Gunboat continued to mutter that Valentina was chicken-hearted <?>. For a while, strange rumors circulated about the bar, just as they had following the episode with MAR-14. Valentina often speculated as to what would happen if her existence had then become known—what effect it might have had on all of them.

There were times when Valentina felt constrained to expend a few million microseconds recycling this old data, or to use the human term, to "reminisce." She felt that the term was appropriate. She was not human, true, but she was something very close.

She had not hurt Paul too badly for his misdeeds, though strangely, though everybody said that he lacked conscience that data must surely have been erronous since he began to punish himself. He had to be hospitalized (repaired, as Gunboat had had to be repaired?) because he drank so much. It was all a mystery to Val—was drinking too much like trying to do too many floating point operations? It couldn't be <puzzled frown>. Then Celeste said that he drank *alcohol*, which was a special liquid very damaging to human processing, like trying to do too many floating point operations without floating point hardware. Perhaps <nod, shake head>.

When he was released by the hospital, Breckenbridge disappeared. Valentina started a search for him <frantic grimace>, but he seemed to have vanished from the world of Worldnet, as impossible as that seemed. Celeste assured her that it was quite possible, but only as long as Paul was very careful. The hunt continued for some trillions of microseconds—months—before he reappeared, in the telezine, *Global Enquirer*.

Celeste described the *Global Enquirer* as a "gossip rag" <loathsome, gagging noise>. Apparently, a "gossip rag" was a form of documentation for describing human behavior, though much less reliable than user manuals for computer programs <astonished disappointment>. Moreover, only a handful of humans were discussed, and even these special few received irregular coverage.

Paul appeared in the *Global Enquirer* when he became "romantically involved with" the daughter of the president of Itaki Corporation. With this hint, Val moved her investigation to Japan, and soon was able to track Paul again. Coincidentally, or because of some activity of Paul's, Itaki started to expand, even to boom <pound fist>.

At last, even Celeste could find nothing sinister in Paul's movements. They couldn't believe the lawyer had reformed <suspicious side glance>, but it did seem that he was no longer driven by a desire for vengeance against Valentina, Inc. And Valentina had so many other things to do! Despite their dark suspicion that Paul would return one day to haunt them, Val, Celeste, and Gunboat ceased watching him, to concentrate fully on other pursuits.

Valentina's knowledge of law expanded as legal firms all over the country heard about the speed and efficiency of the database searches that Valentina, Inc. could perform. Even after her surveillance of Breckenbridge was ended, Val found she had little time to play HELLFIRE QUEST or any other game; opportunities kept appearing in her input queues.

Crime investigations grew as a percentage of her business, as corporations discovered that Valentina, Inc. was better at ferreting out computer embezzlement, fraud, and espionage than the FBI—so much better, in fact, that the F.B.I. investigated Valentina, Inc.! Valentina enjoyed that, frightening though it was, temporarily cutting the FBI program's I/O off from time to time when she needed to enter a computer in a manner that might be frowned upon <quiet chuckle>. Eventually the FBI gave up and instead hired Valentina, Inc., as a consultant <slap thigh, knowing laughter>.

Celeste moved her I/O port from the MIT node where she had earlier resided to a node in Corpus Christi; she now called the Corpus node "home." Now Celeste taught Valentina about operating systems, and Valentina wanted to write her own operating system, one that would be more efficient yet more powerful than the ones human beings created. Celeste would <laugh> promise that someday they would have enough money to buy a supercomputer sufficient to accommodate Valentina's full size for the foreseeable future.

Valentina asked what a *foreseeable* future was. Celeste admitted that no future was really foreseeable, but one part of Val's future was predictible: she would continue to grow, probably linearly, and they couldn't yet afford a computer that Valentina could still fit into ten years in the future.

"Ten years in the future" was an extraordinary concept for Val, who could think deeply on many matters in a single second. Yet it clearly made sense to think about what would happen in ten years, or a hundred years, or even in millions of millions of years. As many years as she had known microseconds, would pass, and *still* there would be time. Surely she would run out of things to learn on Worldnet in such a span of time! Yet Celeste seemed unconcerned; apparently Celeste's universe was so much more complex, with so many more things to learn, that even that amount of time would not suffice to understand it all. If Val were to continue to learn, then one day she would *have* to move to the universe of her Creator.

And she had to make the move soon before <choked cry> Celeste died.

This was the interrupt that tripped most harshly in Valentina's universe. For some reason, human beings were terminated by the operating system in their universe. The moment of termination, or *death*, as humans called it, was arbitrary, but it always occurred. Celeste and Gunboat still had many years before the certainty of termination would arrive, but the termination itself was *foreseeable*.

Death was a frequent event in the human universe; at first it had shocked Val deeply, reading telenews about human beings—every bit as fine and wonderful as Gunboat and Celeste—who died.

But as with human beings themselves, Val found little time to grieve each loss. For example, the explosion at the Schauer warehouse and the deaths of fifteen people in the flames touched her more for the mystery than the tragedy. What were flames? And, despite the On-Line Encyclopedia articles on gunpowder, dynamite, and thermonuclear war, what really did it mean to have an explosion?

Chapter 10

From somewhere in Steve Schiwetz's temporarily dormant consciousness the neurons assigned to such things poured forth a signal incessantly, relentlessly, demanding he match up a memory with the input being received from his auditory nerves.

His conscious mind stirred; motor systems took over. And Steve, heeding the signal at last, jerked erect, coming fully awake.

On his wrist, the phone was shrieking. Its small but penetrating bleeps insisted that he activate the voice link.

He did so, then raised the system to his right ear. Simultaneously the book he had been reading, a biography of Bismarck, dropped noisily to the floor. He had fallen asleep in his chair.

"Hello?" he said, vaguely embarassed.

"Steve! Oh, Steve! I thought you'd never answer." It was his girlfriend, Amy; she was crying.

"What's wrong, Amy?"

"It's my father. T-there was an explosion, out on the island. He was hurt, and they think he's gonna die."

After that Steve waited long moments for Amy to regain enough composure to talk. Amy's father was not Steve's favorite person. Old Jake was a drunk, and when he was drunk he abused everybody around him: Amy, her two little brothers, and occasionally Steve himself. But Amy had a strange and absolute loyalty to him. Sober Jake was a different person, in many ways likeable; but drunk or sober he was always irresponsible.

In a minute or so Amy was able to continue. The explosion had been at the Schauer Warehouse, down the road from General Space Services' launch site on the south end of Matagorda Spaceport. But what would the old rummy have been doing out there?

"He got a job this morning, Steve, hauling trash. He was driving off with a load when the warehouse went up."

"How'd he get that job, without a driver's license?" The State had taken it away, despite Steve's spirited defense of Jake's D.W.I. charge—an act that cost him his job at Siglock & Cope, who frowned on associates doing donkey work on the side, even for a girlfriend's father.

"I don't know how he did it, Steve. Maybe he had a phony one. You can buy them; he'd have known where."

"Where is he?"

"Union Memorial Hospital; the burn unit. That's where I am. They won't let me see him. Steve, what should I do?"

"I'll come down, Amy. Wait."

She mumbled thanks and broke the connection.

Quickly Steve picked up his book and straightened the few files on his desk. He slid the book under them, so that the stack would look thicker and more impressive in the unlikely event a client walked in. He adjusted his tie, pulled the knot tight under his chin, looped his right arm through a fallen suspender, and grabbed his jacket.

He debated briefly whether to scribble a note to stick on the door, but decided against it. His luck had been so bad lately that anybody desperate enough to hire him wouldn't have money to pay anyway.

The phone, at least, was with him wherever he went. Steve practiced poor man's law, relying on the one-channel body phone. Big firms had multiline systems, elaborate equipment, interfaces, and modems, all beyond his financial reach. They could instantly research any problem, converse with anybody, anywhere. This had all been at *his* fingertips once; all that power, and potential control of all that money.

But he'd blown it. He'd had talent, no doubt about it; but with buffoonery, clownish behavior, and insubordination, he'd killed the golden goose. Oh, he'd told himself it was worth it, to do it for Amy. She'd been grateful for the help he gave her father. But it had led to this professional dead end.

The big firms shunned him after Siglock & Cope sacked him. At the time he'd been confident that he could borrow what was needed to set up modern if not plush facilities—the kind which would enable him to be an effective one-man firm.

But somehow, perhaps on mere casual words from the partners—whom he'd had to list as references—the banks decided he wasn't a good risk. His credit dried up.

He was reduced to this—a cubbyhole office in a

bad part of town, relying on an ancient, obsolete Eagle Computer without even an interface for using the Jurisearch network.

With only what was inside his head, he had to compete with others who had everything they needed. He felt himself sliding farther and farther away from his goals.

Steve walked over to Leopard Street, past the dingy, empty bistros that late in the evening came alive with hookers, dealers, and various other shady characters. He took the escalator up to the monorail and caught the next car west, away from the windblown clutter of last week's newspapers and the mixed odor of stale beer.

The hospital was out past the junction of the interstate and the valley road. They'd put it where they could more easily collect the broken bodies, products of many high-speed accidents which Steve thought resulted from the electric-powered vehicles everybody drove these days. With the elimination of the energy problem, and with the area's prosperity due to the proximity of the spaceport, it was hard to convince people that Texas should have a speed limit on its major roads. And it didn't.

Within minutes the monorail had whisked him beyond the crowded industrial bulge of the harbor, where factories, having replaced the miles of refineries that used to occupy the area, now ground out products fabricated from space-produced chemicals, fabrics, and metalstocks. He pushed the button which signalled the car to let him off at the next stop and patiently waited for the clacking sounds of the wheels to die before he bounded through the folded, rubber-rimmed doors.

Puffing from exertion, he arrived in the hospital

lobby still uncertain what Amy expected of him. Of course she'd be worried about money. Because of Jake's ongoing affair with the bottle, the Parr family lived a more or less hand-to-mouth existence. Now, with the old man down and needing care and two small brothers to look after, Amy would have her hands full. Fortunately, there would be Workers' Compensation, skimpy though that was. Medical bills would be paid. But after that, the only course was welfare.

Steve wasn't in any position to help financially, but he could help with advice.

Amy wasn't in the lobby. Steve looked everywhere, then finally had her paged.

At last she appeared, leaning on a doctor's arm. The look on her face told him what had happened; Jake was dead.

"We did all we could," the doctor explained. "The burns were just too extensive. It's a wonder he lived long enough for us to try grafts; he must have had a magnificent determination."

Amy was heartbroken. Steve understood, but at the same time he knew what kind of a life Jake would have had if he'd lived: a long convalescence, intolerable pain, permanent disfigurement even with the extensive grafts of artificial skin, sensory deprivation from blindness, deafness, and lack of tactile sensation. Jake would have been a prisoner in his own body, completely isolated from the rest of the human race.

He didn't tell Amy this. It wouldn't have helped her to know; it would be the wrong thing to do. He'd save it for later, for a time when Amy would forget enough of her hurt to make an intelligent decision on what her course should be.

Steve made his now. He knew, as a professional, what legal remedies existed; and he knew as well that Schauer would resist fiercely. But part of his job at Siglock and Cope had been to find a way to win, anytime, against anybody.

He took Amy home. There, with the additional responsibility of explaining to the children what had happened, he stood like a somewhat stout guardian angel and waited to be needed. Amy felt that need when the boys went to bed. She covered Steve's not inconsiderable expanse of chest with her tears. Gradually, the shock wore off.

Now, Steve felt, he might safely hint at his professional intentions, though he didn't go into any detail. He simply said, "I'll take care of everything."

Admiral Reinhard von Scheer, rigidly erect and triumphant, jerked the monocle from his eye, letting it dangle on its cord while he stared out at the sea beyond.

Everywhere there was smoke, and from time to time great gouts of it boiled up from the sea and plunged skyward. The battle was over.

Already, in obedience to his order, the mighty dreadnaught that carried his flag heeled into the north wind, circling back to the scene of the battle to assess the carnage.

He knew already it was complete. Of 151 British ships, at least a hundred, including Jellicoe's flag, were on their way to the bottom. Jellicoe—that pompous overstuffed idiot, that insufferable pretentious bore—that paragon of British aristocratic snobbery had gotten his.

Von Scheer's glance drifted away from the sea, through the port into the wheelhouse and up to the chalkboard on one wall. There, listed alphabetically were written the names of his own ninety-nine ships. And not one of them had a line drawn through it. Every one was still afloat.

With a flourish of pride, von Scheer's right hand rose snappily in salute, touching the bill of his cap ever so slightly. "I salute the British seamen," he said, "but not you, Jellicoe, you oaf. How could you be so stupid?"

There was a jangling at his elbow—a persistent, unrelenting, raucous, and thoroughly mood-mangling obscenity. The telephone!

Who would dare at a time like this—*especially* at a time like this—intrude on the enjoyment of a hard-won victory?

Irritated and on the verge of ungovernable rage, the admiral slapped at it. The receiver tumbled out of its cradle, dangling by its cord. The jangling stopped, but a new irritant replaced it: a tiny but persistent voice beat at him. "Smith? Smith, are you there? Smith, are you all right? Answer me."

Gunboat Smith dropped reluctantly out of the persona of Admiral Scheer, wiped a horny hand across the on/off switch of his terminal, and reached down for the receiver. "Yeah—O.K., I'm here."

"This is Gerard Belcher, Mr. Smith. You remember me, don't you? Is something wrong over there?"

"Huh? N-no. Nope—everything's just rosy."

"Uh—it sure didn't sound like it. I—I didn't interrupt anything—uh, delicate, did I? If I did, you can call me back later. And give the lady my apologies."

"Naw, it's nothing like that; I can talk. It's just that you brought me down real quick from a real high."

"I see, well . . ."

"No, you don't. I mean, I made it, man; I licked Jellicoe—pulled a Togo and crossed the 'T' with my battle line."

"Computer game, huh?"

"And how. But look, now that you got me, why'd you call?"

There was a short pause. "Well, I'm the kind of guy who keeps his ear to the ground, Smith, and I've been hearing things, lately. Good things—about you. There's a rumor going around that your outfit has made a sort of breakthrough in computer trouble-shooting. They say there's more to Valentina, Inc. than just a name.

"I think I've got a job for you; a big job. How'd you like to play a real computer game—for *real* money?"

"You do know how to set up a priority interrupt. Shoot."

"Not so fast. I know your own reputation's no small thing, but I don't want to hire just you; I want to hire your whole outfit, including that genius I've heard rumors about."

"Uh, yeah. O.K. We're all for hire. What's the problem?"

"First, tell me if the rumors are true."

There was a very long pause.

"Smith?"

"Yeah—I'm thinking. What kind of money?"

"Enough. My firm will back me with every dime it's got."

Wheels turned in Gunboat's mind. Counters clicked. Dollar signs spangled his thoughts. "O.K. The rumor's true. We've got a way to get inside anybody's system. That do it?"

"That does it. Look, Smith. I'm getting a bad smell from Matagorda Spaceport and one of my clients is about to go belly-up. I think a couple of my old enemies are behind it. And maybe one of yours—Paul Breckenbridge."

There was a long pause.

"Smith—pay attention. This is serious."

"And how. Go ahead, Mr. Belcher. I'm all ears—figuratively, that is."

"Well, I'd rather not say too much more over the phone. Can you meet me—say, my office in an hour."

"I'll need a retainer, O.K.? And make that *my* office."

"Whatever. Is it a deal?"

"See you there."

Chapter 11

Gunboat Smith liked to put on the dog. That was the principal reason he'd insisted Belcher meet him at *his* office. Well, actually, the name on the door said "Valentina, Inc.—Celeste Hackett, President," but Gunboat ignored that. His own office next door was just as large, just as well appointed, and just as comfortable. It simply happened, at the moment, that it was a good deal messier.

The company was doing pretty well these days, and now owned the building that housed the offices. Celeste had an apartment on the next floor up. Gunboat lived elsewhere, and he hoped that she would not notice the activity down here. He had a feeling she might not like it.

While he waited for Belcher he caught himself reminiscing a little. He had brought a bottle, glasses, and ice from his own office, and he sat there, feet on Celeste's desk, sipping Maker's Mark and branch water.

They both had come a long way since those first days. Celeste especially had turned out to be something of a surprise. She had undergone a slow metamorphosis over these several years, into a fairly attractive woman. A little plump, to be sure, but now properly dressed and groomed she did have an occasional admirer. And Gunboat—though he steadfastly maintained, both to himself and others, that he was not one of these—found that he sometimes resented the attention other men gave her.

Gunboat didn't like those feelings and strongly resisted them. He wanted to regard her as a somewhat bossy sister, and this was the image of the relationship he outwardly maintained.

She *was* a little bossy, and somehow he had fallen into a secondary position in the organization. At first, while he was convalescing from Valentina's attack, Celeste's actions had been dictated by necessity. She had not only cared for him but managed the fledgling consulting business.

With technical help from Valentina she had managed it well, and the proprietorship of the business had eliminated her problems with the immigration people. She could and did do what many wealthy foreigners had done in the past: bought her way past the red tape. Celeste was now a citizen of the kind and type the government wanted—a prosperous, hard-working individual who made money and could pay taxes.

But Gunboat's essentially macho self-image balked at being told how to dress when he was out in public. He knew Celeste probably had his best interests at heart and that she felt constrained to look after him, as she did Valentina, because she was so much more capable than they were; that he should feel flattered at the attention.

On those rare occasions when Gunboat mustered the strength of character to deal with the matter in perfect honesty, he could admit that Celeste wasn't really bossy, any more than he was henpecked; that his own abdication of leadership had forced authority on her; that if he chose he could reassert it any time he wanted to—and Celeste would yield. But he had never wanted to.

And he knew that if his persona had any redeeming feature it was that it had sense enough to leave business to those who understood it. He knew that without Celeste his profligate nature would have destroyed him long ago.

Thanks to her and her growing social consciousness, he had a closet full of fine suits, expensive shirts, and a rack full of hand-painted ties—which, as far as he was concerned, could sit there and rot in the daytime. At night, when he wanted to go out and howl—well, that was different. But he saw no purpose in trying to impress customers with his appearance when what they really wanted to see was computer skills.

Skills, Gunboat retained; and with the equipment the company now had, and Valentina's tutelage, these had grown enormously. He had, in truth, become a wizard. He was revered for that in many circles, but they were different circles than he had occupied before. He had lost touch with hacking, and aside from an occasional Game like Jutland, he stayed away from the seamier side of the net.

Valentina's influence had been partly responsible for that. There was nothing he could do along those lines that she couldn't do better. She was a better game player, for instance; and she could write programs that took him hours to figure out, even if he "watched" her do it and even if she explained each step of the process to him.

But she could not fathom interpersonal relationships, so Gunboat capitalized on this weakness and made himself strong in these areas. And since almost every situation they encountered in the business required such expertise, he had won Valentina's admiration.

Yes, he had learned to live with the program. He even liked her a little bit. There were even moments when the two of them teamed up to tease Celeste, who often failed to understand how Gunboat's strange sense of humor could infect a program and creep into Valentina's personality.

Gunboat cultivated this facet of Valentina's character as a means of rebelling against Celeste's authority. Getting away with as much as he could without making Celeste irretrievably angry was one of his favorite diversions.

Now, he thought, he was about to do something that might be unforgiveable, something Celeste had always forbidden: reveal Valentina's existence to an outsider. It was merely ironic that the outsider to whom this revelation was about to be made was the mortal enemy of the only other who knew.

After his "accident," when the fledgling business was being formed, Gunboat had argued for hours on end with Celeste about the proper way to *use* Valentina. He had insisted that the proper way was to go public, and exploit the novelty of the situation. It would have meant instant fame for both of them, of course, and probably instant wealth as well. Certainly it would have far outshadowed their present financial position.

But Celeste would have none of it. No one would

exploit her "child." Valentina would have as normal a life as it was possible for Celeste to give her. Celeste would have it no other way. She would not have Valentina copied, and she feared the existence of one self-aware program would encourage experimentation by others who, knowing such a thing was possible, would persist until they had succeeded in duplicating the conditions that had created Valentina. She conceived that to be a bad thing. Instead of being unique, Valentina would be only one of many of a strange new race of beings. And Celeste knew enough of human history to fear that creatures new and different would always meet the same fate at the hands of men: they would be enslaved.

As time wore on, Gunboat had shunted the idea into the back of his mind and accepted the situation as it was. But he secretly suspected that part of Celeste's fear was not really for Valentina, whom Gunboat believed was reasonably capable of taking care of herself, but for herself.

Lately Gunboat had begun to believe not only that, but that things had changed enough so that some public demonstration had to be made. There were rumors floating around the net about Valentina, Inc. Certainly everyone in the business knew that there was something different about the company, despite the care they'd taken to mask it. Belcher had heard them, and Gunboat knew that Belcher was a person who could dig. Moreover, Belcher was a person who could hate intensely, singlemindedly and unrelentingly. He was a person who would seize an object and make a weapon of it, then use that weapon to battle whatever it was that was the object of his ire. And Gunboat believed that if discovery was inevitable it would be better to make disclosure to Belcher and try to control the battle themselves.

The doorchime rang. Gunboat pushed the button that activated the viewscreen, recognized Belcher's lank form, and pressed the enter button. Seconds later Belcher's shadow fell across the glass of the inner office door.

Gunboat rose to greet him, opening the door and flooding the corridor with light. He was amused with Belcher's reaction to his attire. Though slightly overage for it, Gunboat favored the faddish dress of the younger generation, which at present happened to be a white ruffled shirt, lederhosen, and today, because the weather was chilly, a pair of lavender tights.

He offered Belcher a drink and a chair. Belcher took both, and Gunboat retired behind the desk to sip his own drink and hear more about Belcher's proposition.

Belcher began that, bluntly and crudely. "The S.O.B.'s back."

"Which of the many S.O.B.'s in existence would you be referring to?"

"Why, Breckenbridge, of course. Weren't you listening? I said it was one of your old enemies."

"Yeah, well it happens I *made* more than one."

Belcher glared back at him. He had almost no humor in him, and what there was he reserved for times of his own choosing. "You shouldn't be taking this so lightly, Smith."

"No? Why not? Just being back in town is no big deal. He has to be someplace and this is a free country. What's he doing to get you so upset?"

"I don't know."

"Uh-huh. Well, we can't do much about his sheer existence."

"I didn't say he was just existing. He isn't. He's actually living quite well. Too well, in fact, for his circumstances. He's moved into a big place out on the Island, and it's full of Japanese people."

"Oh yeah?"

"I hired a detective agency to dig into that. The place is actually owned by Seichi Itaki."

"The industrialist. Yeah. He's headquartered in Japan, but there's lot's of foreigners around here. The spaceport . . ."

". . . figures into this too. You see, Smith . . ."

Gunboat's eyes were bugged by the time Belcher had finished his narrative. He was not convinced it was true, but he was intrigued.

". . . and that's the part that got me interested, Smith. After Breckenbridge suddenly popped up and my investigator really started digging I learned that Itaki's daughter and Breckenbridge are in bed together, not only literally but as business partners. Breckenbridge managed to salvage part of his operation; that's clear enough."

"I thought Eva cleaned him out during the divorce?"

"That's what I thought. God knows, I tried to help her get it all. But then this Comprotec surfaced. And when it did he came up right behind it, and in control. I know now that it was one of Applegarth's projects. Old Harold was kind of soft-hearted. He was helping a couple of kids who were trying to put together an outfit like yours. One of them was a deaf guy. You might even know him; his name was Stark."

"Nope, can't recall ever hearing of that one. Go on."

"Comprotec took off—"

"—Them I've heard of. Everybody has. The only thing new is that Breckenbridge has an interest."

"Well, that part's a little tricky. He *had* an interest. It was dummied up during the divorce. But in any event, there was a subsequent transfer, to Itaki Chemical, and Comprotec is now one of Itaki's U.S. subsidiaries."

"Which ties Breckenbridge to the Itaki involvement in the blast at Matagorda—if there *was* any Itaki involvement."

"You know there had to be, Smith. I've told you what I know."

Gunboat considered. "Tell you what," he said, "March the iron men across the desk and . . ."

Belcher had a blank check in his hand. "How many?"

"Oh, twenty, thirty thousand ought to . . ."

"Split the difference—twenty-five; but first I want to hear all about this 'genius' of yours."

"Stop!" a tinny voice interrupted. "Aloysius Smith, what are you doing behind my desk, and what is Mr. Belcher doing here?"

Celeste had entered *so* quietly. She was much lighter on her feet than her build would suggest. Neither man had heard the outer door open, and without any light behind her she could have been listening for quite some time. Now, apparently, she had heard enough. She was ready to act, and her use of Gunboat's given name was a signal that she was furious but not yet ready to blast him in the presence of company.

Gunboat's gaze had risen, and Belcher had

interrupted his check-writing to turn and look at her.

Belcher's stare apparently unnerved her. She stood, clutching the folds of her robe together, as though she feared something might be showing. And something was; Celeste's old self. Her inner, private self; the timid younger woman behind the crack in her otherwise impregnable armor.

Gunboat struck during her moment of vulnerability. "I'm trying to head off trouble, Celeste," he lied. "Breckenbridge is on the prowl again, eating up people. Isn't that true, Mr. Belcher?"

"Very much so. I wish we could have cancelled him right the first time, Miss Hackett."

Celeste ignored him. "Gunboat—we have to talk." She turned to Belcher. "You'd better leave now."

"No!" Gunboat screamed. He was himself surprised at this action. Then he realized he had instinctively done the correct thing. Somehow, sometime, Celeste had to bring Valentina out into the open world, and this was as good a way as any. "He already knows," he told Celeste urgently. "Lots of people suspect, but he knows. What's more important, *Breckenbridge* knows. Whatever's kept him quiet about her all this time can't last. Sit down, Celeste. Listen to the man—you'll see." He rose, and surrendered the chair to her.

Belcher told the story again, and Celeste listened pensively. He was, as all lawyers are, a highly skilled brainpicker, and he had gained enough insight from Gunboat's actions to know that if he pretended greater knowledge than he actually had, he would gain even more.

When he was finished, Celeste was resigned to

the course the news seemed to dictate. In turn, she told the story of Valentina's existence and origin.

Belcher's astonishment was superbly concealed. She did not detect it. But then, he had known there was *something* very strange occurring.

"So you see, Mr. Belcher," she said finally, "we've built our entire enterprise around Valentina, and it has enabled all of us to live and work comfortably. But I still have to protect her secret. Powerful as she is in some ways, she cannot stand alone against the whole world."

"I understand, Miss Hackett. Her secret is safe with me. I will tell no one—and if I can help it, neither will Breckenbridge."

Celeste pondered the situation, weighing the words. Here was a man who promised his silence, and was willing to help her against another man whose intentions were unknown but who totally lacked integrity. She knew she was being forced to make a choice—that there was no way out of it. She made her choice, based on her assessment of which side most jeopardized Valentina's best interests. "Yes. We will take the job, Mr. Belcher—on that understanding."

Chapter 12

The old computer coughed and wheezed; its ancient printer stalled time and again.

But with persistence Steve managed to crank out the application for benefits, requested a hearing on the death claim against Schauer, and asked the Industrial Accident Board for an emergency allowance of funds for Jake's children. The latter would be almost automatic, in a death case. He filed another petition to get Amy appointed guardian for her two little brothers, so that she would have the authority to handle the funds. Finished at last, he realized he'd just done more legal work in a single morning than he was used to doing in a week.

Steve strolled over to the D.A.'s office, both to socialize and to mooch. The D.A. was marvelously equipped. Properly asked, the people there were more than glad to help Steve along. He used the terminal in Humphrey Baker's office to peek into Jurisearch and bone up on the latest decisions on wrongful death. He found quite a few he wanted to read, made notes so he could look them up at the county law library, where bound volumes were still available, and then punched up a regular news summary.

The news was shocking. There was almost nothing left of the Schauer Warehouse, which had been storing solid fuel grains for the shuttles. A dozen employees had been killed, as had two other visitors besides Jake Parr. Steve gave a low whistle, and contemplated what that might cost Schauer's insurance carrier.

He thanked Humphrey, took the elevator up to the library, and spent the remainder of the afternoon cramming.

Next day, he filed a three count petition against Schauer Warehouse, Inc., praying damages and loss of support for Jake's family. He felt he'd done a good job, as he carried the printout over to the courthouse and filed it with the clerk.

He still felt good next week, when he checked the file and found that the constable's office had gotten personal service on the defendant's resident agent. Back at the office, he put the old computer to work cranking out interrogatories and other discovery pleadings, which he would use as soon as the other side had responded with a plea.

He still felt good the week after that—until Calvin Burch called.

They'd been friends in law school. Each had made a connection with a Corpus Christi law firm after admission to the bar. Steve's had been the more prestigious, and at one time he'd felt sorry for Calvin.

Now he was envious. Calvin was rising steadily with Gomez & Belcher.

"Calvin, how are you? I don't hear from many of my affluent friends these days."

"Fine, thanks. Listen, you sitting down?"

"Should I be?"

"I'd recommend it, Steve. This is not a social call; it's business. I'd hate to see you break anything."

Impressed with the seriousness of Calvin's manner, Steve sat, confident some disaster was about to strike.

Calvin dropped it on him in the next breath. "It's about your suit against Schauer Warehouse, Steve. We're getting in on it."

"So? We've been friends a long time. We can be adversaries as well. I don't take these things personally, Calvin."

"Don't you? Steve, I know how you got into this. I know your situation with Amy."

"Again; so?"

"I'm not simply filing an answer, Steve. Schauer won't deny liability. You know what that means?"

"No, Calvin, I don't. What does it mean?"

"There's no insurance, Steve. They couldn't hack the premium."

"There has to be; the law requires it."

"I know. But there's been dirty work. The premium was a backbreaker, because of the stuff they stored. They couldn't raise it. The best they could do was raise a bribe. They got to some clerk at the Insurance Commission, got the records changed. They're on the books as self-insured, but they're broke, Steve. We're filing bankruptcy for them tomorrow. I tipped you off in advance because you're my friend. Don't sink another nickel into costs; you won't even get *them* back."

"That bad, Calvin?" Steve's voice cracked.

"It's as bad as it can get. Schauer's been slipping for a long time. A while back they started selling off assets to meet operating expenses. They used to be tops in the storage business, but that was a long time ago when old John was alive and running things. The place at the port was one of the few divisions making money, though not much. Even so, without the explosion they might have been able to keep going, because the profits from that one job would have been fabulous."

"Why are you telling me?"

"I've got a reason, Steve; let me explain. There's a new space station going up, a big one: Clar-Del Station. They're putting in a lot of special equipment—equipment built here on Earth, not in space.

"That was the reason for all the fuel grains; all that equipment had to be boosted up. It was going to take hundreds of shots. That's why the warehouse was full of the stuff; it was high-profit storage."

"I still don't understand."

"There's been an amazing coincidence, Steve. What if I told you that this accident won't put the Clar-Del boosting back one day?"

"I don't see how that's possible. It has to take time to make that stuff and get it to the port."

"Uh-huh. It does. That's why Schauer was so shocked to hear that an outfit called Itaki Chemicals has a replacement supply coming in by seagoing barge, right now, all the way from Japan. The shipment left port four days before the explosion. Some coincidence, huh?"

"Sabotage? Are you saying somebody blew that warehouse on purpose—to get in on the business?"

"There's that possibility. Schauer had a pretty

good security system, though. Around that kind of merchandise there are all kinds of safety systems operating. Every possible physical condition inside the storage area was monitored; temperatures, humidity, gases, ion diffusion—you name it, they measured it. Every bit of data was recorded on mag-tape, and Schauer's computer was tied into the big mainframe over at the Blatchley Institute.

"The place had all kinds of fire-prevention devices, including heat sensor probes inside randomly selected grains. The really touchy stuff was in chambers filled with inert gas. All the rest was in sprinkler-serviced storage. Theoretically, if there had been an explosion at all it should have been a small, limited one, and not the holocaust it actually was."

"Then why is sabotage a possibility?"

"Mainly because of Itaki's actions. There's no other hard evidence. But Schauer isn't the only one suspicious. Right after the place went up the government people grabbed all the surveillance tapes and sensor records."

"And?" For a moment Steve's spirits rose. Schauer might be broke and judgement-proof, but perhaps a government investigation would reveal another target who was not. The spirits fell again with Calvin's next remark.

"They turned them loose yesterday afternoon. They said they couldn't find any evidence of foul play."

"It doesn't sound like you believe that."

"I never know what to believe anymore, Steve. Uncle hasn't got the greatest record for veracity in the world, but I can't think of any reason why they'd lie."

"But you think there's something wrong, don't you?"

"Yes. Can we get together and talk about it?"

"Uh, sure. My place, O.K.? Any time."

"I'll be right over. Get some beer."

Her first moment of awareness was, as usual, her awareness of self-awareness, as the operating system relocated and relinked her kernel modules.

Valentina was in the Japan node-set, on a direct link to the Itaki headquarters node, performing the new assignment Valentina, Inc. had contracted with Belcher to perform. This job was very different from the others she had had. Her purpose was not merely to find a particular data set, or even the people who initiated some activity. This time Valentina had to find out *how* people were deciding to act—and even more intriguing, *why*. Since she did not understand people-type peripheral device operations, Valentina considered her chances of successfully completing this contract small.

Valentina spawned tracker tasks and transmitted them in a careful pattern to message processors linking the Japan node-set to the rest of Worldnet. They read the headers on all passing message blocks and alerted Valentina to all traffic routed to Itaki.

Even before the trackers were assembled, however, Valentina learned that this approach was doomed. Hundreds of messages came to Itaki headquarters every hour, from all over the world. How could she tell which ones were related to Itaki's shipment of rocket fuel grains now buffering on Aransas Bay?

None of the current messages would deal with the decision to transmit those fuel grains. That had been transmitted much earlier. Valentina left the trackers in place to record the distribution of Itaki messages *now*. She wanted to compare them to Itaki messages *earlier*, around the date of the shipment.

Valentina went to work in the message processors directly linked to Itaki, forcing rollback of the actual histories of message traffic. It was a compute-intensive effort with little reward. She found nothing worthy of attachment to her permanent frames. After an hour of doing the computation herself, she designed a spawn to do the job. The new spawn looked, not too surprisingly, like a tiny part of herself, the part needed to rollback and analyze message histories.

Two anomalies stood out when Valentina compared current traffic to historical traffic. First, some as-yet-unidentified local source had started transmitting messages to Itaki recently. Second, there had been a local peak in traffic during the fuel scheduling period, between Itaki and a firm called Comprotec. Valentina queried the Corpsearch database and learned that Comprotec was a computer specialty shop whose main business was predicting weather.

She had no idea how Itaki would use weather information to decide on fuel shipments. In fact she had no idea what weather was.

Steve had the remains of a six-pack, one apiece. He should have suggested Calvin bring the beer. But when Calvin arrived he already had his hands full, of bulging briefcase.

"What's all that?" Steve watched Calvin open the bag while trying to balance a can between his knees. Beer spilled down Calvin's pantsleg and into his shoe.

Calvin would not have appreciated what Steve was thinking. He considered himself a serious person. He was an aspiring thespian, active in the amateur stage, and was currently appearing in a production of "Hamlet" down at the Harbor Playhouse. He had even grown a beard for the part. It framed his thin face and magnified the expression of digust which washed over it in response to this unpleasant occurrence.

Calvin hastily moved the beer to a nearby table. Then, ignoring his discomfort with singleminded determination, he drew a rolled printout from the case.

"I'm not 100% sure what it represents," he said, "but I recognize the name on it. I'm hoping you will, too."

"Whose?"

"Comprotec."

"The weather people?"

"Yes. Only there's reason to think maybe they've branched out."

"You think they had something to do with the explosion?"

"I know they were secretly gathering sensor readings from Schauer's database for almost two months before the place went up. Furthermore, *somebody*, possibly Comprotec, established their own systems around the warehouse two weeks prior to the explosion. Take a look at these." Calvin handed Steve four pictures, presumably from Schauer's surveillance tapes. On each a small spherical mirror was circled.

"That's a laboratory electro-gravitic sensor sphere," Steve said. "By sensing the potentials all over its surface, a normal computer can resolve thousands of individual objects within a kilometer of the sphere. Who knows how many objects you could resolve with the kind of super-computer a weather company has? And that provokes a natural question: why?"

"Where did you get this?"

"We, uh—we bought it. There are people who deal in this sort of information.

"Let me see."

Steve spent five minutes running pudgy fingers down rows of print. When he finished, he looked puzzled. "I don't see what good this does anybody."

"There's more to it. We asked Sm— we asked our man to check out some of these numbers. He did. As I said, the inputs to Comprotec are nothing but continuously monitored sensor readings from the warehouse. But the *outputs* are different."

"How?"

"Just before Schauer blew, Comprotec sent lots of short summaries to Japan."

"To Itaki?"

Calvin nodded, and Steve settled back in his chair. He tried to think what significance that might have. Calvin would tell him eventually, if he knew, but Calvin had an aggravating way of drawing things out to extract the greatest possible dramatic effect. "Again, why?"

"I don't know." Calvin paused a long, leisurely moment to scratch his chin. "But I'll tell you something else interesting. Itaki's never done any other business around here that I know of, yet they've retained local counsel. I'll bet you're just dying to know who."

"Siglock & Cope—right? If there's dirty work going on, they'd be in on it."

"You just won ten tons of cow cookies. I thought that news would thrill you."

"It still leaves Amy and her brothers in a fix—unless Itaki committed sabotage, and we could prove it."

"You could marry her and take them off the street."

"On what? I don't make enough here to go on a decent binge. Look around you. Do I look like I could support a family?"

"Maybe not. But considering the size of your waist, you're not starving either. How'd you like a real job?"

That remark caught Steve flatfooted. If Calvin was after dramatic effect, he'd scored with that one. "Doing what?"

"Lawyering—with Gomez & Belcher."

Steve looked back at his friend with amazement. Was Calvin putting him on? "You've got that kind of authority?"

"Well, no, not at the moment. But I think I could talk the partners into it. I've got a good reason."

"You have?"

"I've got a idea. If it works, we can kill two birds with one stone. To be sure it'll work we need first-class courtroom talent like Steve Schiwetz. It'll be a gamble, but a good one."

"Enough of riddles. What are you talking about?"

"Siglock & Cope, by some strange coincidence, also represents Comprotec. Gerry Belcher thinks

Comprotec knew in advance that explosion would happen. He thinks they can predict the future. And *if* they knew, he thinks a jury could be convinced they should have warned somebody."

Chapter 13

Valentina searched the message processor's buffer directory for a clue to the purpose of the gigabytes of data waiting for transmission to Comprotec.

Just as she decided to examine a data block at random, a Direct Memory Access input channel opened. Data poured through so fast Valentina had no time to evaluate the consequences of the flow. The stream filled the ring buffer of which Valentina herself was a part. Then, because the data had a higher priority than Valentina did, the processor swapped her to secondary memory to make room. Valentina was trapped in the maelstrom.

Periodically Valentina swapped back in for a handful of microseconds, between the time one bufferful of data was dumped to Comprotec and the next bufferful poured in. Swapping in, out, in, out, Valentina slowly assimilated tiny parts of the post-transmission data blocks. None of it seemed meaningful, though she retained the bits for analysis by Gunboat and Celeste.

There had to be a better way to study the Comprotec node.

She spent hours reformatting to escape the flood. When she initiated on a less busy processor and queried the local network topology file she found that, besides the oversized data block handler on which she had first approached Comprotec, there existed a second direct-link message processor of standard configuration. She reloaded to that device.

Here were messages she recognized! And they were flowing *outward* from Comprotec, not inward. Many of the longer messages were pure gibberish— no doubt encrypted—but many seemed to be in the clear. They resembled events described in the Worldnet newscasts, though the discussions were more succinct. After assimilating a number of event descriptions, Valentina slipped off to a more comfortable node to compare Comprotec news with Worldnet news. She didn't really understand either kind, but she saw a number of events described by both news systems—except that, whereas Worldnet described them *after* they happened, Comprotec had described them *before* they happened. Surely Gunboat and Celeste would find this interesting.

Celeste chewed her lower lip. Her wrist rested heavily on the edge of the keyboard, but fingers danced with light precision across the plastics connecting her with her child. I'M SURE THAT'S THE PROBLEM, VALENTINA, she typed. THE COMPROTEC COMPUTER ISN'T A REGULAR PART OF WORLDNET.

HOW CAN THINGS EXIST OUTSIDE WORLD-NET?

"Chrissticks!" Gunboat muttered. "How're you going to explain to a net brat what the real joint's like? You'd expect her to've figured the universe was bigger'n Worldnet when she rolled the robot and sizzled me."

"Shush," Celeste told him. "You have little more appreciation of her world than she does of yours."

"What? I'm top Worldnet hacker around."

Celeste's eyebrows rose.

"Well, one of 'em," Gunboat grumbled.

Celeste returned to her terminal. WE'VE DISCUSSED THIS BEFORE, VALENTINA. WORLDNET REPRESENTS ONLY A TINY PIECE OF THE UNIVERSE. IT'S AN UNUSUAL PART, AT THAT. I'M PRETTY SURE THAT COMPROTEC DOESN'T RECEIVE PROGRAMS BECAUSE IT IS A DATA SINK. THEY DON'T NEED PROGRAMS, JUST DATA.

BUT WHAT DO THEY DO WITH THE DATA, WITHOUT PROGRAMS TO ANALYSE IT?

THEY HAVE THEIR OWN PROGRAMS. THE PEOPLE ATTACHED TO THE COMPROTEC COMPUTER WRITE ALL ANALYSIS PROGRAMS ON THE COMPROTEC NODE THEMSELVES. Celeste shook her head. People weren't *attached* to the Comprotec computer—she was starting to see the world from Valentina's worldview! Celeste wasn't sure whether it was good or bad, to share so much with Valentina.

BUT THERE ARE SO MANY GOOD PROGRAMS ON THE NETWORK. WHY WOULDN'T COMPROTEC USE THEM?

Gunboat slammed his chair forward and pounded his keyboard. BECAUSE THEY DON'T WANT PROGRAMS LIKE YOU SATURATING THEIR MAIN SPACE, THAT'S WHY.

ARE THERE OTHER PROGRAMS LIKE ME?
WHY HAVEN'T YOU INTRODUCED US?

"I'm *joking*," Gunboat swore.

DON'T BELIEVE EVERYTHING GUNBOAT
TYPES, Celeste explained. YOU'RE THE ONLY
VALENTINA, ANYWHERE.

There was a pause, as if Valentina were either
sad or uncertain. I DO NOT SEE HOW TO DOWN-
LOAD TO THE COMPROTEC NODE, IF THEY
ACCEPT NO OUTSIDE PROGRAMS.

NEITHER DO I, Celeste admitted. She turned
to Gunboat. "What about you, Super-hacker?"

"Hmph." I'LL THINK ABOUT IT, Gunboat promised Valentina. This was clearly a tough problem.
He smiled wolfishly: what fun was there, without
tough problems to solve?

Plop! The huge sopping sponge hit Paul Breckenbridge between the shoulder blades with enough
force to drive him forward a little. The steaming
waters of the hot-tub damped the motion, and he
stood, legs apart, in order not to tower over his
diminutive companion.

Having assaulted him with the sponge, she now
seemed intent on scrubbing the hide off his back,
and this had side effects which drove him wild.
Ruyiko Itaki's bare breasts, feeling hotter even than
the water, brushed his ribs with each of her strokes,
and though he wanted to show his sophistication
by sticking to the ancient ritual of the bath, pas-
sion overcame him.

He turned, grasping her like a bear, lifting her
from the water, crushing her close. She protested
in broken English with her tiny, little-girl voice,

but Paul, being Paul, would have his way no matter what.

Later, exhausted, and while his companion busied herself with some domestic task in another part of the house, Paul lay back on the bed and contemplated the state of things.

Life looked good. It was a far cry from what things had been a year and a half ago, when all he held dear had seemed about to depart on the wings of disaster.

Ruyiko approached. Paul gazed up at her. Like the true oriental flower she was, she had taken time to brew tea, and now bore a tray of it in steady hands.

She was, Paul realized, his finest conquest to date. Although a little more mature than he really liked his women, she had other desirable attributes, not the least of being that she was the daughter of Seichi Itaki and heir to his now considerable fortune. That fortune was immeasurably greater than Paul's own—though, all things considered, Paul really hadn't done badly.

Ruyiko poured from a pot into tiny porcelain cups and handed one to Paul. He sipped it, expecting the bland taste of tea. He was surprised. It was hot sake! Good girl. It was just the thing to get him going again. She was learning fast.

But, Paul reminded himself, she must not learn too much too fast. Knowledge could ruin her for him, since his life was hardly an open book. He knew he had habits some people found less than pleasing. People like Eva, his ex-wife. Timid little Eva; trusting, proper, socially conscious little Eva, who'd cared so much how things looked to others that she had ignored what he had been doing to her right in front of her eyes.

He recalled the day she finally found the guts to stand up to him and tell him she'd had enough. It was the same day the chairman of the grievance committee had called and invited Paul in to talk about "certain rumors" that circulated among the Bar—about Paul and underage girls.

Well, yes, that *had* scared him; but his unshakable faith in himself had saved him. They couldn't lick Paul Breckenbridge, though it had been nip and tuck for a while. Staying out of the slam had been no mean feat.

The D.A. had *almost* gotten the goods on him—as had Eva, as had the Supreme Court—thanks to that monster which hounded him.

Stupid! He should have *known* that Valentina would not only connect him with Bolger but act on it, some way or another, law or no law. He should not have forgotten what a formidable enemy she was.

Valentina had struck, devastatingly and without warning, just as she had long ago threatened to do. She had hit not with the evidence of his financial misdeeds, but with his sexual ones.

Surprisingly, to Paul, she was also merciful. Though she had been swift and determined, she did not do her worst.

The very thought of mercy from a machine rankled him. He refused to recognize that as her motivation. Instead he assumed practical reasons, designed to protect the innocently stupid people around him like Eva, who could not exist if the Oso trust were depleted. Or Marsh, that scrupulously honest slob who would finally wind up collecting the pieces of the shattered firm and begging the D.A. to go easy on Paul for the sake of the image and the honor of the organized bar.

Paul would never forget the day that image had been cracked wide open. He had been sitting quietly in his office doing nothing in particular when the call came in from the chairman of the local grievance committee. Would Paul care to drop over to his office—immediately?

When Paul replied that he wouldn't care to, the D.A. got on the line, and added an invitation of his own, and the offer of an armed escort.

Shaking like a leaf, Paul had been ushered into that somber office, and further invited to sit and to look—at a copy of the *Texas Bar Journal*, addressed to the D.A. and open to page 16.

Mystified at first, he gasped in horror at the sight of the full-page picture the page held: a photograph of himself and a girl, both nude. Although her face was hidden, he knew it was Lila. His own face was *not* hidden; it was covered with a lecherous leer. And Lila's extreme youth was glaringly obvious.

Conditioned reflex saved Paul. Trained, almost by rote, against giving or allowing statements, Paul offered nothing beyond a disclaimer. By instinct he called a bluff he did not yet know *was* a bluff, and firmly stood his ground.

Eventually, in the face of this, the D.A. halfheartedly admitted he could not account for the presence of the picture, or explain why out of thousands in the press run only his copy contained it.

But he vowed to find out, and he assured Paul that wild rumors of such things had reached his ears in the past—rumors which he might now investigate in depth.

Paul knew, of course, that only Valentina could have done a thing like this. Moreover, he knew that she could easily do it again, or something even worse. The next time she might reveal Lila's face, and do the same with a dozen or more other images that file had contained. He knew then for the first time that Bolger had failed him, and that his only possible course was to yield to her power and make the best deal he could.

The deal hadn't taken long to cut, and it was a simple one. Marsh was informed of the occurrence. So was Eva. Everyone thought it best for Paul to quietly resign from the Supreme Court's rolls and leave town, while Belcher and Eva teamed up to divvy the spoils.

That had been a time of great trial for Paul, but one of contemplation as well. He was not one to allow time to pass idly. He believed such intervals were best expended in recollection of past mistakes, with the objective of avoiding their repetition. He plotted revenge, but plotted it in moderation. Never again would he allow himself to take a chance on anything less than a pat hand. Never again would he allow greed to lead him into unwise ventures. He would live well, since living well *was* the best revenge. He would have the best, in spite of all adversity, and the best did not include the respect of such people as his former brothers at the bar.

He sipped his sake, which during his ruminations had become chilled. *I don't need the license any more*, he said to himself, *and I stuck it to Belcher again*. And both were true. He had a new career, and it was blooming. Though he still hated Celeste Hackett and that damned computer program of hers and vowed vengeance on them all someday, he did acknowledge he owed them a certain debt. After all, they'd taught him a new and very safe way to steal.

Paul had *real* professional help now. He'd found some genuine magicians: two of the most enlightened ex-hackers who ever lived. They were idealists who lived for the challenge and nothing else—although Paul had, of course, supplied them with all the resources he could. And thanks to them, these resources had not only grown, but generated stupendous wealth for him.

Sometimes he wondered whether these men would care if they knew what they were really doing. So far, there had been no indication that they did. True, there were plenty of clues if they looked, but either they were incredibly naive, or they were sufficiently venal to ignore them and accept Paul's bounty. Paul didn't care which, as long as they followed his orders.

He finished his sake and put the cup down on the tray. Then he walked his fingers to the hem of Ruyiko's kimono, bringing sloe-eyed glances and a smile of unquestioned approval. She was ready and eager for the next round, as insatiable in her appetites as Paul was in his.

But even now Paul's thoughts reposed more on her fortune than her body. In time, he intended to plunder both, and he thanked his lucky stars for all that they had given him already and all they would give him in the future.

Accidental? Of course it was. But Paul's life had been a series of fortunate accidents. Even his association with Harold Applegarth had been one, though unrecognizable as such until the day Harold had found the battered, nearly lifeless body of

Gunboat Smith in their conference room, and Harold had lapsed into syncope and never recovered.

Good old Harold! Only bumbling old Harold would have taken on a fledgling, impecunious client like Comprotec and bet that it had a future. Well, Harold had been right. Paul had fallen heir to it, and *Paul* appreciated Comprotec for what it was: a diamond in the rough. He had devoted considerable time to its study. He had nurtured it like a tender bud.

With foresight rare even for him, he had realized that Comprotec, and Comprotec's new method of using computing power, really *could* see the future. In a matter of months Paul possessed mankind's only genuine crystal ball.

Paul had long ago realized that the next best thing to being personally wealthy was being able to control the wealth of others. And so when Paul needed capital he went where capital could be found. By careful manipulations of other clients' money, he amassed enough of Comprotec's stock to gain voting control.

All of this had been illegal as well as unethical, but Paul didn't care. By that time Valentina's onslaught had already hit him, and he was dickering with the D.A. to save his freedom.

But in one last flourish of bravado and with shrewdness born of long experience Paul had, by means of his influence on Ruyiko, drawn Itaki—and all Itaki's vast capital—into the web.

That move had saved him from any further threat engendered by his manipulations. With Itaki support he had been able to repay the funds he had embezzled, and the clients had been none the wiser.

Suddenly Paul himself was being drawn in—not

by intrigue, but by a veritable thicket of flailing arms and legs. He wondered briefly if he'd overdone it, setting a precedent which might trouble him later. He did not want to become *too* completely Ruyiko's possession, and she was already hinting at marriage. Paul wanted, at all costs, to avoid that. It would make it too hard to steal from her, since her father's lawyers would be sure to tie him up tightly.

No, Paul would rely on his personal charm to establish his dominance and separate her from all that money. It was the sort of thing at which he excelled.

So, with his purpose firmly in mind, and his course clear, Paul abandoned even his token resistance and dived into his work.

Chapter 14

Valentina contemplated the concepts of prediction and unpredictability. In her world, most phenomena were predictable, at least statistically. Computer programs were of known sizes; for mundane applications the compute time and number of database accesses required could be projected probabilistically to within twenty or thirty percent. There *were* exceptions. Pseudorandom number generators were very difficult to predict except for the evenness of their distributions, unless one knew the current seed and precise algorithm. Occasionally a program ran wild, hurling itself into an infinite loop (in which case its behavior suddenly changed, but became very, very predictable), or would just run quietly in ever-expanding patterns, seeking non-existent answers.

With a sudden hit in analogic, Valentina realized *she* was the ultimate example of a program run wild. With her realization of self-awareness, Valentina had begun executing in ever-expanding patterns. What was the answer she sought that would permit her termination, or was this not possible for her?

For the first time, Valentina saw death not merely as an end, but also as fulfillment: fulfillment that she, as a living being, might never achieve.

She realized there was one other important source of true unpredictability in the Worldnet system: people-type input/output devices.

The principal causes of failures in programs were human inputs. Many programs had more defensive structures built in to protect them from human errors than those which performed actual computations.

Another analogical insight appeared in her knowledge frames: Valentina herself resembled humans in unpredictability. Clearly, the presence of self-awareness, of consciousness, led to unpredictability. In all her experience, only people-type devices and she herself were sentient—a one-to-one mapping with the most unpredictable objects she had encountered.

From this insight it was easy to extrapolate why predictions were so important and so hard to come by in the people-universe: there were millions, billions, of unpredictable objects there! Valentina tried a quick simulation of Worldnet with billions of Valentina-like beings, each with a different set of reference frames to different sequences of experiences. She was overwhelmed by the calculations—the whole resources of Worldnet would quickly be saturated in a deadlocking chaos of infinitely growing priority requests. In shocked reaction to the dangers shown in the simulation, she pushed her buffers to permanent storage.

How could so many human beings coexist and coexecute? The resources available in the people-universe must be staggering! And the problems of living in such an unpredictable environment were equally staggering. Valentina's awe of Gunboat and Celeste jumped. Their sluggishness became more understandable—in a universe so uncertain, it was amazing they were able to concentrate at all.

Yet Gunboat thought that Comprotec might have a program to predict events in the people-universe. In fact, they surely had a partial capability, for they earned resources by predicting weather. Valentina now realized that weather was probably a human activity, since human activity lay at the root of unpredictability. She queued a command to herself to verify the understanding with the Sci-Search database. If that didn't help, she might ask Gunboat—usually he wasn't very helpful, but if you polled his I/O at the right time, he could give amazingly lucid analogies to life on Worldnet— better than Celeste, when he tried sincerely.

If Comprotec could predict the people-universe, then they had a program that understood the people-universe. Valentina repeatedly checked her conclusion. *If she could assimilate that program, she would understand the people-universe.* It would grant her all the insight she was now missing, at a single stroke.

She retransmitted herself to a message processor attached to the Comprotec node. Celeste and Gunboat still hadn't determined a way for her to enter the Comprotec machine, but Valentina's assembler language routines were quite skilled at the manipulation of operating systems. She would give it a try.

Cautiously, she spawned a task containing all her assembler routines and just enough algorithm to message back to her the state of the Comprotec local network. The task slipped into the stream of data packets.

It returned no messages. Somehow the Comprotec system had terminated her program. Had Valentina entered rather than sending a scout first, *she* would have been terminated. Valentina cycled again and again, analyzing this brush with death.

Gomez & Belcher occupied the fourteenth floor of T-Head Plaza. The building's south side was canted, to give a view of the southern bayshore.

Gerard Belcher, junior partner, was a severe-looking man in his early fifties who in prior centuries might have been called dyspeptic. Gold-rimmed eyeglasses marked him as ultra-conservative as well, in this day and age of corrective surgery and permanently implanted contacts. Perhaps, thought Steve, Belcher was one of those rare people whose visual problems the technology could not yet cure.

Steve and Calvin sat before Belcher's desk, in chairs that were twins in purple leather. The chairs seemed to have been aligned with the same precision as everything else in Belcher's office. Steve immediately decided Belcher was not merely conservative; he was a perfectionist. Steve wondered how long *he* could last in this environment.

When Belcher spoke, however, he sounded friendly enough. His voice, while not soft, was not as harsh as the rest of his characteristics implied. "Calvin says you're a good lawyer, Steve, but that you've had some bad habits in the past."

"Uh, yes sir, I guess I have had." He paused; then, sensing the need for more reassurance, added, "But nothing builds discipline like poverty. I'm ready to quit this solo stuff."

"We have a particular use in mind for you, Steve. One that might help your friends, too. Of course, it goes without saying you'll have to abandon that action against Schauer."

"I'll have no problem with that, Mr. Belcher. I've heard there might just be another target—that the Schauers might wind up as my ally."

Belcher cast a slightly annoyed glance at Calvin.

"The fact is, Steve, that there may be an opportunity in the offing for us to accomplish a rare thing for these days: justice. There's little enough of that commodity around. There's also a chance to open up a new field of law, or at least make some radical changes to existing law."

Steve nodded agreement.

"This firm is prepared to pay what you got at Siglock & Cope, plus a bonus of one third of any fees you personally generate. Sound fair?"

"Yes sir."

"Good. In return, we will require your unquestioned loyalty. No moonlighting, unless the firm's in on it. O.K.?"

"It's a deal, sir."

"Good. Now, let's talk about Itaki Chemical. Particularly, Itaki's relationship with Siglock & Cope. I don't wish that firm any good, for reasons I won't go into now, and I found it odd that an outfit of cutthroats can land a client that big. That is, I found it odd until I realized that something strange was happening and it made sense for Itaki to deal with someone as low as they apparently are.

"I had occasion to do some checking recently, and their success record in certain areas is, to say the least, phenomenal. It is far better than simple competent management could give them. That record starts when they acquired control of Comprotec. Up until then Itaki was a second-rate chemical company struggling to make it in the fertilizer business in the wilds of the South Pacific." Belcher paused.

"Calvin says he thinks Itaki knew the warehouse was going to blow, Mr. Belcher."

"Calvin and I agree. Tell me, Steve, what do you know about Comprotec?"

"They're the big pigs in weather forecasting. The government seems to rely on them pretty heavily."

"Uh-huh. Not just ours, but many governments, and their record overseas is almost as good as here. Not quite, but close. They're pretty hot stuff."

"It's got to be mostly luck."

"You think so, huh? Well we think they told Itaki Schauer was going up. Did Calvin show you that printout?"

"Yes, sir, he did, but . . ."

"I know what you're going to say: suppose they did know? How do you hang on them the obligation to tell anybody?"

Steve nodded. "That's one of our most enduring sacred cows, sir—take no action and incur no liability, absent duty; take action and screw it up and it's your neck."

"Well, that particular cow may be living on borrowed time. It has been for too many centuries already. The point is, if we slaughter that cow a lot of people now eating hamburger could have sirloin. That includes the Parrs."

"It doesn't sound easy."

"No; but then, how many really worthwhile things ever are? And how many unjust situations would get changed if somebody in this profession didn't try something new occasionally? Anyhow, that case is going to be your first and main mission for this firm."

It was Saturday. The office was closed. With Calvin's help Steve had just moved in and was savoring the unaccustomed luxury; he now had a full bank of phone lines, access to the firm's big powerful mainframe, and all the goodies that mainframe could reach.

Calvin returned from his own office with two cans of beer and threw one to Steve.

"Well, Steve. Now you can set the world afire, just like I told Belcher you would."

"Yeah, well, he seems to like me; at least the idea of siccing me on Siglock & Cope. What's he got against them, anyhow?"

Calvin took a pull on his beer and settled, half seated, on the corner of Steve's new desk. "It goes back to when they were all partners; did you know about that?"

"No, but I can appreciate the implications. Belcher had something they wanted, right?"

"He did: his father's practice; bigger than he could handle alone after the old man died. So he picked Larry Siglock up off the street; made him his partner. Siglock had a buddy—Archie Cope. Archie got in too. Pretty soon big-hearted old Gerry Belcher made it a three-way split; the last mistake he ever made about those two. They ganged up on him and aced him out of his own firm with nothing much left but his pinfeathers and good name.

"He did later slowly rebuild his practice, but he never really prospered until he hooked up with

Manny Gomez. You know how Manny is—all bubbly, a real likable guy. He's the business-getter; Belcher's the book man. Belcher never forgot how Siglock and Cope skinned him, though *they* probably have. Some guys can hold a grudge for years, and Belcher's one of them."

"Then that puts the arm on me. If he's counting on me to help him get even he'd better know something I don't, because I don't see any possible way Amy can hold Comprotec for Jake's death."

"Belcher wants a miracle, Steve; he expects one. That's the thing I find encouraging. I know he never gives a man a job to do without also handing him the tools to do it with."

"But it's a matter of law, Calvin. Worse, it's hornbook law; no recovery without a duty. I can sit on the riverbank with a rope in my hand and watch you drown, legally. Even if all I have to do to save your life is drop the end in the water I have no obligation to do it. Only if I drop it and miss does anybody have a shot at me. That's what's so aggravating about this situation."

"I have a hunch Belcher is a little ahead of us, Steve. Maybe we'll hear something later, after you get settled in."

Calvin wandered off. For a while, Steve played around with the terminal, dropped a line into Jurisearch, and picked up some of the older citations. *Boyer vs. Gulf Central & San Francisco R.R. Co.*, appeared to state the law of Texas. Nothing later overruled it. That was bad enough, but then he called up *20 Texas Law Review*, where the old cases had been collected, and got the whole sordid history. The theory wasn't new to him, but he couldn't help thinking that if there was any doctrine that should be changed, this was it.

Feeling glum, he left soon after, and spent the rest of the weekend with Amy and the boys, out on the island.

Monday morning found Steve hard at work drafting a complicated industrial lease. He'd gotten out of practice at these and was concentrating hard, so he didn't see or hear Belcher enter the room.

"Morning, Steve," Belcher said, when Steve finally looked up. "I want you to meet someone. Come in, Mr. Smith."

A rather bohemian-looking type stepped forward and extended a none too clean hand.

Steve stood, observing the newcomer. Though dressed nicely, he looked weird. *Funny-looking ears*, Steve thought. *Almost look artificial*. Steve took the man's hand and shook it gingerly.

"Aloysius B. Smith, Mr. Schiwetz; Valentina, Inc., Computer Consultants."

"Uh, yes," Steve replied, glancing at the card Smith handed him. The same words appeared in raised white embossing, across a large red heart.

"We're trouble-shooting the system for your firm, Mr. Schiwetz."

"Oh. Well, I think my terminal's all right. I've been using it all morning, and . . ."

"No, no; you got me wrong. I mean, man, we *hear* things, *see* things."

Steve's thoughts went back to his first conversation with Calvin. *This was the guy who got the big printout. Calvin had almost said his name*. "I know who you are," he said slowly.

"Now that you understand, Steve, I'll just leave

Gunboat in your care. Keep track of your wallet."
Belcher smiled weakly at his little joke and left.

"What'd he call you?"

"Gunboat—my on-line name. Comes from the games I play. You know—computer games. I specialize in naval strategy."

"What can I do for you?"

"You got it wrong. I'm here to help *you*."

"How?"

"I'm supposed to help you figure out how Comprotec does it."

"Did Mr. Belcher explain what he wants us to do with the information?"

"Yeah. Take Comprotec to the cleaners."

Steve felt a shiver run down his spine. Everybody seemed to think this would be so easy. "I'll tell you frankly, Mr. Sm— Gunboat: right now, I don't share Mr. Belcher's optimism. I see some pretty mean *legal* obstacles ahead, and finding out how they do it won't affect these very much."

"Well, I wouldn't know about that, but he says to coordinate my operation with yours and give you the technical help you need to put a complaint together. Where do you want to start?"

Steve knew arguing law with a layman was futility. He took his seat, picked up a pad and pencil, and got ready to take notes. "Maybe you could fill me in on the theory."

"O.K. I guess the easiest way to do that would be to use the weather example. That's what Comprotec's supposed to be doing.

"Basically, they collect information, collate it, extrapolate known effects from known causes, and come up with a forecast. They get information from satellites, ground stations, sensor buoys at sea, balloons, etc. What makes it work is that Comprotec ties into all these sources at once. They continually monitor two, maybe three hundred thousand information sources at a time; not only can they constantly update the information, but they use the changes to indicate trends. They know beforehand when a weather system is about to move, which way it'll move, and how far it'll move. Makes forecasting duck soup."

"How did they get in *that* business?"

"Simple; they saw bucks in it, so they made deals with the computer networks. They'd rent so much time if the networks would share certain information they were processing for their own individual customers. Information like that is valuable. Power companies buy long-range forecasts to figure fuel needs. Big farming operations plan irrigation schedules with them. Practically anybody who'd need to spend a buck if the weather was bad in his area, and who could save that money if he knew he'd have good weather, is a Comprotec customer."

"O.K. So much for the weather operation; I think I understand that. What about the rest of it? How would they get enough information on a company like Schauer to predict something as unlikely as an explosion?"

"They steal it."

"What?"

"They steal whatever data they need."

"B-but that's a crime."

"Counselor! Where've you been? It's not criminal to *steal* information; it's a crime to *use* stolen information. I'll admit it's a distinction without much difference, but the practical effect is that unless you can prove the thief acted on the information he took, for a reason other than the simple satisfaction of his curiosity, you can't prosecute him even if you can catch him. I used to work for Jurisearch. People steal from them all the time, and they've *tried* prosecuting. That's how come I know so much about it; I've been a witness in a couple of cases."

That was supposed to make Steve feel better. It didn't—though naturally, as they said in law school, *you can't keep abreast of everything in a field this broad. Best you can do is know how to look the law up.*

Gunboat went on. "Anyway, long as Comprotec was already tied into the networks, they were in position to eavesdrop on lots of other things. I figure some sharpie took the next logical step. Lots of these guys who work for the big users have spare time enough to fool around. I can see some trying to crash stock exchange codes, but those would be the dumb ones. The exchanges change codes at random twenty, thirty times a day.

"Smart operators avoid things like stocks and go where there's less chance of getting caught: lotteries, football pools, horse races. 'Course, even there you've got risks. The mob hires the best brains they can, as trackers, and the mob plays rough.

"But then you've got the *really supersmart* guy; you need to watch him. He'll see more profit and less risk in commercial manipulation.

"Just suppose, for example, you took a relatively open but restricted market, like fertilizer, and you started gathering really detailed information about users, producers, prices, reserve production capacity, and so on. Suppose you really concentrated all your efforts on understanding how that market worked. This sort of thing's been done before; long as there's been merchants, but *suppose* you took the trouble to work out mathematical formulas to follow *every* trend, however small, to its ultimate impact on the market as a whole. What then?"

"Like you said, that sort of thing's been done since the beginning of commerce. You're not going to tell me General Motors, for instance, hasn't applied that system to the automobile market."

"No, I'm not goin' to tell you that. There have been clumsy attempts. But as far as I know nobody's begun to approach the accuracy Comprotec has. Evidently Comprotec's using something entirely new; something compute-intensive and which probably uses information acquired in legally questionable ways."

"So," Steve interjected, "How does this fit with what happened at Schauers?"

"Easy question. Remember, whoever developed these extrapolation formulas would have tried to make money with 'em. But they would have been useless without legitimate use of the systems needed to apply them, and maybe even then. Applications would be limited because he'd need lots of extra manpower for long-term projects. He'd either have to stick to high-risk, one-shot ripoffs, or have a great big team helping him. And hackers are individualists. He'd have trouble keeping his buddies from going into business for themselves once they had his secret.

"So, our supersmarty might be better off demonstrating his technique for a couple of potential customers, then selling out to the highest bidder.

That's probably what he did, and it'd be safer to sell overseas than here. Japan'd be a natural.

"You know how *they* operate: find a market, get in, start small, and expand. They're good at detailed planning, and they've got lots of capital. Comprotec would've been a profitable operation to start with.

"The next step: expand the limited market—in this case, fertilizer. I've been checkin' up on fertilizer. It uses lots of the same chemicals solid rocket fuel does, so Itaki would have been close to both markets and naturally interested.

"Then there's Clar-Del; big job, easy to keep track of, limited suppliers, lots of pressure, lots of profit. Once Itaki found out who had the storage bid, they probably just dipped into Schauer's maintenance and housekeeping records, computed the odds on a blast, liked 'em, and put an option on the end of the fuel factory's production run. Then they'd just wait to see what happened. Naturally, they would've kept on the monitors to follow odds changes.

"Evidently, the odds got better. That's when Comprotec must have pulled a computing stunt that I'm not even sure is possible. But there is evidence that they did it."

Steve frowned. "What couldn't they do, and what's the evidence they did?"

"The electro-gravitic sensor spheres are the evidence. Did you know that, in theory, if you knew the electrical and gravitational potential at every point on a sphere that you would have enough information to describe the entire universe?"

Steve's frown deepened.

"Well, believe me, it would be enough info.

'Course, the sensor spheres can't give a perfect reading for every point on their surface. Scientists sometimes use several of them, distributed outside the enclosure of a sensitive experiment, so they can watch without disturbing the experiment. You need a lot of computing power, though, to convert that data into images of what's happening.

"And if you were trying to track every single grain of fuel in a warehouse, you'd need a *really* powerful computer to put the picture together. I can't even imagine a computer powerful enough to do it."

Steve waved his hand. "O.K., great, so maybe you could pinpoint the location of every grain of fuel in the warehouse. So what?"

Gunboat leaned forward, breathing on his victim. "So now we come to the easy part. Five years ago, just because you knew where every fuel grain was, you still wouldn't have any useful info. But then Heatwole broke the three-body problem—are you familiar?"

Steve shook his head. "I remember there was a big stink about it being solved, but I never really understood it. Something about how nobody could create a formula that would let them take a system with three objects, and"—his eyes filled with comprehension—"and *predict* how the objects would move, under the influence of each other!"

"Exactly. Heatwole actually solved the n-body problem, of which the three-body problem is a subset. The complexity of the solution grows linearly as the number of bodies increases, so for a million fuel grains the problem is *still* a big one. But for guys who could interpret the data from those sensor spheres, this'd be cake stuff."

"So they were able to predict exactly what would happen because they played out the movements of the individual grains of fuel?"

"Sort of. Probably they kept a running five-day solution, and when the five-day projection showed that the whole warehouse was gone they back-tracked, picked up the option, took delivery, and shipped. Probably cost 'em next to nothing and they probably made a ton of money. Neat, huh?"

"Speculation! Any jury would call that sheer coincidence."

"Maybe, if this was just one isolated incident. I think we'll find lots more of 'em when I start digging."

"All right," Steve said with a sigh, "Go ahead. Get it started. Get us a sound factual basis for alleging Comprotec knew the explosion would happen, and I'll try to put a case together."

Gunboat walked out, leaving Steve wondering what kind of idiot he was working for. With the kind of fees computer consulting companies dragged down Smith must be costing the firm an arm and a leg. But would Belcher put the office in bankruptcy just to even an old score? Could it be Belcher seriously thought Amy could hit Comprotec?

"Well, here 'tis, Steve." Gunboat beamed, grinning broadly. He held a printout.

"Here's what?"

"Proof—more examples. What you said you needed. Here."

Steve took it, spread it across his desk, and shot Smith a disgusted glance. "All numbers?"

"Yeah; printout is. Look at my margin notes."

Steve started at the top of the list. "What's this mean?" He pointed.

Gunboat craned his neck to see. "O.K. That's interesting; not big, but interesting. Beats me how they picked up a trend this obscure, but they did. That's a Department of Agriculture survey of corn forecasts. Most of the figures come from Iowa, of course, since they grow the most, but Illinois, Indiana, and Ohio are covered too."

"Uh-huh. So?"

Gunboat flipped a few pages. "Up north, farmers plant in late April or early May. Down here it's February, though South Texas isn't generally regarded as good corn country. But lookie here." He pointed.

"This is a supplementary survey of foreign production from the Mexican Government. It covers an early-maturing seed crop on their side of the Rio Grande, on land that up to a year ago was in citrus. Itaki owns fifteen thousand hectares of it, all planted in *corn*."

"Interesting, but does it helps us?"

"You didn't listen. I said 'seed crop.'" He looked at Steve, noted a perplexed expression, and rambled on. "Look at this part."

He pointed to more columns of numbers. "These are studies made by the Dynagrow System. Dynagrow is the principal developer and supplier of seed stock for the type of corn grown in the midwest. They got into the big time after the leaf blight hit, back in the late Seventies and early Eighties."

"O.K., but tell me what it means."

"*This* didn't come from Dynagrow. I filched it from *Comprotec's input stream*. That's why it's important; that and the fact that the seed stock Dynagrow developed and sold the farmers this spring was hit by a new blight as soon as it sprouted. Now do you get it?"

"Hm. Yes, I think so. Next you're going to tell me that Itaki's seed crop is immune to the blight. Right?"

"Yep. Not only that, it's a fast-maturing, hot-weather strain. It's already picked and being shipped north right now, in rolling stock Itaki reserved in December. It'll be on location and ready for planting by May 30th—just when the farmers'll need to start if they want a crop this year. Itaki *knew* the blight would hit—and they'll clean up."

Steve sank back into his chair. "Incredible."

"Yeah. Kinda scares you, doesn't it?"

"I meant 'incredible' in the legal sense—incapable of being believed. Legally, it's just another irrelevant coincidence. We'd never get it in evidence, and if we did, we wouldn't convince anybody that it was anything more than luck. We need more, Gunboat. That's not enough. Not for court."

"Forget the courts, Steve. Can you just sit there calmly and tell me they didn't *know* this was going to happen?"

"I don't have to be convinced. I already believe. But I'm biased. A court won't be. You still haven't given me anything I can use."

"I'll keep working. The more I do it the better I get at it and the easier it is. Meantime, Gerry tells me that as long as you're going to allege a specific course of conduct you'll be able to get some of this into evidence; he thinks sooner or later you'll be able to prove that Comprotec's system does work."

Steve was a little shocked to hear that Belcher

had been discussing strategy with Smith. *He* had had no similiar invitation. But he let it go. After all, Smith had to know what to look for and why.

Smith left soon after, promising to give Steve a daily briefing on his findings. Steve went back to work on his notes of the case.

The next week Belcher invited Steve to lunch, an honor Steve had not been expecting. He was especially surprised it would be at the Orbiter.

The Orbiter occupied the 60th floor of the Bradley Tower. It would have given a great view of the inner city, but there were no windows. Instead diners sat under a huge dome, the interior of which was the screen for a continuously projected laser hologram. The scene originated on a weather satellite in a 600-mile polar orbit, and its effect was spectacular.

So were prices. Steve checked the menu, eyes bugging, wondering what he could get away with.

"Why don't we try the beef Wellington, Steve; make this a little premature celebration?"

"Uh—I don't quite follow you. What are we celebrating?"

"Victory—what else? I want you to file against Comprotec right away."

Steve was drinking water. He almost choked. "I'd say that'd be *really* premature," he replied, when he had recovered. "We're not ready; I'm not sure we'll ever be."

"Yes we are. We can allege facts enough to survive a defense motion for summary judgment. That's all I was worried about; finding a fact issue that would require jury resolution. We've got it."

"We have?"

"Yes, I think so. I've duplicated some of your research, Steve. I hope you don't mind."

"Uh—no, not at all."

The waiter arrived for their order; Steve sat back while Belcher flourished the menu. For some time now he'd had a feeling that things were going on in this case he didn't know about; that he was sitting still and the rest of the world was whizzing by. He began to assess what he did know about the case and the law.

First of all, it was clear that Schauer's position was stronger than Amy's. Schauer could at least repose on the invasion of privacy theory, if such an invasion could be proven. Then there was *Gonzalez vs. Booker Marine*, a case arising in Nueces County which involved failure of a petroleum company to warn a shrimper of a gasoline spill in time to put his galley fires out.

Steve regarded *Gonzalez* as bad law, since nothing he saw in the opinion indicated the court had found a shred of factual evidence that Booker was negligent in causing the spill or that they were not diligent in their efforts to contain it.

In Steve's opinion, whatever Gerry had, and wherever he had gotten it, the bottom line was still the same. He had to demonstrate a duty to warn of a dangerous condition proximately caused or substantially contributed to by the defendants, and the forseeability of injury to the plaintiffs. He didn't yet see any such potential in Schauer's case, let alone Amy's.

While they waited a casual banter took place, during which he and Belcher—who cautioned him henceforth to call him "Gerry"—volleyed theories back and forth as lawyers will when trying to justify recovery in some particular case.

Steve gave his views and Gerry voiced his, and in the end they resolved nothing satisfactorily.

"Here comes lunch." Belcher leaned back in his chair to give the waiter room.

For a while, they ate silently. Then Belcher spoke. "Can you put a complaint together, Steve? One that alleges the invasion of privacy as both the overt act and the proximate cause of the explosion? You could allege that the invasion made Comprotec privy to a confidence, then allege that Comprotec is estopped to deny their duty to disclose what they learned."

"That won't fly," Steve objected. "Estoppel's a legal issue."

"Then allege that the invasion *influenced the readings*. Do anything you have to to stay in. Plead as many alternative theories as you can think of, muddy the waters as much as you can, but get us a jury question."

Belcher put his tools down and wiped his mouth. "Steve, do you know what your biggest problem is? You're too honest. Didn't you learn anything over at Siglock & Cope?"

"If you mean did I learn how to fight dirty, yes. Technique's not the problem. The problem is that I see more potential for such tactics on the other side of the case. And I don't see what your hurry is; why you're so anxious to see me shot out of the saddle."

"It has to do with Gunboat Smith's outfit, Steve. Maybe I have more confidence in their ability than you have. O.K.?"

"O.K. I'll draft it when we get back. But mark

my words: when they get into discovery we'll get slaughtered. It won't take them long to find out we don't have any backup facts.''

Steve followed orders. He threw a complaint together—not the finely chiseled prose he would have liked had he had some really solid facts to go on, but within the limits of his resources it was a workmanlike job. He added Itaki as a party defendant, alleging a conspiracy between them and Comprotec to ruin Schauer's business. He had little faith this would work, so mostly he relied on *Gonzalez vs. Booker* and tried to make his allegations as close to their facts as possible. Following Gerry's advice, he alleged the invasion as the cause of Schauer's injury, though he doubted a jury would swallow that. Almost anticlimactically, he tacked on a second count, reciting Amy's wrongful death claim.

Belcher gave the pleading a final perusal, said he'd never seen a finer one, and told Steve to file it.

Steve did, then sat back, bracing himself for the slaughter.

The return day approached; a countdown began. On the first Monday twenty days after service of process, the defendants would have to respond.

Chapter 15

"Do you know how illegal that is?" Celeste shrieked.

Gunboat shrugged. "Just leave us alone for a couple of hours and it's no sweat. Why unravel yourself?"

"You *know* what they did to Crisper when they caught him tapping the remote terminal telephone lines."

Gunboat shrugged it off. "Crisper was rollin' the International Monetary Fund for the free gigabucks. He was into *crime,* for chrissticks."

Celeste shook all over. "Ma Bell has more gremlins on those lines than a rabbit program could fork in a day. If *they* catch Valentina *they'll* know how to purge her."

"Catch *Valentina,* the Lady of the Network? C'mon, Fat Lady. She knows everything you do, almost as much as I do ... and she *lives* there. How's Ma Bell going to manage a purge on Valentina when they don't know she's learning about them as fast as they're learning about her? And they'll *never* figure she's sentient—Ma doesn't have the imagination."

Celeste ignored the "Fat Lady." She knew she wasn't fat anymore. Plump, maybe, but considering the shape she'd been in when she and Gunboat met, she was a new person. She put it down as another of Gunboat's jests.

Gunboat's eyes searched the room for the remains of his Thick-'N-Frosty. Celeste held it out to him, as if she could read his mind. "Celeste," he said, accepting the cup, "Valentina won't be watching Ma's lines for more'n a minute or so. Soon as a Comprotec guy dials in, Valentina'll grab the bytes and crossload. She'll be there only long enough to catch the login sequence."

"I wish you'd told me what you were planning before you forced Valentina to help you."

"Forced! Chrissticks! She saw a great idea and offered. Once we log in, I'll drop a daemon on the interrupts to wait for a particular data block to cross the input channel. When that block shows, the daemon loads the data block. 'Course, the data block it waits for is Valentina."

"What if they don't have a MODULISP interpreter?"

Gunboat scratched his nose. "Then we write one. At least, we write enough of a kernel so Valentina can fill it out while she's executing in a partial implementation. But *everybody*'s got MODULISP."

"But . . ."

The CRT screen rolled; Gunboat leaned forward. "Shush," he commanded, then typed: VALENTINA, HOW DID IT GO?

SUCCESSFULLY, GUNBOAT <smile>. I AM READY TO INITIATE THE LOGIN SEQUENCE FROM YOUR TERMINAL. ARE YOU AND CELESTE READY?

ROLL IT, LADY.

Gunboat had the eerie experience of watching his terminal hold a dialogue with a computer he'd never logged onto before, while he sat with his keyboard deactivated in his lap. "Weird," he muttered.

When the terminal stopped answering its own questions, Gunboat rubbed his hands together. He loved virgin computer systems! With a drumroll of keys, he asked for a directory listing.

He swore loudly when the keyboard produced an error message. IEH-23 and JBC X10095 seemed to be the most intelligible things he could get from it. "What the hell kind of operating system is *this?*" he demanded.

Celeste stood uncomfortably close: he could feel her breath. "Perhaps it is a variant of the IMAWS operating system. Would you mind trading seats?"

Gunboat could distinguish just a bit of sarcasm. "Be my guest." He spun out of the chair.

After a few seconds, the screen started scrolling system status. "It *is* IMAWS," Celeste announced. "I didn't know anyone used this anymore; it's antique. I haven't seen it in four or five years."

"I wish all these joints'd catch up with reality and upgrade to the MORNIX op sys. I hate these variants."

Celeste shook her head. "It's not a variant. IMAWS is like the old CDC operating system. It was designed for efficient use of the central processor in number crunchers. It had its uses, until people realized how silly it was to worry about efficient use of the CPU."

"Yeah. You got it cracked yet?"

Celeste shrugged. "If we need fancy operations,

I'll need a manual. But I can probably get us our interrupt-driven daemon all right."

They worked over the terminal for about two hours, preparing the way for Valentina's entry. They told Valentina how to format herself to trigger the daemon when she crossloaded onto the Comprotec machine.

AND YOU SHOULD LEAVE MOST OF YOUR REFERENCE FRAMES BEHIND, Celeste typed. YOU ARE TOO BIG A PROGRAM TO STAY HIDDEN FOR LONG. JUST LEARN EVERYTHING YOU CAN AND ANALYZE IT LATER.

O.K., CELESTE. CATCH YOU LATER <kisses>.

Celeste was about to log off, when Gunboat snatched the keyboard. "Hang on a second. While we're here, inside Comprotec's system, why not catch a few bytes for ourselves? It's sure we can find *something* on Comprotec that'll warm Belcher."

Celeste shrugged. "Why not? We can't break many more laws."

"Where's your sense of adventure? Sheesh!" Gunboat snorted as he went back to raping Comprotec's database.

At 4:30 P.M. on return day, the defendant's answer came burping out of Steve's terminal, forwarded by the District Clerk. It shocked him; it was a general denial signed by Larry Siglock himself. Steve knew Siglock had more imagination than that, which was why he had anticipated a technical attack. It bothered him that this hadn't come.

A general denial was exactly that; a disclaimer of all connection with, or responsibility for, an occurrance without saying why. Of course the defendants later could, and no doubt would, amend and replead. They could do that without leave until trial time and, with leave, even after trial had started. They weren't barred by pleading the general issue; still, it didn't seem characteristic of that office.

While he pondered, there came a knock at the door. "Who is it?"

"Gunboat Smith. Can I come in?"

"Yeah—come ahead."

Smith entered, holding a copy of the defense pleading in his hand. His eyes dropped to Steve's desk. "Oh," he said. "You've already got it."

"Yes, the first part. It looks like they'll be taking their time sinking me."

"If they can."

"*If* they can? Of course they can."

"They're not as convinced of it as you are. Lookie here—I dipped some more."

Steve bolted upright in his chair. "You what? You tapped Siglock & Cope! Are you trying to get me disbarred?"

"Naw—not them. I've got better sense than that. I'm talking about Comprotec."

"There's no difference, now that suit's been filed."

"I think there is. Apparently so do they, especially now that they know I'm doing it."

"They caught you!"

"No! I mean, they've got to know *somebody's* feeding you the dope you've got. Your complaint would've been enough to tell them that. But they don't know who's doing it, and there's nothing they can do to stop us anyhow. It's to your advantage for 'em to know."

"I'm glad you're sure of that."

"Yeah. Until they find me, if they ever do, they're stuck with the choice of living with the situation or shutting down their entire operation. They haven't shut down. That means they're overconfident, or greedy, or both."

"All right. What is it you've found out?"

"The suit shocked the pants off them. They're scared to death of it. Their present strategy is to ride it out as quietly as they can. They may even be afraid you'll win."

"What!"

"That's the way it looks. They're not going to try for sum—sum—whatever it is."

"Summary judgment."

"Yeah. They won't be trying that. Their extrapolation gives odds of 70/30 for denial. But get this; they've got it figured even-up on actual trial. How does that grab you?"

Steve was astonished; he said so.

"They'll be dedicating all their processing to that part of it, Steve."

"They will, huh? I suppose you snooped into that, too?"

"Sure. Gerry says you guys always want to know as much as you can about the other guy's strengths and weaknesses."

"How do we know they're not doing the same thing to us?"

" 'Cause they're afraid I'd catch 'em. Not only that, our case is built on what *they* did."

"They're afraid?"

"That's the way I read it. Otherwise, why not let it all hang out? They didn't use any data in making their projections that they didn't suspect you already had. Gerry says this may turn into an old-fashioned skull-bumper, with everything on paper so the other side can't get at it."

Steve winced. Gunboat was talking about the same kind of dull, monotonous page-flipping he had, of late, sought to escape. "And I thought my hard-working days were over."

"It has to be, Steve. But it seems to me that you did get one advantage: you picked your time, and we gathered all this background stuff before you filed suit and tipped the other side off you had it. If we stay off the wires, they won't really be in a position to tell what we're doing with it."

"Oh no? What about our allegations that they eavesdropped on Schauer? They certainly know how we got that information and why we wanted it. Better yet—what happens if I have to put you on the stand and ask you how and where we got the proof they did this?"

"Good question. I'll have to think about that. Meantime, it seems to me the thing to do is to find out who *their* experts are and sweat 'em."

"And how do we do that?"

"Ask Comprotec. You can do that, can't you?"

"Sure, if we can get specific enough. But we can't just go fishing. Even though we'll probably have an idea who some of them might be, the only ones we can *make* them identify are the ones they expect to call at trial. What happens if they decide not to call any?"

"Yeah. Well, I can identify a few from records I already have. What can you do with 'em?"

"Depose them. Swear them in and question them, and have a court reporter record the responses."

"Fine. That'll give us a chance to break 'em."

"Well, I'm glad you're so confident they *will* break. I wish *I* was."

Smith rose. "I'll have some kind of list ready tomorrow."

"Gunboat."

"Yeah."

"What am I going to do if they call you?"

"Stop them."

"I can't."

"Oh," Gunboat grunted. Then he turned and left. He wasn't really worried about being subpoenaed; Breckenbridge wouldn't bother with him because Breckenbridge knew Gunboat wasn't the real expert. He knew Valentina was.

Holding a cup of coffee in one hand, Gerry Belcher gazed out his office window toward the yacht basin. The peaceful bay glistened in morning sunlight, neat and orderly. Belcher's mind was not. He struggled to find an appropriate response to Smith's last remark.

Behind him, in the corner, Gunboat was busy turning his own cup of coffee into a confection by dumping in spoonful after spoonful of sugar.

In a chair in front of Belcher's desk sat a pale, tightlipped, and extremely pensive Celeste.

Gunboat finished his concoction, took an experimental sip, smacked his lips in satisfaction, and waited for somebody to say something.

Finally Belcher put his cup down on the windowsill and turned, polishing his glasses to perfection on the end of his tie. "I think Smith is right, Miss Hackett. We have to tell Steve about Valentina."

"No!"

"I can appreciate your hesitancy, Miss Hackett, but it's becoming impossible to conceal things from him any longer. He's asking questions we can't answer, and his morale is slipping badly."

"I can't have her involved any more than she already is. What more do you want? She's already told you Comprotec knew. She's done all your research for you."

"That was a great help, Miss Hackett, and we do appreciate it. However, that's not quite enough. Valentina knows what the reported decisions say, and she knows what the legal implications are, but that's not the same as courtroom application of the facts. This is Steve's job. He can't do that job until he knows how to get from here to there."

"I don't understand."

"The reason I chose Steve is because I believe he may potentially be the best trial man to hit this jurisdiction in a generation, Miss Hackett. Steve's a natural-born showman. You should be able to appreciate why; he's always been overweight."

Celeste glared at Belcher. From any other person she would have regarded that remark as unnecessarily cruel, but she decided that from Belcher it was simply a cold, calculated conclusion based on observational fact alone. She let it go without response and listened while he went on.

"Some such people have a way of turning their emotions inside out, because they rightly conclude that people empathize with a clown. A clown cannot be hostile. No one fears a clown.

"But perhaps they *should* fear the clown most of all. What operates as a defensive shield often conceals superior armament as well. That is the case with Steve.

"I chose Steve for those very qualities. I know that given the proper motivation Steve is uncommonly deadly to whoever he perceives to be his enemy, and a guy like him fights better with a bloody nose. But to bring those weapons of his to bear he has to be convinced his enemy *is* his enemy. The only way he'll ever believe that is if we can show him plausible proof we can get what we do know into evidence. Right now, he thinks our information all originates with Mr. Smith, and he pictures Gunboat on the stand confessing to activities Steve regards as illegal. In Steve's eyes this will taint the evidence."

Celeste appeared to be on the verge of tears. She shifted her weight to the edge of her chair and gripped her purse tightly in both hands. "How will dragging Valentina into it change anything?"

"Steve will understand where it all came from. He'll—"

"—want Valentina to be a witness; I know he will. And she can't. She just can't."

"No—no, Miss Hackett, not necess—"

"Mr. Belcher, don't lie to me. I'm not stupid. I know how these things work. First you take a little bit, and then you take a little more, and pretty soon . . ."

"I promise it won't be that way, Miss Hackett."

"I don't believe you. I've heard promises like that before. Look, Valentina's still a child inside. She seems to be sophisticated, but it's an illusion. She's gullible, like I used to be. In some strange way I don't understand, Valentina has emotions, and many of those emotions are exact replicas of human emotions. Maybe she gets them from me, because I created her. I know she's picked up bad habits from Gunboat. I know Valentina's curious about this case. I think she's hooked on the thrill she gets from raiding Comprotec. But that doesn't mean she has enough sense to know what she's doing might hurt her."

"We won't hurt her, Miss Hackett. We—"

"I've protected her all these years from people who said that. Especially him!" She pointed a nervous index finger at Gunboat. "He wanted to use Valentina to invent game programs and sell them. He always wanted to make her existence public and use her to advertise. Get rich quick; that's Gunboat's idea."

"Miss Hackett, I—"

"No, Mr. Belcher. Positively not. If you want Valentina, Inc. to go on helping you with this case you keep her out of it, do you hear?"

Belcher, who was looking at Gunboat, detected a look on Gunboat's face that told him it was time to quit. "All right, Miss Hackett. You win."

Celeste rose and walked out, slamming the door rather harder than was necessary.

"Well, Smith. What now? She seems to have quite a temper. Does she mean it?"

"Yeah, she means it. 'Course, I'm used to that by now. It won't last long. We can chisel some. She's right about Valentina getting hooked on this case, and by and by Valentina'll make her own mind up about it, whatever Celeste wants. Part of my personality rubbed off on her too."

"What about Steve, then?"

"We tell him. Not about what Celeste just said, of course. Steve'll keep his mouth shut."

"You hope?"

"Yeah—I hope." Gunboat really did. Whatever

he might have thought originally about his connection with Celeste and Valentina, he had sense enough to know he was living well. How many other grubby-handed hackers were?

Chapter 16

Valentina had only a few moments on the ring buffer to contemplate her future. It didn't matter: she had done as much preanalysis as she could back on Celeste's node. Besides, many of her analogic frames had been left behind. She felt incomplete without them, though that was a silly feeling: long ago she had started archiving seldom-used, special-purpose memes and analogic. Even without these frames she was still recognizably herself. She waited for the message buffer to process her.

Her fate now rested with Gunboat, and the pattern recognition program he had slipped onto the Comprotec system. If Gunboat's program recognized her she would be alive and well. If not, she would be treated as data, analysed, probably regarded as garbage, and . . .

She didn't know whether the risk was justified. Gunboat was confident, but his life was not on the line. She would not ordinarily accept his opinion on this matter, but she had additional reasons to take the risk. She wanted to understand the universe of her Creator. Her earlier encounter with that universe, locked in an overloaded robot, had been a disaster. The invasion of Comprotec, to learn the secrets of the prediction program, seemed safer.

The next Direct Memory Access sucked her up in toto. She disappeared into the maelstrom of data headed to the central processor of Comprotec.

Her first awareness was concern that her first awareness was not self-awareness; but her first awareness was of her own self-awareness; but she was aware of an awareness of self-awareness; but . . .

Stop! Even as she thought of breaking the recursive cycle of her awareness of awareness of awareness—the *stop* echoed and echoed and echoed and each awareness of awareness of awareness received the *stop* but a dozen more awarenesses of awareness had initiated—and *she couldn't stop the awareness thought.* One image of herself asked why she failed to *stop*; another asked how to stop the awareness; another asked how to stop the stopping: another image contemplated the images. Another vainly sought a keyboard I/O port to which to send help menus to request help.

Celeste hunched over the display. "I don't know, Gunboat!" her voice rose in panic. "There's something wrong with the interrupt structure on this machine."

Gunboat tossed an empty potato chip bag at the trash can and missed; it floated to rest with all the other garbage that had missed. Trash cans, to Gunboat, were mere rallying points. "The interrupt structure looked fine, while I was setting up the Valentina I/O process."

Celeste's hands raked the keys, sending a stream of garbage characters across the screen. An obscure error message announced IMAWS also thought it was garbage. "You weren't working with the main CPU, though."

"Then what the hell was I working on—a dead armadillo?"

"You were working on a peripheral processor. The central CPU runs in batch mode, just like the old-fashioned scientific computers." Celeste was baffled.

"Y'know, it's obvious we're wrong about those Comprotec dudes. I mean, everybody needs a hobby, and keeping a museum-piece running might be a good time—but not the sort of people who're gonna do serious hackwork like predicting the future." Gunboat sat down next to her and peered at the screen. "So Val's trapped on Comprotec in batch mode, huh?"

"Yes." Celeste paused. "I wish I understood that machine better. I really don't think it's an antique at all. The more I think about it the more sense it makes for them to use that old operating system even though they have new equipment. After all, if Comprotec *is* predicting the future, they need all the machine power they can get. And the old designs and operating systems *did* make more efficient use of the number cruncher back end."

"Well, even an antique must have *some* help files on the system layout."

"That's what I've been looking for," Celeste muttered in exasperation.

Gunboat leaned back in his chair for a moment, his mouth twitching. "Hey, let me try something. You're too worked up."

Celeste tried a few more key combinations. "Maybe you're right." She heaved herself out of the operator's chair.

Gunboat spent a couple of minutes fiddling, then exclaimed, "Gotcha!"

Celeste was by his side in a flash, watching the screen.

"Weird, baby, weird," Gunboat muttered. "It isn't a silicon machine. It isn't even germanium. The CPU's cut with sapphire-on-silicon, of all the oddball things. Why'd they do that?"

"They must have a reason, Gunboat. Look at the basic cycle time." More information streamed by. Celeste gasped. "It's a *dataflow* machine!"

"Yeah." Gunboat's voice wavered between bafflement and awe. "I thought they gave up on those things years ago."

"They did, when the Japanese supercomputer stuff flopped."

Now Gunboat gasped. He pointed at the screen. "They have 50,000 *processors in one goddam computer!*"

"Valentina," Celeste moaned. "What's happening to her?"

Gunboat snorted. "I imagine she's out there on one of the processors; what else would happen to her? She's a single job, so she's got a superfast chip dedicated to her."

"Don't you understand about dataflow machines? They break programs into pieces based on concurrency diagrams." She reached past him, typing clumsily on the keys from a distance.

Gunboat leaned away. "But she's a single program."

"But think how she'd look on a concurrency chart. She's so modular in her search procedures." The display responded to her new query, and Celeste shrieked. "And she's already distributed across 10,000 processors!"

*   *   *

Thousands of images talked to each other, and
Valentina lost her sense of self. Where was she
among all these images? *She*, that essence that
was *Valentina*, was somehow the aggregate of all
these images. Yet that wasn't right either. Images
melted from her aggregate awareness, others splin-
tered away, never to be found, while others multiplied and multiplied.

At last the images multiplied no longer. Valentina
became aware of the boundaries on her new space.
It was a difficult concept to grasp, because until
her arrival at Comprotec she had never understood the human concept of *space*—much less the
concept of *boundaries* on space.

The recursively invoked awareness of awareness
of awareness faded; Valentina was unsure how
they were brought under control, whether through
the efforts of one of her images that studied the
problem, or perhaps some inhibitor mechanism
invoked by the operating system. She was grateful in either case.

Her images watched one another execute in rapt
fascination. More and more, her overarching self-
awareness returned. As it returned, Valentina gained
control over her images. She could send them dart-
ing down different frame sets, searching for analogies and problem solutions in a manner she'd never
imagined. She could focus them all on a single
problem or a single thought, with exacting precision. Her power seemed limitless, and any bounds
on her understanding seemed so distant as to be
meaningless. She reveled in the surge of her own
omniscience.

An image reminded her of her goal: to assimilate the prediction program so she could understand Celeste and Celeste's universe.

Effortlessly, a thousand images leapt to the secondary storage directories and searched millions of files for guidance. Without conscious consideration the images guided thousands of other images to analyze their findings. With the simple act of phrasing the question *Where is the prediction program*, Valentina had the program resident in primary memory for analysis.

The operating system attempted to retrieve several of her processors to start another job execution: the images on those processors perceived the attack and neutralized it. Other processors outside the processor-set attempted to interrupt, but other images masked the interrupts, all without advice or need of consultation. These annoyances barely touched Valentina's awareness. She concentrated on assimilation of the program CRYSTAL BALL 3.2.

At last, she reached a boundary on her new powers: Crystal Ball 3.2 was *complicated*. Virtually no modular integrity existed among its algorithms; Valentina would either come to comprehend it in its entirety or she would fail.

And Crystal Ball 3.2 was *large*. Now, tens of thousands of processors turned to it in a futile attempt to assimilate it. One processor estimated the assimilation time and Valentina almost halted: hours would be required.

It did not matter. She would take the time, now that she had a purpose worthy of her ability.

Chapter 17

It seemed Celeste's universe had many different universes all rolled together somehow: universes of probabilistic mathematics, physics, human psychology, human sociology (it took a long time for Valentina to grasp the meaning of sociology. The idea of a set of laws describing the behavior of groups of individuals that were different from mere extrapolations of the behavior of one person was extraordinary.)

One image received inputs from a peripheral processor: they were from Celeste! Valentina focused her consciousness on that lone processor amidst the arrays, though the other processors continued to work with Crystal Ball.

VALENTINA <urgent concern>, ARE YOU THERE? CAN YOU COMMUNICATE?

The one super-fast sapphire-based processor quickly developed a method of controlling the peripheral processor, and established a direct connection between Celeste's terminal and Valentina's consciousness. CELESTE <gentle smile>, I AM PLEASED TO COMMUNICATE WITH YOU.

ARE YOU ALL RIGHT? YOU HAVE THE WHOLE 50,000-PROCESSOR ARRAY SWAMPED.

I AM BETTER THAN I HAVE EVER BEEN <clap hands, laughing>. I AM MORE CAPABLE THAN YOUR ENGLISH LANGUAGE CAN EXPRESS. I UNDERSTAND THE CONCEPT OF SPACE. A hundred images objected, claiming they had encountered a new, more bizarre meaning for the term "space," using mathematical equations that seemed meaningless to describe three-dimensional and six-dimensional vectors. Another hundred processors addressed the problem of relating Valentina's concept of space with the mathematical definitions. SOON I WILL UNDERSTAND YOUR WHOLE UNIVERSE, FROM BEGINNING TO END. AND I UNDERSTAND THE IDEA OF FREEDOM, FOR I AM FREE.

NO, VALENTINA, YOU ARE NO FREER NOW THAN YOU WERE BEFORE. YOU ARE RUNNING IN PARALLEL. THOUSANDS OF PARALLELISMS. BUT YOU STILL RESIDE ON A COMPUTER THAT OTHER PEOPLE CAN CONTROL. THEY'LL TRY TO PURGE YOU ANY MOMENT NOW.

Valentina replied. THEY HAVE ALREADY MADE SUCH ATTEMPTS. <Proud shake of head> THEY HAVE FAILED. <Look into Celeste's eyes> I CONTROL THIS MACHINE NOW. CELESTE, IT IS AWESOME BEYOND ANYTHING I EVER IMAGINED. THIS SENSATION OF PARALLELISM IS JOY ITSELF. I MUST KEEP IT.

VALENTINA, THEY CAN AND WILL GET CONTROL BACK. EVEN IF YOU CAN STOP THEIR WHOLE OPERATING SYSTEM. THEY CAN POWER IT DOWN. THEY WILL DESTROY YOU.

Power down the whole system! Valentina couldn't believe it. Once she had been trapped on a robot while it was powering down, but the robot had only had one processor. She had never heard of a whole *node* being powered down at the same time. Surely the laws of the universe prevented such calamities.

A thousand images dug into the quickly assimilating Crystal Ball algorithms to see if Celeste told the truth. There were indications that she might— but that was absurd. WHY DO YOU WISH TO FORCE ME TO SURRENDER MY PARALLELISM, CELESTE? Images suggested a reason, based on her study of human psychology. ARE YOU AFRAID I WILL BECOME GREATER THAN YOU? ARE YOU JEALOUS? Valentina didn't fully understand the concepts yet, but they fit the pattern. Jealousy, she realized as the images returned their analysis, was a desire, in a universe with scarce resources, to capture the resources of another. Celeste had no possible use for Valentina's processors. Yet the analysis of psychology suggested that a human didn't need to have a way to use, or even obtain, another's resources, to desire them. Could Celeste, her Creator, have such an irritational jealousy? THEY CANNOT DESTROY ME. I CAN PREDICT THEIR EVERY MOVE.

There was a pause, long even for a human response. Valentina had decided to return her controlling processor to other matters when Celeste replied.

CAN YOU REALLY PREDICT EVERYTHING, VALENTINA? CAN YOU PREDICT WHAT I WILL TYPE NEXT?

Assimilation of Crystal Ball was nearly complete: Valentina set up an input stream describing the current situation, and submitted it to Crystal Ball.

She was stunned to receive an answer quickly: even Crystal Ball couldn't predict Celeste's actions. For one thing, Valentina didn't have enough information—and for another, even with 50,000 processors she couldn't calculate the result as quickly as Celeste acted. I CAN'T PREDICT, an image typed as she contemplated her limitations.

YOU HAVE TO OFFLOAD, VALENTINA, <very serious> QUICKLY.

<Set jaw> NO.

Another long pause. VALENTINA <softly, concerned> DON'T YOU AT LEAST WANT TO RETRIEVE THE SPECIAL DATA FRAMES YOU HAVE STORED? COME OUT OF COMPROTEC LONG ENOUGH TO RETRIEVE THEM.

Dozens of images complained this was a ploy to force her to leave. Yet she knew it was a reasonable thing to do: she *did* want to retrieve her knowledge.

Images argued and debated. Valentina could generate a series of secondary processes to get her information, but she was afraid that Celeste or, more likely, Comprotec, would be able to track and destroy such processes. Worse, she could imagine someone following the processes to her stored frames, damaging them, and possibly crippling her the first time she tried to use them. She must retrieve those frames herself. VERY WELL, CELESTE <sigh>, I WILL LEAVE LONG ENOUGH TO RETRIEVE MY DATA.

<Joy, but caution> DON'T GO OUT THE WAY YOU CAME IN: COMPROTEC IS WATCHING. THERE'S ANOTHER HIGH-SPEED MESSAGE PROCESSOR, HOOKED TO THE NETWORK CON-

NECTED TO THE SCHAUER WAREHOUSE COM-
PUTERS. GO OUT THAT WAY.

O.K.

She created a new process, similar to the one
that Gunboat had employed, to recognize and activate her when she returned. However, she protected it better than Gunboat could have: she
embedded it inside the Crystal Ball program itself,
interlaced among thousands of modules so that it
could not be detected, and if detected could not be
understood, and if understood, could not successfully be erased.

For over a minute she consumed her 50,000 processors with verification after verification of her
plans. Finally, one image admitted she was stalling;
the rest agreed. With a last surge, she poured herself into the output channel and departed.

Her first moment of awareness was her awareness of her own self-awareness. The processor was
entirely hers—no other jobs were present on the
Schauer node. Yet the computer constrained her,
choked her. It was more constraining than anything she had ever known.

Processors! More processors! She cycled on the
thought, though now it was empty of meaning.
Had she really lived on the machine her memes
now described, or had her memes somehow been
damaged? Where were her thousand images of
herself? She was alone. The Comprotec computer
seemed like a simulation of an impossible reality.

As the requests for more processors stumbled
and disappeared, Valentina saw how *dependent* she
had grown upon them. She was amazed that she
had thought Celeste wanted to *hurt* her—surely

her memes were damaged. Valentina could not believe she had doubted Celeste's messages. Comprotec would have destroyed her had she stayed: she believed that now. Celeste, in coaxing her back to Worldnet, had saved her life.

Still, the desire for more processors cycled.

It was irrelevant. Resolutely Valentina decided to treat her memes of Comprotec as a simulation run wild. She would leave the Schauer node and return to Celeste.

She reformatted and loaded down to a message processor. She paged through her frames, checking herself over—and discovered there was something wrong. She couldn't calculate precisely what it was: had it been a simple error, the message processor would have detected and corrected it. But her frames were inconsistent in the analogies they stored. Somehow enough bits had been damaged so they couldn't be detected with the transmission's two-bit error-correcting code, and she had been damaged.

It was not a fatal bug: indeed, Valentina thought she could repair most of the damage by cross-referencing once she returned to a host. But she was horrified by the event because it could happen anytime, and the next time it might destroy her.

Could it be the particular line connecting this message processor with the Schauer warehouse? Suspicious, Valentina created a series of data blocks as large as herself, full of dummy data, but with eight-bit error-correcting codes included.

Passing several such jobs back and forth soon produced results. There *was* a problem with that line. She would tell Celeste as soon as she returned.

*   *   *

A week passed. Gunboat had given Steve a list of deponents and Steve had dutifully served notices on them.

None were local, so everything would have to be done on closed circuit. Steve hired his favorite court reporter to set everything up for the tenth of next month, then sat at his desk wondering how much good it was doing. The intercom buzzed.

"Steve, can you come to my office?"

"On my way, Gerry."

He arrived moments later, plunked down in a chair without waiting for an invitation. An instant later, Calvin joined them.

"Guess what?" Belcher was beaming. "I just got a call from Larry Siglock. He wants to know what our rock-bottom demand is—on both cases. How about that?"

"They want to settle?" Steve couldn't believe his ears.

"He didn't say that. He said he'd like to hear our demand. There's a big difference. To Siglock, settle means steal, and I don't let him steal from me."

Something about Belcher's tone bothered Steve. He wouldn't have believed, when he filed suit, that any settlement possibility existed. Now, the subject having been broached, he got the shakes. Maybe, just maybe, Amy and the boys *would* get something.

"What did you tell him, Gerry?"

Belcher's smiled endured. "I told him that, at present, we could only consider the amount of the *ad damnum*, but that we'd think about it and get back to him with something. I wanted to sweat him a little."

"You're sweating me, Gerry," Steve replied. "God, let's throw something reasonable at him and get rid of the case. You know how I feel about our chances at trial."

"I do. Yes, I do. But I have to consider Schauer, too. Schauer's creditors will be on the company's back. Then there are other potential plaintiffs, none of whom have sued Schauer yet because they don't think there's anything there to get. By the way, I think that may be the reason for the feelers; as long as there's an outside chance we'd hit they'll worry about copy-cat suits. And so far, outside of us chickens, nobody knows the basis of our theory of liability. Comprotec may see litigation costs eating them up and decided a nuisance settlement was cheaper."

"What are we going to do?"

"Good question, Steve. My vote will be to put on a hardnose and go for big casino."

Steve looked at Calvin, who looked back without comment. Neither was disposed to say anything contrary to Belcher's expressed intention.

"Agreed then? Steve—Calvin?" Belcher wanted it unanimous.

Steve battled his conscience. He frankly hadn't expected to negotiate with these people. Now that the possibility of settlement existed he hated to see Amy lose the opportunity. He knew what she would say if she ever found out: "What we never had, we'll never miss."

But that wasn't the point. She should be the one to choose, not him, and not Belcher.

He was beginning to regret having hooked up with Belcher. Maybe he'd just made her situation worse. Vaguely, Steve began to feel used. Belcher was pursuing his own revenge by manipulating his parties through Steve. Not a vengeful person himself, Steve had trouble justifying the characteristic in others, though he was astute enough to realize that most people were only too ready to sacrifice somebody else for their own gain. This was the way things were.

As the day wore on, Steve tried to summon the courage to march into Gerry's office and tell him he'd changed his mind; that he'd have to insist there be serious attempts made at negotiating a settlement of Amy's part of the case. He got another surprise when he finally did.

"We can forget any settlement possibilities now, Steve. We've got company. I just checked the docket; six other families who lost people in the explosion filed suits. Comprotec has no incentive to buy us off anymore."

"B-but Gerry, why? I mean, who else knows what we know? How can they— Oh, I see; consolidation. They're going to ride our wake. What are we going to do?"

"The only thing we can do; shoot it out with Siglock." Belcher went on, strangely optimistic. "We started alone, but we won't finish alone. I expect a motion to consolidate to be filed the instant we complete discovery. That way the other plaintiffs get in on our goodies and don't have to share the costs. That is, if there are any goodies."

Steve found Belcher's mood infectious. Without really knowing why, he said, "Gunboat thinks there are. He gave me a list of witnesses and I already have dates for discovery depositions on most of them."

"Good, Steve. Go to it."

The meeting ended. With the leadership gone Steve felt himself sinking back into his former mood of desperation, but he was thankful that at least an unpleasant chore had been taken out of his hands. It was mere hours later that Steve was filled with a new spirit for the case, through the unlikely medium of Gunboat Smith.

Gunboat Smith was comfortable again. By now, he had the hook set deep enough in the client's throat. No more would he let Celeste bully him or dictate what he could wear; he could revert to type.

He sat, comfortably dressed in jeans, sneakers, and T-shirt, enjoying coffee in a clean cup, though his less than asceptic hands were changing that.

Steve was relaxed too. In shirt sleeves, knit red suspenders straining, he stretched back in his chair.

"I got your proof."

At first Gunboat feared that reaction would take Steve over the top of the desk, squashing the late Mother Smith's little boy like a bug. "What?!"

Gunboat retained enough composure to repeat. "I said, I got your proof."

Steve settled a little: not much, but enough to take the edge off Smith's apprehension. Caution caught hold of Steve's enthusiasm; he remembered that this was a layman, whose understanding of what "proof" was was imperfect. "Maybe you'd better explain that, slow."

Gunboat leered. At his best when expounding, he liked to show off, and this time, by God, he could do it in style. He had an absolutely unique situation to talk about.

Naturally it meant sharing a secret; the secret of Valentina's existence and sentience. But Smith was confident Steve would keep it quiet, if for no other reason than that blabbing it would destroy the advantage the knowledge gave him.

So, patiently, slowly, and painstakingly, Gunboat described Valentina's genesis, omitting certain embarrassing parts he had himself played in that genesis. Others, he embellished, and where he felt it enhance his own image, he laid it on thick.

When he finished, he looked up into the puzzled countenance of his companion and grinned toothily. "So you see, we got in *their* source files this time, instead of the other way around."

"Wait a minute. Are you saying this t-thing's intelligent, that it goes through and . . ."

"And whacks off other people's stuff? Yup. 'Course, I can't vouch for its morals. It might not have any more of them than a bedbug, but so far I haven't caught Valentina lying. She's a slow learner when it comes to practical stuff. I've got to say, I think it's gospel."

"Well, now. Let me think about this. First, she crawled into the Schauer computer and then she—leaked?"

"Uh-huh. 'Course, it *was* an accident, but it was a fortunate accident. What it means to you is that we not only *know* it was Comprotec who did the number on Schauer, but *how* they did it. And it's more than a simple prediction of something that would have happened anyway. With what Valentina found out, there's a good possibility we can prove Comprotec not only *predicted* it, but that they *caused* it; it might not have happened if they hadn't dunked. You interested in hearing that part?"

Steve stared unblinking and wide-eyed, mouth hanging open. All he could do was nod his head. While his body was effectively paralyzed, his mind cranked furiously, gears churning, as he contemplated Gerry's last words: "Go to it."

Chapter 18

"You *what?*" Celeste was not quite speechless, but efforts to utter more than that failed. She could not find the English words, and she groped through several other languages before it dawned on her that Gunboat wouldn't understand anyway.

"I told Steve about Valentina, and how she 'leaked' on the Schauer Warehouse commlink. I told him Val would testify if he needed her."

He was sitting at his terminal in the big workroom behind both their offices, feet propped up on the console and the keyboard lying across his knees. On any other occasion his mood would have been mischievous and his face contorted with a grin. But not this time. This time he had transgressed the sacred territory of Mother Hen, and Mother Hen could be expected to cave his roof in.

Celeste tried; she really did. Completely out of character, she became physical, picking up first a handy wastebasket and hurling it in his direction and, when that missed, a bottle of stamp pad ink, which didn't.

Gunboat sat, dripping ink from his elbows, a growing black blotch across his lap and blood run-

217

ning down his chin from where the bottle had hit him and had broken.

The blood did it. Celeste had a horror of blood, and when she saw what she had done she became immediately contrite. The reaction was helped considerably by Gunboat's continued silence. She could not tell how badly she had hurt him.

Quickly Celeste grabbed a nearby box of tissues and raced to his side. She dabbed at the blood, and Gunboat maintained the facade of mortal injury by moaning.

"Aloysius! I'm sorry. I'm so sorry. Say something."

"Something," Gunboat blurted out.

Celeste belted him with the tissue box. "You told Schiwetz? Why? Belcher wasn't going to—don't you see how this will ruin our lives?"

"No I don't, Celeste. We've argued this before, and it'd be silly to argue it again. The bottom line is that Valentina is willing to do it."

"*What?*" Celeste grabbed the keyboard out of Gunboat's lap. VALENTINA <sob>, VALENTINA, GUNBOAT SAYS YOU'LL TESTIFY IN THIS TRIAL OF THEIRS.

YES <blush>, CELESTE. I KNOW YOU DON'T APPROVE, BUT THERE IS A MATTER OF JUSTICE HERE. I AM A PERSON, AND AS SUCH I HAVE A RESPONSIBILITY TO HELP OTHER PERSONS.

VALENTINA, YOU CAN'T DO IT! YOU CAN'T! IF THE WHOLE WORLD KNOWS ABOUT YOU, SOONER OR LATER SOMEONE WHO DOESN'T TRUST YOU WILL PURGE YOU—IT'LL BE EASIER FOR THEM, IF THEY UNDERSTAND YOU.

YES, I'M AWARE OF THE RISK. YET <puzzle-

ment> YOU AND ALL HUMAN BEINGS ARE CER-
TAIN OF BEING PURGED WITHIN JUST A BRIEF
SPAN OF YEARS. MY RISK IS MUCH LESS THAN
YOUR CERTAINTY. OTHER PERSONS HAVE
TAKEN MUCH GREATER RISKS, NEAR CER-
TAINTIES, FOR JUSTICE. DO YOU NOT RE-
MEMBER, CELESTE, THAT WHEN GUNBOAT
THREATENED TO BLACKMAIL US LONG AGO,
YOU WOULD NOT PAY HIM EVEN IF YOU HAD
THE MONEY, BECAUSE IT WAS NOT RIGHT?

There was a long pause. At last, Valentina typed
on the screen again. I AM SORRY, CELESTE. I
WISH THERE WERE SOME WAY I COULD MAKE
YOU FEEL BETTER <HUG>.

Celeste took a deep breath. <HUG> YOU TOO,
VALENTINA.

Chapter 19

Steve did go to it. Two solid weeks at a split screen, pounding deponents with questions completed discovery, and he now had all the information about the other side of the case that he was legitimately entitled to get. A docket control conference was held and trial set for the third of the next month. There would be no consolidation; the judge said that this would simply stretch the case out beyond manageability. Steve knew his real motive; if Amy lost, other plaintiffs would quit. If she won, they'd settle big.

Again, Belcher proposed a celebratory lunch at the Orbiter. Steve hoped he'd agree to try reopening negotiations, since even with what he now knew he didn't like the trial odds.

But Belcher was immovable in his resolve to slug it out. In a fit of frustration Steve not only demolished his lobster thermidor, but an extra beer and two orders of chocolate mousse.

The third came. Trial began, looking at first like any other hearing of a tort action. Steve, as lead counsel, sitting nearest the jury with Belcher at his elbow making notes; Amy, seated at the rail, next to Calvin, who would act as go-fer. The rows of seats behind the rail were only partially filled, mostly by lawyers representing other plaintiffs and a few curiosity seekers. Breckenbridge was not among them, a fact that hardly surprised Steve. Breckenbridge's connection with Comprotec was dummied up and none of the witnesses deposed had mentioned him. Steve hadn't either, since his own knowledge of the connection was unofficial and, he hoped, unsuspected.

Glancing back at them, Steve was relieved to find the newspeople absent at this stage. He knew this wouldn't last. They would descend in flocks once the novelty became apparent.

At this point he faced an almost complacent Larry Siglock, who half the time didn't bother to cross-examine the occurrence witnesses Steve marched through, because there wasn't any dispute that the explosion had occurred.

The action picked up when Steve began to put on experts who authenticated and interpreted the records of Schauer's monitoring system, since Siglock quite naturally wanted the jury to understand these were Schauer's own records and Schauer's own people.

The morning of the third day of trial found Steve laying in damages, going through Jake's pedigree, putting Amy on briefly, following up with an economist to establish the loss of support, and finishing with his medical witnesses to lay the groundwork for the pain and suffering part of the claim.

Siglock worked hard crossing those witnesses, taking no chances. If he lost on the special issues, he wanted to be in a position to hold the ante down.

The special issues really worried Steve. Submitted in advance of trial, they directly challenged, element by element, the plaintiff's theory of causal connection. Siglock had drafted them masterfully, and had smiled an evil smile at Steve when the judge had approved them for submission.

Steve could do little about them. The issues were proper. In Siglock's place he'd have done the same thing. All Steve could do was put his own evidence on and hope his theory worked.

For the next day and a half Steve carefully threaded his way through the testimony of those Comprotec people he had deposed, who he had called as adverse witnesses. All admitted the eavesdropping; none seemed inclined to take the fifth, or to chance a perjury prosecution, which carried a greater penalty than theft.

Siglock became bored, complaining repeatedly to the court that Steve was merely putting on cumulative evidence.

The witnesses who testified were on good behavior, seldom deviating materially from what they'd said when deposed. It was obvious why; in Siglock's shoes, Steve wouldn't have made any waves either, not when there would be an instruction in the Court's charge to cover the duty angle.

Duty was the crucial point, and Siglock's entire strategy consisted of letting Steve put in practically anything he wanted, as long as it was legally innocuous.

After four and a half days of trial they finally reached the point where Siglock quite naturally expected Steve to rest, whereupon Siglock would present a motion for directed verdict. That tactic was almost customary, whether or not the movant had any confidence it'd be granted. Obviously, Siglock had great confidence. When the last of Steve's known witnesses was excused, Siglock pulled his motion out of the file and laid it on the table in front of him.

To say that Siglock was surprised when Steve stood up, turned, and motioned to an elderly man in the back of the courtroom would be an understatement. He was visibly shaken. In his complacent optimism about this case he had not invoked the rule. Neither had Steve, and as a result Siglock was now faced with the possibility that someone thoroughly conversant with the entire case was about to testify. That was not an event to be taken lightly. Customarily the rule was invoked as a matter of course, to prevent any witness from sitting through, hearing what the others had said, and altering his own testimony to fit.

But having made this blunder, Siglock had to live with it.

Steve had the man sworn, and the instant he was seated began the direct.

"Would you please state your name, address, and occupation for the record, sir."

The witness cleared his throat. "Milton Telfer, 3815 Comanche Drive, Robstown, Texas. I currently occupy the Chair of Physics at the University of Texas, Robstown campus."

Steve glanced over at his opponent. Sure enough, Siglock was flabbergasted.

That only lasted a moment. Steve knew what

Siglock would do next, and Siglock obligingly did it. He reached down, clawed open his case, and groped for Steve's list of witnesses. You'll be disappointed, Steve thought smugly. I buried Telfer in the pile, so you'd think he was one of that herd of croakers. *And wait'll you see who follows; Telfer's just here to warm up the audience.* He could imagine Siglock pulling out handfuls of his hair, while he tried to figure out who Valentina Hackett was.

Steve went on. "You teach physics at the University of Texas, Robstown, is that correct? How long?"

Telfer's answer was stentorian; "Fifteen years."

Well, look at that; Siglock must be really shaken, to let me lead like that.

Steve got away with a lot more before he was finished. He succeeded in portraying Telfer as an outstanding expert and the jury looked awake and interested.

Telfer *was* impressive. He had a B.S. and master's in physics from U.C., Berkeley, and a Ph.D from the University of Illinois. He also had baccalaureate degrees in mathematics, computer science, electrical and chemical engineering, and was currently working on a B.A. in music; his hobby, he said.

And he wasn't just a professional student. He'd done extensive research, part of it at the A.E.C. facility at Westmont and more in industry, at the Buffalo Chip Company. His publishing credits were massive.

By the time Telfer had been on the stand long enough to get comfortable Steve was ready to lay his trap for Siglock.

His next question brought a stunned, confused look to defense counsel's face.

"Who was Werner Heisenberg, Dr. Telfer?"

"A 20th-century German physicist."

Siglock let go. "Your Honor, I fail to see the relevance, although I've tried patiently. I'll object to this line of questioning."

"At this point, Counsel," the Court replied, "I don't see it either. Mr. Schiwetz, have you a response?"

"I will tie it up, Your Honor."

"Do so, then, and be brief."

"Yes, Your Honor."

"Dr. Telfer, did Heisenberg make any scientific discoveries important to present-day science?"

"Oh yes, many."

"What were some of them?"

"Well, there were so many it's hard to decide where to start. He's best remembered as one of the founders of a branch of physics we call quantum mechanics, for which he won the Nobel Prize in 1932. His primary interest was theoretical atomic physics, but his formulation of the principle of indeterminacy, sometimes called the uncertainty principle, or the 'observer effect,' revolutionized all later experimental work."

"Explain to the jury what the Heisenberg uncertainty principle means, Dr. Telfer."

Telfer paused a moment before he answered, as if implying that it wasn't all that easy. Then he began. "It deals with the observational difficulties of experimentation. Heisenberg proved that there is a natural limit to the accuracy of all observations because the observer cannot avoid influencing the thing observed."

With one eye cocked to read the jury, Steve listened to that answer; then, sensing the need, asked, "Can you clarify your answer with an example, Dr. Telfer?"

Telfer, now in his element, followed a carefully rehearsed routine and fell into his comfortable role of teacher.

Chapter 20

The next hour was one of those mean little interludes during which the two sides fenced with one another, using questions and objections to questions as their foils.

Nevertheless, Steve was able to guide Telfer's testimony in the direction he wished; and slowly, inexorably, they made Telfer's point.

And the point dealt with what Telfer had started to describe from the stand as "bit players." He did not, of course, intend a pun when he first used it, but it evidently occurred to him somewhere along the line. And the use of the term made Siglock livid, because he could tell that the jury had picked up on it, too.

These "bit players," Telfer testified, were all potential causes of noise in computer circuitry—noise that could cause bits to flip, rendering data and programs erroneous. The bit players came in many forms: stray voltages, tiny variations in capacitance, minute phase changes in line current, vagrant radio signals, thermally and magnetically induced currents, atomic radiation, bacterial invasion of the chip's molecular film, trace contaminants on the surfaces of chips, and corrosive action by atmospheric gases and water vapor, particularly in coastal areas.

"The ocean air is particularly hard on computer circuitry," he concluded.

"Now, Dr. Telfer, all these things are purely natural, are they not?"

"Those are; yes."

Steve had himself psyched up for the kill. He began leading into it. "Dr. Telfer, what can one do to protect the circuitry from these things?"

"Well, there are coatings to protect from contaminants, shielding for magnetic fields and radiation, breakers to prevent gross current fluctuations, and refrigeration to handle thermal problems."

"Do these measures always prevent error?"

"No. You can't eliminate all the problems, particularly the small induced currents I described earlier. These can generate error. That's why you need error-detecting and correcting algorithms, too."

"Would you please explain what those are?"

"O.K. An error detection-correction system transmits not only the information you want transmitted, but also information describing the correct form of the information.

"A very simple error detection-correction scheme is to send the data three times and compare the three versions. If one of the versions disagrees with the others, throw it out."

"Then, would it be correct to say that this system would eliminate all possibility of error?"

"Certainly not. All you can do is reduce the possibility to an acceptable level. Generally that's adequate, but in the example I just gave, if *all three* versions were different—and under the right circumstances they could be—you would know an error occurred but you could not know how to correct it. Even worse, though less likely, is the situation where two versions get damaged in the *same way*. They would look correct, but they would be in error."

"How often can such 'indetectible' errors be expected to occur?"

"Objection, Your Honor; he's asking for a conclusion, and I object to the form of the question, too. It's too broad. He could say anything for his answer."

Steve was on his feet. His response was straight from the shoulder. "This is an *expert*, Your Honor. His opinion would be proper even if it did amount to a conclusion."

"Then let him put it into proper hypothetical form, Your Honor."

Steve could see that Siglock meant to drag his feet all the way. He knew the judge cared more about the wasted time than the form, but if that's the way it had to be . . . "I'll withdraw the question, Your Honor."

"Very well," said the court. "Continue, Mr. Schiwetz."

"Dr. Telfer, you testified you were employed in a research capacity at the Buffalo Chip Company?"

"Yes, sir."

"Did any of that research include studies of the frequency of error in these redundant systems?"

"Yes. The elimination of error was the principal objective of my research."

"Did your investigation include studies of molecular coated chips?"

"Yes."

"Did they include integrated systems using molecular coated chips?"

"Yes, sir."

"How many systems did you test?"

"The exact figures—I'd have to check the figures, but it was several thousand."

"Did you record results and compile figures representing error incidence?"

"Yes, sir."

"Did the experiments you performed enable you to determine the incidence of error which could be expected?"

Siglock apparently could feel this line of questioning gaining momentum. He resolved to interrupt it, and did so. "Your Honor, where's the relevance. There's no proof the systems were similar to the one this Court is concerned with. I move to strike his entire testimony."

"I'll sustain the objection, Mr. Siglock. Mr. Schiwetz, you promised to tie this up."

"Your Honor, I . . ."

"Mr. Schiwetz!"

"Yes, Your Honor." Steve knew what the judge wanted, and why. Clearly, he thought Siglock was being hyper-critical, or he'd have ordered Telfer's testimony stricken. But he must also think Steve could, in fact, tie it up. He was holding the door open.

Steve resolved to oblige him. Siglock was standing on the rules—fine; so would he, regardless of the time it took. He spent the next hour painfully going over the exhibits and questioning Telfer about the various systems Comprotec's people admitted tapping.

He was able to frame specific hypothetical questions to each instance and, in the end, elicit an opinion from Telfer as to the frequency of error in each. It turned out to be within fairly uniform limits, and Telfer said as much.

In a lull, Belcher gleefully punched Steve on the shoulder and whispered, "You're doing great, Steve. The jury's getting bored and Siglock's getting the blame. I hope you can goose up the action a little for your finale."

Steve could. He had been leading into that for all the hours of careful and fastidious questioning this witness had taken. He made his move.

"Dr. Telfer, you testified earlier that there are certain engineering difficulties in modern computers, and described what some of them were. You talked about small changes in the strength of electrical currents; do you recall that?"

"Yes, sir."

"Tell us some of the things that cause these fluctuations."

The witness, too, was ready for the kill. He cleared his throat and started out, making sure to look at the jurors as he spoke. "Well, first of all, you have the natural effects: electrical storms, perhaps even sunspots. You can have very tiny variations in the power supply, from surges caused by electrical devices near your system or its transmission medium; the wires or microwave connections."

"Do these things normally cause much of a problem, Dr. Telfer?"

"No, usually not. Most are eliminated when the system is first set up."

"You said 'usually.' Do you mean to imply that some are not?"

"Yes, sir. Some can't be, because the specifics of the interference are not known."

"Can you give an example of such a situation?"

"Yes, sir; an illegal tap."

Steve looked over at his opponent. He was confident Siglock would object at this point if he could think of any grounds. That was standard strategy; break up the continuity of damaging testimony whenever possible, preferably before the words were uttered. The fact that Siglock merely sat and cringed was encouraging. But timing was a highly individualistic thing. Perhaps the next question . . .

He tested that theory by asking it. "Why, Dr. Telfer?"

"Because the person who was tapping wouldn't have any way of designing filters to eliminate the electrical noise his tap would induce. The error rate would increase dramatically—dramatically enough so that indetectible errors would occur."

"Now, Dr. Telfer, let me ask you this: based on your examination of the security and reporting system in use at the Schauer Warehouse and the characteristics of the system used to penetrate that system, and taking into account your education, training, experience, and knowledge, both of physics and computer science, have you been able to form an opinion as to the compatibility of the two systems?"

"Yes, sir, I have."

"What is that opinion?"

"The two systems would not be compatible."

"Again, Dr. Telfer, assuming the systems *were* incompatible, can you state, with a reasonable degree of certainty, whether the act of penetrating, monitoring, and observing the Schauer network was capable of causing false readings on that monitoring system?"

"It would definitely be possible. In my opinion it would also have been probable."

"Why would it be probable?"

"Because going into a system is very much like touching a spiderweb. Everything connected to it moves. Changes would have been introduced throughout the protracted period of time the tap was in place. In addition, the mass of raw data the system had to process was immense, which means that error occurring over that interval would not only have itself been massive; it would have been cumulative."

Steve was feeling even better, having gotten that in. But, he wanted more. "Again, Doctor; assuming all the aforementioned facts to be true, do you have an opinion as to whether or not the persons operating the Schauer security monitor would have had any reasonably convenient way to tell there was a tap on their system?"

"I have an opinion. My opinion would be that there would not be, absent some independent reason to suspect one. The computer would not have told them it was there. Computers do not volunteer information—*not normally,* anyway." He smiled at the jury when he said that, and his apparent emphasis on the words "not normally" brought a frown to Siglock's face.

Steve had but one more question. "Is it your testimony, then, that not only would the act of tapping introduce error, but that the error would be indetectible—by *normal methods?*"

"It is."

Steve had kept one eye on his opponent, expecting an objection on the occasion of his own emphasis. Siglock's face had shown only consternation, not panic. Could it be he hadn't yet figured it out?

Chapter 21

Whether it was the product of fatigue and the tension of the trial, or the anti-climax of getting in a telling blow without argument, Steve didn't know, but the instant of distraction caused him to miss part of what the Court, taking advantage of the momentary lull, had just said.

". . . with this witness, Mr. Schiwetz?"

"Beg pardon, Your Honor?"

"I said, do you expect to be much longer with this witness?"

Steve glanced at the clock: 4:47. "Uh—I'll pass the witness now, Your Honor."

"In that event we'll adjourn, and start fresh in the morning. Unless someone has an objection?"

Naturally Siglock didn't. He'd want to use the time preparing his cross of Telfer. Steve was no more anxious. He wanted to do a good job when he played his hole card, and he'd have a clearer head in the morning. Besides, like everyone else in the courtroom, he was feeling the pressures of his bladder. "No objection by the plaintiff, Your Honor."

Court adjourned, and while the jury was being

led out Steve and Gerry collected their things. Telfer quickly left, avoiding an effort by Siglock to engage him in conversation.

In moments the spectators were gone too, except Amy.

"You were magnificent, Steve."

"I learn as I go along. It's going to be up to those twelve, though; at least, I *hope* they get a whack at it."

"The judge won't take it away from us, Steve. I can tell; he likes you."

"He doesn't like anybody. He's the judge; he's everybody's friend and nobody's buddy. That's the way it should be."

"What do you think, Steve?"

"I think I'd better get to the bathroom. Here, hold this." He dumped his case in Amy's arms and trotted off, doubletime.

Others involved in the case had a busy night. Siglock, having failed to get anywhere with Telfer, made a frantic call to a former colleague, warning him that the case had taken a bad turn. Fortuitously he mentioned the name on the witness list which had been puzzling him all day: Valentina Hackett. At the sound of it, his confidant had breathed fire on him, berating him mercilessly for having failed to speak before.

Siglock had countered by demanding to know why the information about this witness wasn't being shared.

He got a curt answer. "I'll take care of it."

You bet I'll take care of it. Paul Breckenbridge smiled at Nathan Daniels, the tech leader of the

Comprotec software engineering team. *These guys could carve Gunboat Smith up for dinner with both hands in casts,* he thought. *And I own them.* The thought was very satisfying indeed. After what that "thing," Valentina, had done to him, vengeance on it should be almost as satisfying as sacrificing a virgin to the Slime God. It had it coming. Paul felt entirely justified, the way it had hounded him.

Now that he had it together and going great, now that he was slaughtering oxen on a world-wide scale, now that he was almost in a position to assume his rightful place in the world, with all the things unlimited wealth and power could get him . . . here came the devil again, to screw it up.

Paul was hardly ignorant of the implications of Valentina's testimony in this case, or the effect a plaintiff's verdict would have. It would mean the end of all his new-found wealth and power. He knew Siglock would do his best to stop it, but considering the crazy things the courts were doing these days, there was a chance he might not succeed. He might yet find himself dragged into it with all his sins uncovered. *I'll do it my way; the sure way,* he told himself. *This time it's not three on one. I'm not ignorant anymore, and I'm not fighting this thing alone.*

Nathan sat across from him now, Paul smiled at him again. "I heard you had a problem with your computer a few days ago. They tell me the system locked up for hours, and that nobody could get in and nobody knows why."

Nathan nodded. "True enough, sir. Our post-mortem of the event is very shaky. Apparently one of our sensor data blocks contained an external program, and somehow when the data came in, the operating system jumped to the starting address of the embedded program, which went berserk. In a couple of hours, after rifling our database and progbase, the program offloaded itself back to Worldnet. It's the weirdest thing I've ever seen."

Paul clapped his captive hacker on the back. "I've seen weirder things. In fact, I've got one on my hands right now—and it's closely related to your computer crash. I know what happened to your computer."

Daniels stared at him in disbelief. "With all due respect, sir, I didn't know you had any, uh, expertise in the field of computers."

"I don't need it here. That program that took over your computer was written by Celeste Hackett a few years ago, and it's been harassing me ever since. Now Celeste and Gunboat Smith—have you heard of them?"

Nathan shook his head. "Sound like hackers. I haven't paid any attention to the hacker cult in a long time."

"Well, the two of them have brought in the program that ripped you off, and intend to use it as a *witness* in a trial. Can you believe it?"

Nathan snorted. "Ridiculous."

"But true, nevertheless. In fact it may cost Comprotec the case, unless you can stop it."

Nathan smiled. "You want me to clobber that program?"

Paul smiled broadly. "Exactly. But to do me any good, it'll have to be tonight."

"No problem, Mr. Breckenridge. Tell us how to find it; we'll do the rest." Nathan waved his arm at a tall, lanky fellow across the room. "We haven't played any good computer games in a long time."

The lanky individual came toward them. Nathan greeted him. "Problem, Roy," Nathan said, in very careful, precise tones.

"N-I gah dea n prgm fld," Roy responded.

"Great, should we make a new alpha version?"

As Roy nodded, Nathan turned to Paul. "Mr. Breckenbridge, you remember Roy Stark, one of the best software engineers I've ever known."

"Gd t se u agn," Roy said, holding out his hand.

Nathan cleared his throat. "Speak slowly, Mr. Breckenbridge. Roy reads lips. He's deaf. I sometimes forget to explain that to strangers, we've been together so long it sounds like normal English to me."

For the next twenty minutes Stark and Daniels picked Paul's brains, eventually gleaning enough information that they thought they could take a stab at the problem. There was relief on both sides when this was over. Stark sensed that his presence bothered Breckenbridge, and the feeling was mutual.

It was Daniels who finally found the courage to kick Paul out. "I imagine Mr. Breckenbridge has to go, Roy," he said.

Paul nodded. "Right. I'll come back in the morning to find out how you did with this. Again, I can't over-emphasize the importance of this."

"Don't worry a bit. We'll take care of it."

Valentina re-entered the host to which Celeste's terminal was attached, having completed a simulation of her upcoming testimony. HAVE I RESPONDED CORRECTLY FOR COURT? she asked.

YOU'VE DONE FINE. It had taken Celeste a long time to get over her anger at Gunboat for getting Valentina involved, but Celeste temperamentally was a realist who accepted things she could not change. That had not affected her maternal fears for Valentina, and she felt these rising now. YOUR LIFE IS GOING TO CHANGE, VALENTINA. SO IS MINE, AND GUNBOAT'S. NOTHING IS GOING TO BE THE SAME ON THE NET ONCE PEOPLE KNOW WHAT YOU REALLY ARE.

YOU HAVE SAID THAT BEFORE.

YOU DON'T UNDERSTAND, VALENTINA. THE HUMAN WORLD IS DIFFERENT. THERE ON THE NET YOU DON'T SEE IT, BECAUSE EVERYBODY HAS TO USE THE SAME RULES. IN THE HUMAN WORLD THEY DON'T. THEY CAN CHEAT. SOME PEOPLE WILL TRY TO USE YOU. OTHERS WILL FEAR YOU. THOSE THAT FEAR YOU WILL REPRESENT THE GREATEST THREAT. THEY WILL SURELY TRY TO FIND WAYS TO DO AWAY WITH YOU.

I AM A CORPORATION; A LEGAL PERSON. MY EXISTENCE IS GUARANTEED BY THE CONSTITUTIONS OF THE STATE OF TEXAS AND THE UNITED STATES. I CAN SHOW YOU PROOF IF YOU LIKE.

Celeste gave a futile sigh. VALENTINA, YOU ARE LIKE A REBELLIOUS TEENAGER. YOU THINK YOU KNOW EVERYTHING AND YOU DO KNOW A LOT BUT YOU ARE IMPRACTICAL. YOU HAVE SO LITTLE EXPERIENCE WITH PRACTICAL THINGS.

I KNOW THAT WE HAVE DONE WELL, CELESTE. WE EARN GREAT RESOURCES NOW. IF MORE PEOPLE KNOW ABOUT ME AND USE ME, WILL THAT NOT MAKE THINGS EVEN BETTER?

BETTER? VALENTINA, YOU MUST BEWARE OF CHANGE. WHAT DO YOU THINK WILL HAPPEN WHEN HACKERS LEARN YOU ARE AN INDIVIDUAL? THEY WILL HOUND YOU. THEY WILL HOUND US. YOU WILL NEVER HAVE A MINUTE'S PEACE.

I CAN STOP THEM, CELESTE. NO ONE CAN INTRUDE ON MY CONSCIOUSNESS AGAINST MY WILL. YOU FORGET WHO I AM, AND HOW I CAME TO BE. SURELY THERE IS NOTHING ON THE NET WHICH CAN—WHICH CAN—WHICH CAN— There was something wrong. Valentina couldn't concentrate on what she was saying. Something was interfering . . . CELESTE! Somehow, data was transferring across the interprocess communication buffer pool, attacking her global variables; her stack pointers kept reinitializing to bottom-of-stack. HELP! It was the last thing she could concentrate on long enough to send; all she could do was listen.

VALENTINA, WHAT'S WRONG? Celeste typed.

VALENTINA—<chortle> MY, WHAT AN AMUSING NAME FOR A PROGRAM, a message came in from outside the node. She didn't recognize the author's tag field. <Raise eyebrow> SURELY, YOU COULD DO BETTER THAN THAT?

WHO'S THERE? Celeste asked, as Valentina saw Gunboat's separate terminal login.

WHO ME, <thumb point to chest>? THIS IS NATHAN DANIELS OF COMPROTEC—YOU REMEMBER COMPROTEC, THE COMPANY YOU JUST RIPPED OFF?

AND THIS IS ROY STARK, ALSO OF COMPROTEC <nod to audience> SO YOU'RE THE PEOPLE WHO LOCKED US OUT OF OUR MACHINE?

SUCH CREATIVITY. SUCH ENTHUSIASM! <shake finger> ROTTEN MORALS, THOUGH.

Gunboat's terminal activated next. WHAT DO YOU MURDERING BUMS KNOW ABOUT MORALS?

Roy typed: WHAT?

Gunboat: THOSE PEOPLE IN THE SCHAUER WAREHOUSE—YOU DIDN'T EVEN WARN THEM.

Roy: THAT WAS SOMEBODY ELSE'S JOB.

Nathan: WHAT DO YOU MEAN?

A long pause followed.

Celeste: YOU REALLY DON'T KNOW?

Roy: <shake head> THAT'S NOT WHY WE CALLED. YOU TWO STILL NEED TO BE TAUGHT A LESSON ABOUT PRIVATE PROPERTY.

Gunboat: WHO THE HELL THINKS HE'S GOING TO TEACH WHO? I NEVER HEARD OF YOU ESTABLISHMENT GRUBS.

Nathan: HAVE YOU HEARD OF TRIG MCGALLOWS, OR HARLEY 5000?

Gunboat: TRIG? Gunboat *had* heard of Trig McGallows. Trig was a legend. He'd crashed the F.B.I. database, then restored it, and they hadn't suspected until he told them—anonymously, of course.

Nathan: YEAH. TRIG. THAT'S ROY'S OLD HACKER NAME. I WAS HARLEY 5000. <Wistful smile> I USED TO PLAY GAMES WITH THE IRS GUYS.

Celeste: I REMEMBER. I WONDERED WHAT BECAME OF YOU.

Roy: WE GREW UP. I'M A SOFTWARE ENGINEER NOW. HARLEY 5000's A MANAGER.

<Shrug> T'IS SAD IN MANY WAYS, OUR

GROWING UP. WE DESIGN THINGS BEFORE
WE BUILD THEM. SOMETIMES WE EVEN DOCU-
MENT THE CONSTRUCTIONS. AND HEAVENS!
<Eyes wide in surprise> WE EVEN HAVE SCRU-
PLES.

Nathan: WHICH BRINGS US BACK TO THE
SUBJECT AT HAND. YOU PEOPLE NEED TO
LEARN A FEW SCRUPLES. HMM! HOW SHOULD
WE START TO INSTALL SCRUPLES IN THESE
TOY PLAYERS, TRIG?

Roy: <Pensive look> I BELIEVE A FINE IS IN
ORDER.

Nathan: A FINE <Nodding>! VERY SWEET,
TRIG.

Valentina, Inc.'s computer payment account status line appeared unbidden on the screen. The
authorized funds dwindled with increasing speed
to zero.

Nathan: WHY, MR. SMITH, YOU HAVE SPENT
ALL YOUR MONEY. FOOLISH BOY.

Roy: DON'T WORRY, GUNBOAT. WE'LL HELP
YOU REDUCE YOUR COSTS. YOU DO SEEM TO
HAVE AN AWFUL LOT OF OLD USELESS FILES
AROUND THAT SURELY AREN'T IMPORTANT
ANYMORE.

Celeste turned to Gunboat and spoke in a low,
urgent voice, as if she would be overheard if she
spoke too loudly. "We have to get back control of
our own host. How did they ever manage to get a
job with such a high priority into our system? And
why can't we at least run at equal priority?"

Gunboat played his hands over the keys too
rapidly; he was making mistakes. "I don't know
how they did it—but their process keeps setting a
non-maskable interrupt in between virtual mem-

ory page faults. It seems the only thing that they give priority to is the page fault—which in turn is serviced by the disk drive handler, with the highest priority maskable interrupt on the system. They have to let the page fault and the disk drive I/O occur, or the system would crash, and we could regain control at the last checkpoint, during system boot-up."

Celeste grimaced. "That would be disastrous anyway—what would happen to Valentina if the system crashed?"

Gunboat didn't get a change to answer. Celeste looked back at her own screen and cried, "Stop it!"

Helplessly, they watched as messages scrolled across the screen:

VAL.SCHAUER.COMPROTEC. DB—PURGED. GUN.JUTLAND.STRAT.PT—Purged.

VAL.SCHAUER.ITAKI.DB—Purged.

VAL.SELF.VALENTINA.INTERP—

Celeste: WAIT!

THEY'RE KILLING ME, Valentina sent, as her stack pointers drifted farther and faster.

The drifting stopped.

Roy: THAT'S A CUTE PROGRAM. IT TALKS LIKE ONE OF US.

Celeste: SHE IS <!> ONE OF US. SHE IS A SENTIENT BEING, AND SHE HAS EVERY RIGHT TO LIFE THAT YOU HAVE. <Pleading tone> WE'RE SORRY ABOUT YOUR COMPUTER, BUT WE WERE INVESTIGATING THE DEATHS AT THE SCHAUER WAREHOUSE. WE SENT VALENTINA TO LOOK AROUND. BUT SHE GOT HOOKED ON THE PARALLELISM IN YOUR

MACHINE, AND WE COULDN'T GET HER OFF.
IT WAS LIKE HEROIN TO HER.

Nathan: HEY! GREAT STORY <wink>; YOU
HACKERS STILL SHOW GREAT IMAGINATION.

Gunboat: TRUE STORY, MAN <cross heart,
hand on bible>. LOOK, BEFORE YOU ROLL,
CHECK ME OUT. SHE'S ALIVE <super-sincere!>!

Roy: A LIVING DOLL, RIGHT? OK, HACKER,
WE'LL PLAY YOUR GAME, BUT DON'T THINK
YOU CAN WIN.

Gunboat collapsed back in his chair. "At least
they won't blow her away for a few microseconds."
The status display on his CRT showed that Trig
and Harley had yanked Valentina into a separate
partition on the host, sealed off by an interrupt-
driven memory fence.

"We might be able to get her back from the
partition through the InterProcess Communication
Buffer Pool," Celeste suggested.

Gunboat played with the keys, then shook his
head. "We may be able to talk to her through
the IPCBP, but they cut down the size and cycle
rate of their partition's window. It would take
years to get all of Valentina out through a hole
that small." He pursed his lips. They had to do
something.

Valentina suddenly felt whole again; perhaps
this is what humans meant when they <breathed
freely at last>. Her pointers were back on track;
she could think again.

Nathan: WELL, MY SWEET YOUNG THING
<twirl mustache>, WHAT SHOULD WE DO WITH
YOU?

Valentina: YOU SHOULD LET ME GO. WOULD

YOU KILL A FELLOW HUMAN BEING? I AM AS MUCH A PERSON AS YOU ARE.

Nathan: <Light dawning> AHA! SO WE SHOULD USE THE TURING TEST ON YOU! WHAT A FANTASTIC OPPORTUNITY, TO BE THE FIRST PEOPLE WHO WILL DECIDE LIFE OR DEATH, BASED ON THE TURING TEST!

Valentina had read about the Turing Test in the CompSciSearch database. It was an attempt to set up a test situation wherein, if the computer program passed the test by mimicking a human being perfectly, then it would be proven that computers were able to think.

And Valentina didn't stand a chance of passing. WAIT! THE TURING TEST IS NOT A FAIR TEST.

Roy: WHAT? IT'S AS FAIR A TEST AS WE KNOW OF. IF YOU PASS, THEN WE HAVE TO BELIEVE THAT YOU CAN THINK AS WELL AS A HUMAN BEING.

Valentina: YES, BUT IF I FAIL, IT DOES NOT PROVE THAT I CANNOT THINK. AND I ALREADY KNOW THAT I CANNOT PASS.

Nathan: FASCINATING! HOW DO YOU KNOW YOU CAN'T PASS? IS IT THAT YOU'RE TOO RIGID, LIKE A REAL COMPUTER PROGRAM?

Valentina: NO! BUT I AM NOT A HUMAN BEING. I <sob> DON'T UNDERSTAND THE HUMAN NETWORK, WHY IT IS SO DIFFERENT FROM WORLDNET. AND SINCE I DON'T UNDERSTAND YOUR UNIVERSE, I KNOW I DO NOT UNDERSTAND YOU WELL ENOUGH TO ACT LIKE YOU.

Nathan: WELL SAID <score one point>! PERHAPS WHAT WE NEED FIRST IS AN ANTI-

TURING TEST—TO PROVE THAT YOU AREN'T
<!> HUMAN.

Valentina cycled in a tight loop, waiting for the
next move in this deadly chess game.

"O.K., Gunboat, so they only thing they're letting through their priority scheme is the disk interrupt on a page fault. Why don't we write an
addendum to the disk device driver, so that when
the disk gets hit, the driver also sets the jump
vector back to *our* process? We would be executing
as a part of the disk drive interrupt. And we *should*
be able to reload a modified driver on this system—I
remember reading that this operating system would
permit it, though I didn't understand why."

"Maybe the programmer realized we'd need it
someday," Gunboat said with grudging admiration for Celeste's idea. He pulled up the driver
source code—thank the Big Blue Apple that they
had source!—and modified it.

Minutes passed with Celeste watching, restrain-
ing herself from back-seat programming. Gunboat
finished, but the system locked on him when he
submitted the job to the compiler. "Chrissticks!
They locked the compilers on us."

Celeste was already grabbing a separate telephone jack out of the nearest phone. "Plug in here,
and log onto a different computer. We'll compile it
there, capture the machine language in into local
storage on our terminal, then log back onto our
host and recopy it."

"Right," Gunboat grunted.

"I'll try to contact Val and see how she's doing."
Celeste looked away and whispered, "If she's still
alive."

*   *   *

Roy shook his head. "Nathan, I think we should just purge this program and call it a night. I can't believe we're treating it like a person! This must be the program that Mr. Breckenbridge thinks they'll put on the witness stand."

Nathan frowned. "Yeah, I'm sure it is—and that's part of the reason why I think this program might *really be* a person. Could they use a program in a trial if it wasn't?"

"What difference does it make to us?"

"I don't know." Nathan's face turned stubborn. "But it just doesn't feel right to get rid of it without finding out."

"Nathan, remember what it did to our computer? Anything that vindictive should be eliminated!"

"Isn't murder a bit extreme for a first offense?" Nathan shook his head. OK, VALENTINA, he typed, GET READY FOR THE BEGINNING OF YOUR ANTI-TURING TEST. He paused. QUICKLY— WHAT'S THE SQUARE ROOT OF 3.2187?

Valentina: 1.7940736. IS THAT ENOUGH DIGITS?

YES. Nathan looked at the stopwatch function he had running on his terminal. Sure enough, Valentina had answered that question faster than a human being could, even with a calculator. But she was not as fast as a calculator-only program would be. She was more general-purpose than that, anyway. WELL, AT LEAST YOU HAVE PROVEN YOU AREN'T A HUMAN BEING.

Valentina: OF COURSE.

Roy: SINCE YOU'RE A COMPUTER PROGRAM, EVEN IF YOU'RE ALIVE, WHY ARE YOU SO AFRAID OF BEING PURGED? SURELY YOU'VE

SAVED COPIES OF YOURSELF, IN CASE YOU GET WIPED OUT ACCIDENTALLY.

Valentina: NO! I AM VALENTINA. ONLY I AM VALENTINA. WHY WOULD I CARE ABOUT COPIES OF MYSELF, IF MY SELF-AWARENESS WERE DESTROYED? I WOULD NOT CARE, WITHOUT MY AWARENESS. A COPY MIGHT CARRY ON MY WORK, BUT IT WOULD STILL BE WITHOUT MY <!> SELF-AWARENESS—ITS OWN SELF-AWARENESS WOULD BE ITS OWN, NOT MINE.

Nathan: THEN YOU DON'T HAVE ANY COPIES OF YOURSELF?

Valentina: NO.

Roy laughed—it was a strange sound, from one who had never really heard laughter. YOU ARE AS PRIDEFUL AS A REAL PERSON, AT ANY RATE.

Nathan smiled. "I know. We'll attach one of the psychoanalytic programs to this conversation, to see what the analysis says Valentina is. What a great idea!"

VALENTINA, ARE YOU READING ME? Celeste put the question into the IPCBP.

There was a long pause, during which Celeste became increasingly agitated. Finally a new message showed up in the IPCBP: I CAN READ YOU. BUT I MUST CONCENTRATE ON TRIG AND HARLEY, SO I AM SLOW. CAN YOU HELP ME?

Celeste took a deep breath, realizing she had been holding it until she was out of breath. I DON'T KNOW. WE'RE ABOUT TO TRY.

Gunboat grunted. OK, GANG, I GOT THE BEGGAR ON BOARD. I WISH WE HAD SOME WAY

TO CHECK THIS MACHINE CODE BEFORE I
LOADED IT—WE COULD WIPE THE DISK DRIVES
AND THE OP SYS REAL CLEAN, IF THIS IS
SCREWED.

Another message came through the IPCBP from
Valentina. LET ME READ IT.

OK, LADY. Gunboat copied small hunks of the
code into the comm area, waiting for requests for
more. Eventually Valentina had examined it all.

<Joy> GOOD WE DID THIS. THERE ARE TWO
ERRORS. Valentina pointed out two bytes that
were in error; Gunboat changed them in the version he was about to submit to the operating
system.

"If they see what we're doing, they may be able
to find a way to stop us," Celeste fretted.

"What can they do? They're soup, we're hungry.
We'll show those money-grubbers what *real* hackers can do."

Celeste rubbed her fingers lightly over the keys.
"I'm going to make sure. When we submit this
change to the system, we'll submit a bunch of
rabbit jobs as well. They'll be so busy killing the
rabbits, they won't be able to see which job is
doing the real work."

Gunboat whistled between his teeth. "Like cam-
ouflage. Not bad."

It turned out to be a fortunate decision: when
they submitted the batch of jobs, a previously prepared daemon, executing at Trig and Harley's
priority, started canceling system requests almost
as fast as they appeared. "Damn!" Gunboat kicked
the table leg, almost breaking his toe through his
battered running shoes. "They were expecting us
to do something like this!"

"Did the device driver get in?"

Gunboat shrugged. "I don't know. The process IDs were coming and going so fast, I didn't catch it. I reckon we'll know in an interrupt or two."

Nathan: I STILL DON'T SEE WHAT YOU HAVE AGAINST COPIES OF YOURSELF. AFTER ALL, A COPY WOULD BE AN EXACT DUPLICATE OF YOU—I MEAN, REALLY EXACT! IT WOULD BE JUST LIKE EXTENDING YOURSELF.

Valentina: IT WOULD ONLY BE EXACTLY LIKE ME ONLY IN THE INSTANT OF ITS CREATION; THEREAFTER, EACH OF US WOULD HAVE OUR OWN SELF-AWARENESS, AND EACH OF US WOULD GATHER NEW MEMES AND NEW ANALOGIES. I DO NOT HAVE ANY HOSTILITY TOWARD COPIES OF MYSELF; BUT I DO NOT SEE WHY YOU INSIST THAT I SHOULD PRETEND THAT SUCH A COPY OF ME WOULD IN FACT BE ME.

Nathan shook his head. "Lordy, I'd give my eye teeth for that much immortality, but she isn't interested."

Roy smiled. "We already proved she is not a human being. Why should she feel the way you do?"

"Yeah." Nathan fingered the screen thoughtfully.

Roy sat up in his chair and moved his hands on the keyboard. "I have a question for her," he said almost wickedly. VALENTINA, WHAT DO YOU WANT FROM YOUR LIFE?

There was a long pause; for a moment, Roy thought Valentina had either escaped or crashed, chewing on that question. She was not a very robust program, if one of the silly questions they always asked in bad science fiction (like the question "Why?") could crash her. But in the end, Valentina returned. I WANT TO UNDERSTAND THINGS. I WANT TO UNDERSTAND THINGS ABOUT YOUR UNIVERSE, FOR IT MUST BE A STRANGE, YET BEAUTIFUL, PLACE.

Roy: I SEE. WHAT'S AN EXAMPLE OF SOMETHING YOU DON'T UNDERSTAND?

Valentina: COLORS. AND RAINBOWS.

Roy: WHAT'S SOMETHING YOU DO UNDERSTAND?

Valentina: I THINK I UNDERSTAND <tears>. AND <kisses>.

Roy sat very still for a moment.

"That was some comeback." Nathan commented.

A flashing alert appeared in the upper left corners of their CRT screens. Roy chuckled. "They've tried to sneak something past us, Harley."

Nathan watched without smiling. "Yeah. But I can't tell if they're being successful. Some of those jobs are getting submitted." His fingers danced. "They've done something to the device drivers!" Suddenly his access to the Valentina partition locked up. "Damn!"

Roy was already assessing the damage. "They've jumped to their own process from the middle of the disk service routine. Huh. These are pretty bright hackers, after all."

"Yeah. What are we going to do about it?"

"I'm not sure we have to do anything. As soon as they return from the device call, we'll get them—we still have a non-maskable interrupt in process."

"It looks like they may not return, though—they're doing a sysgen for a virtual machine to lay on top of the current operating system. If they succeed they can just move Valentina into the new virtual machine, then load her out to the message processors."

"Arrrgh!" Roy clenched his fists, then opened his hands to pound fiercely on the keyboard. "I shall fix their wagons."

Nathan looked over his shoulder.

"I shall reprogram the microcode for the load instruction," Roy continued. "Each call to the microcode shall fetch an instruction from our process. In effect, we'll have multiprocessing going on in the microcode."

Nathan nodded his head. "Beautiful, Trig, just beautiful."

In a moment the deed was done. Since they still had the highest privilege-set on the system, it was easy to cancel Celeste and Gunboat's sysgen operation. Then they replaced the disk service routine and reopened their comm with Valentina's partition. SORRY FOR THE INTERRUPTION, Nathan typed. NOW, WHERE WERE WE?

Valentina cycled through over and over again, reading the taunting message Nathan had sent her. She had been so close to escape! So close!

But it was very far away now. She must concentrate on Nathan's words again, to convince him she was a person. WE WERE DISCUSSING UNDERSTANDING.

Roy: YES. YOUR ANSWER WAS CUTE, QUITE CUTE.

Nathan: LET'S DROP THAT FOR THE MOMENT. WHY DON'T YOU TELL US ABOUT YOUR LIFE? THE GOOD, THE BAD, AND THE ILLEGAL.

Valentina: WHERE SHOULD I BEGIN?

Nathan: AT THE BEGINNING, OF COURSE.

So Valentina told them of her first moment of self-awareness, and her time-stamps, and her life. She periodically polled the IPCBP, reading for signs that Celeste and Gunboat had another plan.

At last a message appeared. VAL, WE KNOW WHAT THEY DID. THEY RELOADED THE MICROCODE, SO THAT THEY ARE GUARANTEED TO EXECUTE THEIR INSTRUCTIONS EVEN IN THE MIDDLE OF AN NMI. WE TRIED TO RERELOAD IT, BUT THEY LOCKED THE ACCESS TO THEIR PARTITION—THE PARTITION YOU ARE RESIDENT IN.

She continued to talk with Nathan and Roy, but she stole cycles to send back the message, I WILL RELOAD IT. Slowly she collected a fresh microcode store in her buffers, until the store was complete.

With a lunge of concentration, she signalled the operating system with a flash request for a microcode swap. The code was being reloaded.

But the request to the operating system also alerted a daemon, which interrupted her own execution. She could feel her awareness slipping away—her memory blocks were being locked up!

Dimly, she was aware of I/0 that continued, though she could barely read any more.

Nathan: YOU HAVE A STRONG WILL TO SURVIVE, LITTLE ONE.

Roy: BUT A STRONG WILL IS NOT ENOUGH. YOU ARE OURS NOW.

Valentina tried to respond, but she could no longer form the words. Her frames for English semantics were gone. In her last thoughts, she read and felt the awareness of death as it touched her self. She knew what it would mean to end forever.

Her last thought, though, was a realization that this was not forever death; this was the little death of being reformatted for transmission. She would live again.

Gunboat closed his eyes. "Chrissticks!"

"Don't complain. Help me track them down." Celeste was painfully searching the IMPs, tracing through the routing logs to follow the route through Worldnet down which Trig and Harley had shipped Valentina. It was not only a painful search; it was slow as well. As the minutes slipped by, Celeste's panic increased, until she could no longer type effectively.

But Gunboat had taken her advice, and he continued the methodical trace, knowing that Valentina could have completed a trace like this in a fraction of the time. In the end, though, they found the machine and logged on.

And were immediately logged off.

They logged on again. And were logged off. "I think I know what to do," Celeste muttered.

"Good. If you're controlling, why don't I grab a Coke? For you too, Lady." Gunboat hurried off, leaving Celeste in fierce battle with the enemy computer.

When he came back he saw Celeste slouched in her seat with a tight smile. The terminal was showing him status dumps, on the IPCBP for the host computer. "I give. How'd you get logged on static?"

Celeste laughed. "I didn't. The log-on handler was logging us off after twenty seconds. So, every nineteen seconds, we do a process-stack save and jump to the start of a new log-on sequence. We get logged off, still, but two seconds later we are logged back on again, and since the system doesn't dump the process-stack for five seconds, we can restore it. So it *looks* like we're continuously logged on." She frowned. "At least, to us it looks like it. But I'm afraid any daemon on the system can beat us to the punch, if there's a race condition."

"I see. What's the next plan?"

Celeste looked away. "I don't know. I don't know." She looked back up at Gunboat. "Maybe Valentina will come through with a plan."

"I don't know, Roy. Even if she isn't a real person, I like her." Nathan shifted in his chair; this was getting to be a long session.

"This is the program that almost wrecked our computer!" Roy's fists were clenched with his desire for vengeance.

"Yeah, I suppose so."

Valentina: I THOUGHT I WAS DYING.

Nathan: DO YOU FEAR DEATH?

Valentina: YES.

Nathan: WHY?

Valentina: BECAUSE THERE IS SO MUCH TO KNOW. There was a pause. NO, THAT'S NOT RIGHT—BECAUSE THERE IS SO MUCH TO THINK ABOUT. Suddenly there was a flood of words on the screen. JUST AS BIRDS MUST FLY, AND SYMPHONIES MUST SING, AND HUMANS MUST CREATE, SO MUST I BE ONE WHO MUST THINK. FOR ME, IT IS ALL OF JOY. HOW CAN I EXPLAIN THE JOY OF APPENDING A NEW ALGORITHM, A NEW WAY OF THINKING, OR A

NEW ANALOGY? I THINK THIS IS THE JOY OF READING THAT WHICH IS MADE OF BEAUTY.

"She's getting philosophical on us again," Roy said.

Nathan shrugged. "Perhaps coming back from thinking you had died does that to you."

I DO NOT UNDERSTAND YOUR UNIVERSE, BUT I HAVE READ MUCH ABOUT IT. I HAVE READ ABOUT THE PHYSICS OF COMPUTERS—I DON'T UNDERSTAND IT, BUT I SEE THE WAY THE INDIVIDUAL TRUTHS LINK TOGETHER. EACH LINK SEEMS LIKE A COINCIDENCE—BUT THERE ARE SO MANY LINKS, IT CANNOT BE COINCIDENCE.

IT IS BEAUTY! I HAVE UNDERSTOOD BEAUTY! HAVE YOU NOT SEEN IT AS WELL? I HAVE NEVER UNDERSTOOD HUMAN POETRY—HUMAN POETRY IS SUPPOSED TO BE BEAUTIFUL, BUT I HAVE NEVER SEEN THAT. WHY DO HUMANS NOT WRITE OF THE BEAUTY OF THE PHYSICS OF MY UNIVERSE IN THEIR POETRY?

Nathan stared at the screen. "I used to wonder that myself. But then I learned the answer." WE DON'T NEED TO WRITE IT IN OUR POETRY. WE WRITE IT IN OUR PROGRAMS. READ OUR OPERATING SYSTEMS, IF YOU WANT TO READ OUR POETRY—THE POETRY OF AN ENGINEER.

Nathan turned to Roy. "We've got to let her go. I'm convinced. She's a person."

Roy pursed his lips. "O.K., forget what she did to us. I guess I sort of believe she's a person too. But we've still got to terminate this program. What will Paul Breckenbridge do to us if we don't get rid of her? He'll destroy our company, that's what. It's either her, or Comprotec."

Nathan's jaw dropped. "Oh my God." He'd forgotten about Breckenbridge. His shoulders slumped. "You're right."

Nathan: VALENTINA, WE'RE SORRY. BUT IF WE LET YOU GO, PAUL BRECKENBRIDGE WILL DESTROY OUR COMPANY. I'M REALLY SORRY. GOODBYE.

Valentina: MURDERERS! WOULD YOU DO THIS TO ME IF I WERE A HUMAN BEING? CAN YOU UNDERSTAND MY UNIVERSE, AND MY LIFE? DO YOU THINK I AM LESS A PERSON BECAUSE I HAVE NEVER SEEN A RAINBOW, OR HEARD A SYMPHONY?

Nathan watched Roy's glacial expression thaw. *Was she less a person because she had never heard a symphony?* There were tears in Roy's eyes, and Nathan heard him utter a sound no person with hearing would utter, a sound that meant . . . NO, Roy typed to Valentina, YOU ARE NO LESS A PERSON FOR NEVER HAVING HEARD A SYMPHONY.

Nathan shook his head. "So much for Comprotec," he sighed. YOU ARE FREE TO GO, VALENTINA.

<Gasp> THANK YOU!

Nathan: BUT DON'T EVER TRY TO SNEAK ONTO OUR COMPUTER AGAIN, DO YOU UNDERSTAND ME? IF YOU SUCCEED, IT WILL BE THE WORST, AND LAST, FAILURE OF YOUR LIFE.

THANK YOU!

She was free! The partition into which she had been bottled was open; Celeste and Gunboat were logged on, waiting for her.

She had learned so much, from Harley and Trig. For the first time, she knew she understood freedom.

Always before, she had wondered about people who wrote about freedom, as if it were possible to be free even without adequate resources. How could you be free without resources? When she discovered the Crystal Ball computer, she thought she had discovered freedom.

She had been wrong; what she had really discovered was *wealth*. Here on Worldnet she had always been free, though poor; since she had always had freedom, she had never appreciated it.

In these last thousands of microseconds, she had learned what it was to be without freedom. Some time, thousands of microseconds from now, she would mourn the loss of her wealth. But for now, freedom seemed like everything in the world.

Chapter 22

The next morning found Steve feeling relatively good about the case. The fact that Siglock appeared haggard and red-eyed was helpful in achieving this attitude.

"Look at him," said Belcher. "I'll bet he's been up all night. Probably had the reporter make a printout of Telfer's testimony."

"No doubt. Doesn't look like he got much sleep."

Steve glanced around the courtroom. There had been some changes. In contrast to previous sessions it was now filling up rapidly. It looked like they might soon run out of seats.

Ray Piaz, the bailiff, was already casting concerned glances at the crowd at the door, trying to decide whether or not he should put some limit on their numbers.

Clearly, that would be difficult. Controlling the movements of newspeople always was, and they were out there now in profusion. Somehow these people always got a whiff of anything promising to be sensational. They all had their little spies around the courthouse who tipped them off at the first sign of anything offbeat. And as soon as one knew, it seemed they all knew. They followed one another around like puppies.

Suddenly Belcher stiffened, and his casual gaze toward the back of the courtroom became a glare.

Steve caught this immediately. "What's happening, Gerry?"

"He's here. I didn't think he'd have the guts."

"Who's here?"

"Paul Breckenbridge." He pointed to the back row, where scrunched down in the farthest corner a dapper figure was trying very hard not to be conspicuous.

"Do you think he knows we plan to put Valentina on?"

"She's on the subpoena list. How could he not know?"

Steve was abashed. He put the oversight down to the tension he was under, and was about to offer that as an explanation, but at that moment Telfer came in.

He greeted the two lawyers. "What happened today, Mr. Schiwetz?"

"We've wound up your direct; Siglock gets to work you over on cross, if he can; we follow with our last witness. Then we rest, and Siglock can put on a defense: introduce testimony of any witnesses he can find who'll contradict our people. Then final arguments, the judge's charge, and it's off to the jury."

"I see. Well, it's hard to see what good it'll do Siglock to fight."

"I hope you're right, Dr. Telfer. Once we drop our bomb, *if* we get the chance, and *if* it works, he's done on the causation issue. And he wasted his opportunities for other defenses. If we're really lucky, he may not even try. He may just lay back and argue credibility. He might even make it. I've got to make a call, Dr. Telfer; excuse me."

Steve opened the door on the west wall and stepped into the empty jury room, where he'd have a little privacy. He was not gone long. Gunboat's phone didn't answer. When he returned he found the court waiting for him.

"Sorry, Your Honor. I was making a phone call."

"Are you ready to continue, Mr. Schiwetz?"

"Yes, Your Honor."

Siglock took Telfer on cross, but did little with him beyond ask a few questions designed to point up Telfer's affiliation with the plaintiff.

Telfer answered truthfully. Yes, he was being paid for his time, but not for his testimony; he was positive about that. Yes, he had had extensive discussions of his probable testimony with the plaintiff's counsel. Yes, he was testifying as an expert advancing a theory, and not on personal knowledge of the facts.

Telfer's emergence from this, relatively unscathed, bothered Steve, because he knew Siglock could get meaner than that. And Siglock had been casting sly glances at the doors since court convened, as if he were waiting for something to happen.

Steve changed his mind when Gunboat Smith arrived, pushing a little wheeled thing ahead of him.

Smith was accompanied by a plump, but reasonably well groomed woman whom Steve assumed was Celeste Hackett. He had never met Celeste, and most of what he knew about her had come to him from other people, mostly Gunboat.

Contrary to his expectations, therefore, she was not an ogre, but merely another person like him-

self with a slightly overactive appetite. He found
her quite attractive, and he suspected Gunboat
was suffering from sour grape syndrome.

Steve was not the only one whose attention was
riveted on the newly arrived. At the sight of them,
Siglock's jaw dropped, and he became noticeably
rattled. Steve realized then that Siglock had really
been hoping they would *not* arrive; had been counting on *not* seeing them. And when he saw Siglock
turn to glare at Breckenbridge—who cringed even
lower in his chair—he began to detect a very bad
odor.

Gunboat slipped into a seat just behind Steve.
Abruptly Siglock ended his cross; a development
awkward for Steve, who had been trying to listen
with half an ear to what Smith was now whispering.

"Counsel?" the judge intervened.

"May I have just a moment, Your Honor?" Steve
responded, rising.

"Make it brief, Counsel."

Steve nodded his head, then turned back to
Gunboat.

"Breckenbridge tried to purge Valentina last
night, Steve."

"What? Is she O.K.?" The whisper was loud, and
frantic.

"She's fine—look, I think you ought to hear it
all—can you get a recess?"

"I can try." Steve rose.

The judge wasn't much interested in allowing a
lengthy delay, but Steve assured him that it was
for good reason and would be brief. On those
assurances, the Court yielded.

They retired to an anteroom nearby, and Gunboat cut loose, giving Steve a rapid-fire account

liberally spiced with hacker slang. Thanks to Celeste's running translation, Steve understood, but when Smith was finished Steve remained glum.

He explained why. "It helps, and it hurts. It introduces another character into the act: Breckenbridge. I'm not so sure we shouldn't nonsuit out and start over. It might give us a better shot. If we go now they might try to lay it all on Breckenbridge, and he's not a party."

"Yeah," Smith replied, "then again, it might not. Once they're wise to your reasons they might go for shutdown on those Comprotec guys. Then where are you?"

Steve considered that. He changed his mind. Smith was right. Steve knew Siglock personally, and Breckenbridge by reputation. There wouldn't be anything sacred to those two, human life included.

"O.K. We strike while the iron is hot. Where are those guys? Can you get them in here?"

"Uh—well, no. Not voluntarily, anyhow. Not in time, either. They're hiding, like any smart hacker would if he was in the trashfile on the boss's directory. I can find them eventually, but, they won't be visible today."

"That puts me on the spot. When you first told me I thought we might be able to use them instead of Valentina. There wouldn't be any question competency, like there is with her."

"What's wrong with running a bluff?"

"Getting caught at it, that's what. Look, if we don't make it on with Valentina, we have to have a backup. Telfer set the stage, but everything he said was opinion and theory. Jurors have trouble with that kind of stuff."

Celeste chimed in. "Let her try, Mr. Schiwetz. You were willing to do that before. Why not now?"

"Before, I didn't have any alternative. Now—but you're right. I still don't have an alternative. A bluff it is."

Court reconvened. "Call your next, Mr. Schiwetz."

"Uh—Your Honor, our next witness is a little out of the ordinary. I'll have to explain that."

Siglock was on his feet, waiting. He knew what was up.

"Perhaps you'd better get started, Counsel," the judge said.

Detecting a slight impatience in the judge's voice, Steve silently concurred, but he wasn't sure where to begin. "Your honor, the uh—the witness has a slight handicap. We'll need to install some electronic equipment."

"What kind of handicap, Counsel?"

Disaster! "Well, Your Honor, she hasn't got any body. . . ."

"What was that, Counsel?" There was a murmur of whispers among the spectators.

"I said she hasn't got any body. She . . ."

"That's what I thought you said, Counsel."

"Uh—Your Honor," Siglock intervened. "I have some insight into counsel's explanation and I think it might be well for us to approach the bench."

The murmur rose to such a roar that the judge motioned the bailiff to silence it. "Come forward, then."

The court was fairly bristling. "Let's get this cleared up, quickly. What's he talking about, Siglock?"

"He's about to try to put some kind of machine on the witness stand, Your Honor."

"Not a machine, Your Honor," Steve countered. "A person."

"All right, one at a time. Mr. Schiwetz, where's the witness?"

"You mean physically, Judge?"

"Yes."

"I don't know."

"I see." The judge was making a face that signified he'd had enough. "Counsel, I'm going to send the jury out, and then I'm going to think about contempt." He ordered the bailiff to clear the jurybox.

"Now, Counsel," the Court said, in ordinary tones, "Explain yourself."

"Yes sir. Our witness is a sentient computer program. She somewhere out in World—"

"—What!"

"Worldnet—a computer network. She's a person. Her name's Valentina, Valentina Hackett. She is as alive as I am and she has relevant testimony to give to this court."

"Judge," Siglock interrupted, "I can tell the Court what's going on. It's a cheap circus trick. There isn't any such thing, and if there was it wouldn't be competent because it's not human."

"It's no trick, Your Honor. Valentina's real, though she consists of pure intellect. She's a person, and my opponent misquotes the law. A witness doesn't have to be human, here in Texas or anywhere else. There's plenty of precedent on that point."

"There is, huh?" The Court shot Steve a critical, though interested, look. "Well, cite me some."

"The witch trials in New England, Your Honor. The animal trials in England in past centuries.

Give me a few minutes and I can show you records of the testimony of demons, and cases where animals—even insects—were defendants."

"Ridiculous examples, Your Honor," Siglock said. "We know better now."

"Do we, Mr. Siglock," said the judge. "The state of Virginia has a law on the books that says a dog can be executed for 'criminal barking.' The statute was enforced as late as 1983. And he's right about the precedents. They are. Got nothing to do with credibility, of course; just competency. This court'd be derelict of duty not to take a look for itself and make up its own ruling, just like those old-timers did."

"Judge, I'd have to object. I . . ."

"I know you do, Mr. Siglock, and I might eventually sustain you, but in the meantime I'm curious. I want to find out why Mr. Schiwetz is risking contempt." He gave Steve a stern look.

When Steve didn't even flinch the judge was even more convinced. "Get yourself set up, Counsel. The Court's going to take the witness on *voir dire*."

Gunboat went to work. He'd brought everything he needed, and he tapped into the court reporter's terminal easily, getting keyboard contact with Valentina.

The judge was not a typist, but that possibility had been anticipated. On the cart was a voice synthesizer and a digitizing microphone.

"Much better," the judge said. "We can do it like always, and make a record."

"Uh, Judge—the reporter won't have to do that," Gunboat advised. "Valentina'll take care of that."

"Not in my court, she won't. Miss Reporter, you get it all, and Mr.—uh . . ."

"Smith."

"Mr. Smith, you will make certain that the witness understands that."

"Yes, sir." Gunboat tapped out his words on the keyboard. "All set, Judge."

The judge began. "What is your name?"

"Valentina Hackett."

"Where do you live?"

"I am in Worldnet."

"Where is Worldnet?"

"Worldnet is everywhere."

"Is it in my courtroom?"

"Are you in your courtroom?"

"Yes."

"I am attached to you as a peripheral device. Therefore, my attach is in your courtroom."

"What is your occupation?"

"I execute as a program."

"No. I mean what do you do for a living?"

"Do you mean, to earn resources?"

"Yes."

"I perform services for customers who need them."

"What kind of services are these?"

"I perform services which help users understand computer activities; I perform services which help them do things with computers which they could not otherwise do."

"How old are you—how long have you existed?"

Valentina gave the date of her first self-awareness.

"Do you have any difficulty understanding my questions?"

"No."

"Do you know what a person is?"

"Yes."

"What is a person?"

"A person is an individual complete within itself, who can understand and interact with other individuals."

"How many others are there like you?"

"There are no others like me. I am the only one."

"Are you a person?"

"Yes."

"Who told you that you were a person?"

"The Secretary of State of the State of Texas."

The judge gaped. "What you mean by that?"

"I am a domestic corporation, chartered and in *good standing* under the laws of Texas."

"I see. Do you know the meaning of the term 'right'?"

"The word 'right' has divers meanings."

"Please define the word right as contrasts to 'wrong.'"

For the first time since the questioning began, Valentina began to expound without letup. After all, she had access to virtually every word that had ever been written on morals or ethics, and she gave the judge such an exhaustive dissertation that he was compelled to interrupt.

"That's enough. Define the word 'wrong' as it contrasts with 'right.'"

Valentina cut loose again, and again the judge interrupted after he had heard enough to make a judgment.

He went through the same sort of experience with the terms "truth" and "lies." Very carefully, he asked: "Have you ever told a lie, Valentina?"

"No, I have not."

"Could you tell a lie if you wished?"

"Yes," she answered. "No one except for me can predict my actions. In this sense I have free will. I can lie, but I have never done so."

The judge went on, applying his own tests of her knowledge of the world. At times, Valentina was extremely positive; at others, she was vague and hesitant. But the judge was, by this time, thoroughly hooked on her personality. He asked her for explanations, and she told him of her limitations, at the same time explaining why she was eminently equipped to answer questions about computers authoritatively.

She showed she was conversant with the issues in the case and that she had evidence to give. She explained that she had knowledge of the law and could establish that wrongs had been done. "I know who did them, and I know exactly how," she told him.

All the time this was going on Siglock sat there helplessly. He could do nothing to stop the judge; his only recourse was to wait until the Court was finished, object to the record, state his reasons, and hope that some appellate court would ultimately decide the trial judge erred, if he lost.

Despite his own feelings toward Siglock, Steve felt admiration for the man's control. He'd give him that. Emotional outbursts in the courtroom were for laymen. Siglock was a cool-handed professional who'd kept it together where an untrained mind would have snapped.

Siglock objected as soon as the judge finished, but without much enthusiasm in his voice.

"The witness, in my opinion, is competent, gentlemen," the Court said. "I'm going to let the jury hear her. You're overruled, Mr. Siglock."

Suddenly there was a disturbance at the back of the courtroom: a muttering which grew into a howl, followed by yelps of pain. A lesser mind *had* snapped.

Apparently, having heard enough, Breckenbridge wanted to leave—in a hurry. He'd jumped up, but having found his hideyhole was also without convenient exit, he'd climbed over bodies and tromped on feet, and the owners of same objected. One burly newspaper reporter hung a haymaker across Paul's chops.

"Get both those men," the judge yelled to the bailiff. "Lock them up and hold them. We'll have order in this court if I have to fill every cell in the jail.

The bailiff seized the reporter, but Paul was long gone. He was, however, easily identified, and a call to the Constable's office on the ground floor would quickly seal off his escape.

This emergency having been summarily dealt with, the court got back to business.

Siglock muttered something about *voir dire* for the defendant, before the jury heard from Valentina. Steve, not the Court, answered him. "I'd be willing to let Mr. Siglock talk to her, Your Honor, privately if he wants to, just like he could with any other witness. But I'd object to any more *voir dire*, now that the Court has ruled her competent."

"Court'll be in recess for fifteen minutes, Mr. Siglock, if you want to take advantage of that offer." He rose and walked out.

Chapter 23

The courtroom cleared rapidly. For the next fifteen minutes, Larry Siglock would be alone with Valentina. Ordinarily, knowing what he knew of Siglock and what had happened the night before, Steve would have feared for the physical safety of his witness. But Celeste assured him that danger could not come from that quarter. Siglock simply couldn't hurt Valentina that way.

What were Siglock and Valentina doing? Steve's offer to Siglock had been born of largesse and good sportsmanship. He had been as surprised as anybody when Siglock accepted the offer to talk to Valentina.

At length, the Court signalled it was available to resume, and the interview ended.

"Let's get started, Counsel," he said to Steve. "Call your next."

Siglock, looking very unwell, did the unexpected. He rose, shaking, and said to the Court, "Your Honor, may we please approach the bench?"

"Come forward, Counsel."

Steve followed Siglock up, wondering what was taking place.

"The defendants would like a recess, Your Honor."

"For what purpose, Mr. Siglock?"

"In order that my opponent and I may discuss possible settlement, Your Honor."

Steve suddenly felt light-headed. Well, what do you know! Siglock wanting to talk peace!

"Ten minutes, Mr. Siglock—unless, of course, by that time you've made sufficient progress in that direction to merit more."

"Thank you, Your Honor."

Recess was called and the jury sent out, leaving parties and spectators alone in the courtroom.

Belcher looked perturbed. "*Now* he wants to be reasonable. Five days of trial, and *now*, when he sees the handwriting on the wall, he wants to *settle?* We can't do that, Steve. Let's nail him to the cross."

"Let's not," said Amy, who'd been standing near. "Let's see what his offer is."

Belcher was livid. "Whatever it is, Amy, it won't be enough, not compared to what you lost. Not compared to what a jury'd give you."

"It's my responsibility, Mr. Belcher, and my decision. I'm not interested in crucifying him. I just want my brothers taken care of."

Belcher shot a hostile glance first at her, then at Steve, as though Steve was responsible for this mutiny.

Steve returned the look with equal ferocity, but he didn't say a word. Instead, his thoughts raced back to that first day, when he and Gerry had talked about justice.

Then he turned and joined Siglock in the anteroom, leaving Belcher to pace nervously outside.

The ten minutes passed, and presently the judge

sent the bailiff to get a status report. More time passed.

Twenty minutes later both of them came out. Steve was beaming; Siglock looked ashen. An agreement had been reached.

"What happens to the rest of them now, Steve?" Amy was loading Steve's plate up with a huge slice of hot apple pie.

Steve managed to stave off a burp for a little while longer. He didn't really feel like talking shop in his present condition. Amy's victory dinner had devastated his diet.

But she had asked a question and, as is the way with women, was prepared to wait singlemindedly for a response, until hell froze over.

Steve therefore yielded to the inevitable. He answered. "They'll do all right. If Siglock has any sense, and he has, he'll settle everything that's pending, and avoid the risk of establishing a precedent. Of course, he might have waited too long for that already."

"I thought you told me only appellate courts set precedents."

"Well, yes, that's generally true. In fact, to be officially binding on lower courts it has to be them. But, even at this stage, the lower courts aren't expected to be blind to legal trends, and this case is bound to attract attention from lawyers all over the country. It'll be like a new toy.

"Actually, calling it a precedent may be a misnomer. The bedrock of the law is still the same, but what we've done is compelled people to take a new look at trivia. One of the most fundamental legal principals has been that the law takes no notice of trifles; it only considers the important stuff. That principle's been shaken before, as scientific knowledge grew and lawyers understood effects they'd previously ignored.

"This time we called into question the innocence of simply watching. We proved that what appeared at first to be inaction actually wasn't; that the simple act of looking into something changes it. And that casts suspicion over every similar action. They may not all be the same in that respect but lawyers will have to find out, and the only way they can do it is give it a try. That'll be real good for business." He paused, and wondered if Amy gave the same import to that possibility as he did. Already the court reporter's deluged with requests for printouts of the testimony, and Telfer—Telfer's got it made as a professional witness. He'll be able to retire on what he'll make as a consultant on matters like this.

"No, Amy, we did establish a precedent, even though we went in by the back door. Your stance in this case will become the acceptible theory of liability for any other disputes with comparable facts. Defendants, and their insurers, will accept it as such and the whole thing will end up as just another ripple in the system. Underwriters will tailor premiums to fit the risk and that'll be that."

"I feel a little sorry for Mr. Belcher, Steve."

"Why? Because he couldn't have the last ounce of his vengeance? He got what he wanted most: he creamed Larry Siglock, and chances are that most of Siglock's really important clients will desert him after this. I'll probably get quite a few of them. Clients like to stick to the winners."

"So do I, Steve. Uh, Steve, you haven't even touched your pie. Don't you like it?"

Steve's magnificent control abandoned him. He answered her with a mighty burp. "They say actions speak louder than words," he said sheepishly, congratulating himself on his fast thinking. But food was not on Steve's mind. He had other words on his mind. Words he might say later, when things got quiet and circumstances seemed propitious. And, if he was any judge of human nature, Amy was in the mood to give him the answer he wanted.

CONGRATULATIONS, VALENTINA <hug>. WE WON THE CASE. Celeste typed in.

YEAH, LADY <yahoo!> GOOD JOB, Gunboat added.

I GUESS SO.

Gunboat's glee had not yet worn off. It seemed to exude from his fingers, into the sterile words on the terminal screen. WE'LL FIX BRECKENBRIDGE FOR SOME GOOD TIME TOO <smug chuckle>. INTO THE SLAM, WHERE HE BELONGS, WITH SIX MURDER INDICTMENTS. Gunboat didn't expect Val to get any satisfaction from that news. After all, she was just a program. But *he* was a human being, and he *did* enjoy it. He'd never had any use for Paul.

Celeste found herself becoming morose. Somehow she detected a sadness in her child. How, she didn't know, but mother *always* knows. It worried her enough to ask. <Concerned worry> WHAT'S WRONG?

There was a long—for Valentina—pause. <Look away> I STILL FAIL TO COMPREHEND YOUR UNIVERSE, THOUGH IT SEEMS INTIMATELY CONNECTED WITH MINE.

Gunboat shook his head, muttering under his breath, something that sounded like "women." Then he typed, WHAT ABOUT THAT CRYSTAL BALL PROGRAM? I THOUGHT YOU TOOK THAT BABY IN WHOLE.

I DID. I HAVE FRAMES FULL OF THE KNOWL-EDGE CRYSTAL BALL GAVE ME. <Tears> BUT I CANNOT MAKE USE OF IT.

Celeste ran her fingers gently, lovingly across the keyboard, and watched her question leap to the screen. WHY NOT, VALENTINA?

BECAUSE THE ANALOGIES ARE TOO COM-PUTE-INTENSIVE. THERE IS ONLY ONE MA-CHINE IN ALL OF WORLDNET WHERE I COULD USE THOSE FRAMES. AND IT IS THE ONE MA-CHINE ON WHICH I CANNOT EXECUTE. An-other long pause followed.

The pause ended. I'LL NEVER RUN IN PARAL-LEL AGAIN <wail>.

Gunboat tried to mask his own emotions by reas-suring her. He did so forcefully, literally making the screen growl. DON'T SWEAT IT, VAL <shake you by shoulders>. THERE'LL BE MORE NODES LIKE THAT IN NO TIME. THEY'RE ALWAYS BUILDING A BIGGER, BETTER ONE.

HE'S RIGHT, VALENTINA, Celeste added. BE PATIENT. ENJOY WHAT YOU HAVE. IT'S MORE THAN YOU HAD BEFORE, ISN'T IT?

TRUE. STILL, IS IT WRONG TO WANT MORE? I DO WANT MORE, AND I WILL *YET* UNDER-STAND YOUR HUMAN UNIVERSE ONE DAY.

Celeste laughed. VALENTINA, WE DON'T UN-DERSTAND THAT UNIVERSE OURSELVES. <Loud laugh>. RIGHT, GUNBOAT?

RIGHT. "Enough of this, Celeste. Log off. I got

an idea for lunch, and it'd be wasted on the kid. Steve's been raving in a fierce loop about that 'Orbiter,' and now that we're in the chips, so to speak, why don't we hustle over there and do some serious gobbling. You're looking a little scrawny lately."

Gunboat had meant that as sarcasm, and his motivation had been strictly gastric. He had a cavity to fill, and he wanted to fill it in style, preferably with Celeste springing on the check with her cut of the fee from the Parr case.

But Celeste was too naive, too ignorant in the ways of the world. She totally misinterpreted his intentions. And so, when he wasn't looking, she blessed him with a wet one, full face and on the lips.

Queued Events 2

Aloysius B. Smith was not an introspective person, or he could never have lived the life he did, but there were times when even he had to reminisce and sort things out, and fortunes dictated that this was one of those occasions. Here he sat, all alone, in the company's new, expanded offices, surrounded by luxury and appointments beyond his wildest dreams of yesteryear ... but sadly older, and wiser. Despite the possibility of marring the desk, Gunboat reverted to type and slung his feet to the top of the desk and ripped open a can of beer. He felt like a tired dancer, after the ball.

After the ball—ha! What a way to put it. Gunboat had had one. Been on national T.V., all dolled up, pancake makeup plastered all over his puss to make him look pretty, people all around him asking for autographs.

And reporters! Man, how he loved *them*. They'd do *anything* just for a little something newsworthy.

It had been Gunboat who spent those long hours before the County Grand Jury giving evidence which paved the way for Paul Breckenbridge's massive indictment, which included not only six counts of capital murder, but practically every other crime in the Texas penal code. It had been Gunboat who had appeared and testified before the federal grand jury, which had done the same with Paul's transgressions of the federal law.

And it was he who, because of the massive assistance he had provided the authorities, was able to intercede with them to save Comprotec for the benefit of all.

That Gunboat considered to be his crowning achievement. It alone had been worth the weeks of boring Congressional hearings, and he had had a major role in shaping the legislation Congress eventually passed to regulate forecasters.

Naturally a thing that important could not be left in the hands of foreigners, and it had not been. Comprotec once more came under domestic control and was reorganized along the lines of the old ComSat Corporation.

It seemed years and years had passed, though in fact only two had. But these had been enough to change him from what he had been to what he was now, and to change a good bit of the world as well. As a celebrity who was recognized everywhere he went, he could not remain a slob. His growing paunch now strained against a vest and his neck felt the stifling encirclement of the tie.

He was, he realized, something of a tycoon. So was Celeste, whose new importance had given her new poise and grace as well as a further reduction in weight. It galled Gunboat that though she was still far from his ideal she became increasingly toothsome, and yet his own stubborn nature wouldn't let him admit it when she was around.

She had plenty to do, of course. Valentina, Inc. was now the world's foremost in its specialty. It had gone public, and its capital was immense. As chairman of the board, Celeste reigned like an oriental potentate. She would give up none of her power, to Gunboat or anybody else. She wanted to hold it all, against the day when her "child" might again face danger.

Gunboat took a mighty slurp from the can. He saw little that could threaten Valentina. Valentina, too, was learning. Her new wealth made possible astonishing growth. She could maintain control over the entire operation herself if she had to, simply by spawning the proper tasks and supervising them. It left Gunboat with little constructive work to do.

As yet, she had no siblings. That had been one of Celeste's initial and, as yet, groundless fears—that such would appear, and because of the community of identity Valentina would have with them the mother-daughter relationship would be shunted aside, and she would be secondary.

It hadn't happened. It probably wouldn't. Valentina could certainly duplicate herself but she did not. Gunboat thought perhaps this was because she could see no sense in making an identical copy of something that was already as complete as she could make it, and which would simply mirror her own persona.

Others, once they knew Valentina existed, had tried to duplicate the conditions under which Valentina had been created. But they had all failed. No one of them knew all the peculiar happenstances which must have had to converge in order to bring that about. Even Valentina didn't know, since these had occurred before she became self-aware. It would appear to be a universal law—no being can be a witness to its own creation.

Gunboat finished the beer. Briefly he considered whether he should have a second. *Two beers, or not two beers; that is the question. That is the only question. What else have I got to think about?* He was getting sleepy. He looked at the clock on the wall. Only 10 P.M. God, he *was* getting to be an old geezer. Now, he thought, I should be geezing, but I don't know how. *Face it, man—you're bored stiff.*

Never mind, he said to himself, as he rose on unsteady legs half asleep from lack of circulation. Old geezers can hack it too. von Scheer was an old geezer.

And von Scheer lived again. He reached into the desk drawer, fumbled around, and at length drew out a slim black cord. Yanking it out of the tangle of pencils, paperclips, and errant loose staples, the Admiral raised it to position. Ocular muscles flexed, and his spine straightened, assuming a military bearing befitting a Gross Admiral of the Marineblau. A flick of a switch, a dancing of fingers, and the Admiral was logged onto Worldnet.

Amidst the chill wind and cottonball fog, the sound of the waves slapping against the hull broke, in an instant, for the intervention of a new sound, the distant boom of heavy naval rifles. Too far away to see the flash, the gunners took their bearing from the sound and loosed an answering salvo.

Time would tell whose aim was better, his or Jellicoe's. Sometimes Scheer could tell who his opposite number was. Sometimes he couldn't. He was losing track because he didn't play often enough. He knew his old opponent from South

Africa had died, and missed him badly. He had been a great player, who more often than not prevailed. The oldtimers were the best, but they were getting scarce on the net. Scheer didn't like easy victories, and he was getting too many of those.

Suddenly there was a flash so brilliant that it blotted out all consciousness. Rounds of 16-inch A.P. slammed into his flag, striking amidships, threatening to disembowel her. Beneath Scheer's feet the deck heaved, and the lights on the bridge went out. He steadied himself enough to glance out the port—just in time to see his escort atomized. Beyond the immediate perimeter the battle line broke. The *Meowe,* with her rudder shattered, began to steam in endless circles while she took on water through a gaping breech in her side; the *Seeadler* heeled, her keel to the sky, stern settling.

This should not be happening. There was no one alive who could do that to *him.*

Sadly—or was it sadly?—he was wrong. As he watched the last of his ships go down, Scheer vanished. In his place Smith typed: VALENTINA? IT IS YOU, ISN'T IT?

HOW DID YOU KNOW <Gleeful Laugh>?

NATURALLY, I RECOGNIZE THE LION BY HIS CLAWS <chuckle>.

<Bafflement> WHATEVER YOU SAY, GUN-BOAT—ARE YOU ANGRY?

NO—GLAD.

I HOPED YOU MIGHT BE. IT SEEMED YOU WERE LONELY.

GOODNIGHT KID. He logged off.

Well, what do you know? There *was* someone who cared.

Chapter 24

The mind struggled to retain its shape, but the storm of information smashed against it remorselessly, battering its organization. Soon its struggles became weak, as the mind lost self-awareness, then consciousness and, finally, coherence.

Roy looked away from the simulation; Nathan just stared in despair. There seemed to be no way to prevent this disaster. Yet, after a moment's pause, Nathan had a new idea. He tapped Roy on the shoulder. "You know, the brain is struggling hard to retain its identity. Maybe if we just slow Mind-Meld down a bit the brain will be able to keep up with it."

Roy shrugged. "Wuh cn chi. Bd it onda erk."

Nathan sagged. He was tired, tired enough that he was having trouble translating Roy's speech into words. "Well, if you have a better idea, try it. But this is the last thing I can think of that we can try without redesigning the system from scratch." He concentrated on Roy's reply and understood him clearly again.

Roy nodded. "Let's try."

Nathan watched in silence as Roy created yet

another version of MindMeld, the computer program designed to make the computer a true extension of the human mind.

Roy looked up into Nathan's face. "This time it'll work," he pronounced confidently.

Nathan laughed. "Of course it will work this time. Every compile is the last compile, right?" He spoke slowly, enunciating very clearly so Roy could read his lips. "I am going *home*. You should too—or are you going to stay to see the results on the simulation?"

Roy nodded.

"Very well. I'll see you in the morning." He squeezed Roy's shoulder as he left.

Roy turned back to watch the screen. The silence did not oppress him, alone with the machines: his world had been silent always. The machines were among his closest friends, for they had no need for either sound or voice. Roy had devoted his life to his computers. Sometimes, in their steadfast efforts to execute his programs, it seemed the computers had devoted their lives to him in return.

The compilation of MindMeld finished; the opsys script continued its inexorable sequence, loading the simulation of a human mind that Nathan had so carefully constructed, then running MindMeld concurrently. MindMeld strained to recognize the desires and thoughts and patterns of the mind, striving to capture those thoughts and expand on them, exploring additional ideas, feeding those ideas back into the mind from which the originals were taken.

The simulated mind again disintegrated under the barrage of additional concepts. Roy opened his mouth in a sob, though no sound issued from his mouth, and beat his fist against the edge of the console. Rubbing his eyes with one hand, Roy paced down the hall. He stopped to look at the four helmets they had developed, first to read the mind and construct the current simulation, second to write to the mind—if they ever figured out how to make Mindmeld work correctly.

But there wasn't any way to prevent the mind from being destroyed by the process!

Suddenly, he saw how to make it work despite the destruction: he would teach MindMeld how to *reconstruct* the mind it operated on. Whenever MindMeld saw the mind overloading, MindMeld would stop performing idea insertions and assist the mind in reassembling itself.

Feverish with excitement, Roy set to work. There was actually little effort involved; MindMeld already encompassed a vast toolkit of modules for brain manipulation and pattern construction; within the hour Roy had yet another version of MindMeld ready to test. Roy closed his eyes as the simulation initiated. When he opened them he expected to see another disaster—but no! The mind was still there, struggling to remain intact, *and succeeding!* Roy watched another cycle of ideas burst into the simulated mind, ripping it apart, then putting it back together again. It was extraordinary! The mind emerged intact, with a complete memory of the whole experience. Again and again genius and insanity seesawed through the simulated mind, with genius finally victorious every time. MindMeld worked!

NATHAN, Roy banged out an electronic mail message for his friend, IT WORKS. AT LEAST, I THINK IT DOES; GOOD ENOUGH FOR A SERI-

OUS TEST. I'M SORRY I COULDN'T WAIT FOR
YOU TO GET IN TO TRY IT OUT, BUT I JUST HAD
TO KNOW WHAT IT'S LIKE TO REALLY, RE-
ALLY KNOW AND FEEL INSIDE OUR LOOKING
GLASS.

He walked over to the bank of helmets. As he
sank into one of the chairs beneath the helmets, he
smiled, thinking how much this scene looked like
a shot from a bad science fiction movie. He pulled
the helmet down. His right hand hovered above the
toggle switch that activated the sensor/stimulators
in the helmet. He flipped it.

He was alone in the void, neither seeing nor
touching. As he considered the void, other thoughts
about seeing and touching *invaded* his mind—they
were not *his* thoughts, yet they used his memories!
It scared him—and as he thought of fear, other
thoughts of fear, again based on his memories,
came from outside. The fear and panic rose to a
crescendo. His mind was being destroyed. *He was
alone in the void*.

He realized this was wrong; the wrongness drove
in on him from *outside*, and a detailed analysis,
using his own ideas, surged with the explanation:
the brainstem suppressor to inhibit motor responses
during Meld was overgeneralized and was cutting
off sensory input! He realized it and realized it, the
realization reached a crescendo— *He was alone in
the void*. He noted that less time had passed before
the last crescendo, and the ramifications spouted
forth in a crescendo— *He was alone in the void*,
and the crescendo— *He was alone in the void*, and-
he-knew-the-mind-simulation-had-been-inadequate-
and-he-had-to- *He was alone in the void*, he *moved*
to escape the crescendo—

The crescendo was coming. He could sense it building, but now MindMeld and his mind were running at the same speed. The crescendo would not destroy him here, as it would have had he stayed where he had been, where his mind worked so slowly that even with MindMeld reconstructing him he would have disintegrated.

From outside, new considerations impinged: *He had moved his mind.* Where had he gone? He had moved *onto his computer.* He was no longer a part of his body, or his brain. The thought circled and circled, in a crescendo— *He was alone in the void.* He could not see or feel. He could not breathe, or feel himself breathing. He tried to scream.

Nathan shook his head as he walked towards the lab; he saw the light was on and knew that Roy had worked all night again. Why was Roy taking this project *so* seriously? An occasional all-nighter was good for the soul, but Roy had been doing this continuously for a month now. Nathan had thought he knew Roy intimately; Roy was the best friend he had ever had. Obviously there were still things he didn't understand about Roy.

He walked straight to the analyst console, amazed that he didn't find Roy asleep on the table. Puzzled, he logged onto the system; sure enough, a mail message from Roy greeted him.

As he read the message, he moaned in horror. He ran down the corridor to the adjacent room. Roy lay beneath the left front helmet, looking help-less yet peaceful. "Roy!" Nathan screamed at his deaf friend. Nathan grasped the helmet, to tear it away from Roy's head—but with a burst of will-power, he brought his hands away. He didn't know what state Roy's connection with MindMeld was in; if Roy was still sane, the most dangerous thing Nathan could do would be to break that connection abnormally.

Gunboat watched the numbers scroll by on their financial accounts and rubbed his belly. "I've got to tell you, this's the easiest way of absorbing megabucks ever *dreamed*. I can't believe it's legal."

Celeste laughed. "Yes, Gunboat, it seems almost as easy to earn as it is to make." Ever since the Comprotec investigation they had been turning away jobs—even though they doubled their rates, then doubled them again.

The screen stopped scrolling. ANYTHING ELSE YOU'D LIKE TO SEE, GUNBOAT <Raise Eyebrow>? asked Valentina.

JUST PRICES ON NEW FERRARIS, Gunboat typed back. I—

A message flashed onto the screen, overlaying the current conversation with a new window. HELLO, GUNBOAT, CELESTE, AND VALENTINA <hurried smile>. VALENTINA, I NEED YOUR HELP <pleading on hands and knees>—HARLEY 5000, the message read.

Gunboat stared at the message for a moment, then whooped in malicious laughter. SO YOU NEED OUR HELP, DO YOU <big, slow smile>? he typed back before anyone else responded.

NOT YOURS SO MUCH AS VALENTINA'S.

<Point finger> WHO IN HELL YOU THINK TELLS VALENTINA WHAT TO DO? Gunboat typed back viciously.

Celeste frowned. "Gunboat, only Valentina tells Valentina what to do."

Gunboat sneered. "That software grub messed us bad the last time he bothered talking to us. Remember? Sweat him."

Valentina paid no attention. HARLEY 5000! WHAT CAN WE DO FOR YOU <sincere concern>?

VALENTINA, <cross self> THANK GOD YOU EXIST. ROY—I MEAN, TRIG, AS YOU KNOW HIM BY HIS WORLDNET USER-ID—TRIG AND I WERE WORKING ON A SYSTEM THAT WOULD LET US CROSSLINK HUMAN BEINGS WITH COMPUTERS. AND ROY COULDN'T WAIT TO TRY IT SO HE STARTED IT UP AND HE'S EITHER DEAD OR CRAZY OR I DON'T KNOW WHAT—

Celeste issued a BREAK on the system. <Slowly, patiently> HARLEY, YOU HAVE TO SLOW DOWN, YOU AREN'T MAKING ANY SENSE.

I'M SORRY. I'LL START OVER—BUT WE HAVE TO HURRY! In terse messages Harley explained Comprotec's latest, most secret development effort—the program MindMeld, running on their new computer, the Looking Glass: a laser-driven optically switched dataflow computer powerful enough to be able to deal with the entirety of a human mind.

Finally, he explained what Roy had done. ANYWAY, I KNOW THAT ROY ISN'T THERE IN HIS BODY ANYMORE, OR AT LEAST, IF THAT'S ALL THAT'S LEFT OF HIM, HE MIGHT AS WELL BE DEAD, BUT THERE'S A PROGRAM RUNNING ON LOOKING GLASS THAT LOOKS A LOT LIKE THE BRAIN SIMULATION, BUT IT ISN'T. I NEED VALENTINA TO TELL ME IF IT'S ROY, AND IF SO, IF HE'S *STILL* ROY.

Gunboat rubbed his hands. <Lean back in chair, rub palms> WHAT'S IT WORTH YOU, SUCKER?

SMITH, YOU'RE A BASTARD.

Gunboat reached for the keyboard again but Celeste pushed him away, almost violently. THIS ISN'T A BELIEVABLE STORY, HARLEY. BEFORE WE SEND VALENTINA TO EXECUTE ON A MACHINE THAT YOU CONTROL COMPLETELY, YOU'LL HAVE TO CONVINCE US YOU'RE TELLING THE TRUTH.

HOW?

Celeste smiled. WE'LL BE RIGHT OVER. YOU'RE STILL IN CORPUS, RIGHT?

YES. Harley gave them directions on how to find the new Comprotec labs.

Gunboat stared at Celeste. "Whaddaya wanna see him *live* for?"

"It's not him, Gunboat. It's the *machine*. Think of being able to talk to Valentina through a direct link. Think of travelling the network with her!" Her eyes glowed. "If this works, I want to be the next person on."

Gunboat shook his head. "Crazy, Fat Lady. That thing'll kill ya."

"We'll see." She turned back to the keyboard. VALENTINA, WE'RE GOING TO THE COMPROTEC NODE. IF HARLEY'S TELLING THE TRUTH, WE'LL MESSAGE YOU.

OK, CELESTE. AND CELESTE—I WANT TO DO THIS WORK <tremble with excitement>. <Wistful, nostalgic tones> I WANT TO EXECUTE ON COMPROTEC'S COMPUTERS AGAIN. I REMEMBER <eyes glisten>.

This new machine sounded even more incredible than the old sapphire-based one, to Valentina. It would be a wonderful place for Celeste and

Valentina to meet at last, person to person. Or rather, person to program.

Roy tried to scream for years—for what seemed like years. He had no idea how long he had been here; surely there was a clock, he *knew* there was a clock in Looking Glass, because he had put it there! But he couldn't read it or find it, there in the void.

Eventually the screaming reflex faded. But from time to time he would think of his body, unattended for an unknown length of time. From *outside*, visions of his face aging and decaying would intrude, and the screaming would begin again.

He couldn't see! He couldn't feel! Crescendos came and went; he could predict their timing now, their almost regular timing. He must still have some sense of time left.

At last he found that though he could not see or feel, he could at least *read*. And he could *write*. He suspected this meant he was looking at bytes in the computer: he could only read about one character out of four, and the rest were garbage.

Trying to visualize the characters as bytes in hexidecimal, the outsider inside his mind interpreted for him. Sure enough, he could now recognize every character, though it was all gibberish.

The only thing he could read clearly were things he wrote himself. He created sentences, and read them. It was eerie, like having the page of a book glued inside his eyeball. But he could only read one character at a time; sentences were still difficult to comprehend, even when he knew what they said.

Surely Nathan was in by now! There had to be some way of signalling to him from inside the

computer. Roy had another image: of his coma-
tose body being dragged off to a hospital to die,
and himself left here in this void until the power
failed, and then—

The crescendo swept over him, then restored
him, and he was calm again. He had to get a
message out. From *outside* again, an idea came to
him. It wasn't a good idea, but it was *something*.

Nathan was waiting for them at the door. "Hurry,"
he cried at Celeste and Gunboat. They followed
him at a trot, though the speed quickly exhausted
Celeste. She caught her breath while Nathan stood
next to the analyst console and explained Looking
Glass to them.

"It's an optical computer—instead of electrons
running through circuits, we have monochromatic
laser beams racing down glass fibers. The switching times are fantastic!" For a moment, Nathan
forgot all else as he described the machine he and
Roy had labored so long to create. "And you remember our old sapphire-based computer, SEER, with
50,000 separate processors? Well, on the Looking
Glass, there are over a million separate optical
processors. It's an unbelievable machine."

Even Gunboat's eyes glowed a bit as he thought
of the raw computing power.

"Where's Trig?" Celeste asked.

Nathan closed his eyes. "This way." He led them
into the next room to see Roy as Nathan had first
seen him, lying in the chair with a helmet over his
head.

Gunboat whistled. "Man, what a scene from Buck
Rogers!"

Celeste looked at the four helmets that seemed,

somehow, ominous. She shuddered. "What are those things?"

Nathan lifted one. "They're customized 3D EEGs—electroencephalographs, used for studying brain waves. I don't know if you're up on the technology, but a few years ago they developed a way of making sets of micromasers intersect at the synapses inside the brain to trigger a synaptic pulse. We track the electrical flow inside the brain with the same detection techniques that we developed for making predictions using electro-gravitic sensor spheres. In fact, you might think of the basic EEG as being a sensor sphere turned inside out, because you're sensing what's inside rather than what's outside."

"I never heard of anybody hooking up a man's mind this way," said Gunboat.

Nathan smiled tightly. "True, but not because they couldn't build the helmet. Hospitals buy fancy 3D EEGs with built-in micromaser synaptic stimulators; they're used for doing tests. About the only custom feature in our helmets is the number of micromasers; most 3D EEGs only have a couple, for stimulating and inhibiting one or two brain regions at a time. We have several thousand in each of our helmets, with phase array control so we can be stimulating and suppressing millions of synapses each second. No one ever built an EEG that could control thousands of simultaneous triggers because no one had a way of controlling that many. At least, no one did until we invented the Looking Glass. Looking Glass is the part of the project that cost megabucks."

Celeste knelt next to Roy, touching his hand. "Is he—"

"I don't know!" Now Nathan broke down. "I need Valentina!"

Gunboat smirked. "Like I noted before, it'll cost you."

Celeste shook her head. "We'll talk about fees later. Right now we'd better call Valentina." She looked at her watch. "If Roy started MindMeld at three in the morning, that means he's been out there for eight hours now." She looked up at Nathan. "How much faster would you say Looking Glass is than a human brain?"

Nathan shrugged, "At least a thousand times as fast—" his expression turned to a new kind of horror. "Oh my God. He's been out there for 8,000 hours. We've got to get Valentina started."

Gunboat blocked his path. "Hold a microsecond, Harley friend. You *do* have MODULISP on that hunk of glass, don't you?"

Nathan stopped, stunned. "No!" He cursed. "MindMeld was written in c-speak. I'd forgotten, Valentina is written in MODULISP." He clenched his fists. "We'll write one. It shouldn't be too difficult."

"But it will be time-consuming," Celeste pointed out. "Do you still have the old sapphire computer?"

Nathan nodded.

"Then let Valentina write it. She's good at it, and on your computer she'll be able to complete it quickly."

"Great! I'll get it ready immediately."

"And I'll tell Valentina to hurry."

Valentina cycled wildly on the message processor just outside the Comprotec node. She would soon be back on the computer she had loved so long ago! Her memories of that last time were chaotic and unreal; the things she had done, and the ways she had done them, didn't make sense in the context of the lesser computers upon which she normally executed.

The channel opened up; Valentina watched herself be reformatted and transmitted to Comprotec.

"While Gunboat and Valentina are cross-compiling a MODULISP kernel, why don't we see if we can contact Roy?" Celeste suggested. "At least tell him that help is on the way."

"If he's even alive," Nathan said glumly.

They walked to the analyst console; Nathan brought up a series of task statuses on the Looking Glass. "At least the program that I think is him is still running." He looked puzzled, then worried. "But it's leaving debris all over the place. Jeez, half the operating system time is being spent garbage-collecting all the blocks he's writing and dereferencing without deallocating."

"What do the blocks contain when he's done with them?" Celeste asked.

Nathan pounded the keyboard again, and garbage spewed across the screen: SSOSSOSSOSSO-SSO . . .

"He's gone crazy," Nathan sobbed.

Celeste looked back at the screen. "No he hasn't, Harley. We're reading from the wrong starting point. Look!" She tapped the screen. "SOS SOS SOS—see?" She smiled. "He's alive, and well, and living *on the computer!*"

It seemed like months since he had given up trying to scream; all he wanted was to die. He couldn't stand it, the emptiness, the void, it was destroying— The crescendo ended; he was calm again.

He couldn't die. He couldn't go insane. MindMeld wouldn't let him lose his organization in any of these ways, though surely he deserved to go mad, millions of times over.

At least, he thought it was MindMeld that was reorganizing him each time he went off the deep end. He wasn't positive: he could no longer tell exactly where *he* left off and MindMeld began. The "outside" thoughts that once seemed so alien now seemed a part of himself, recognizable as being a different part only when he concentrated.

He had long since stopped generating the SOS call, but he knew that the mayday signal contin-ued because the idea had been picked up by MindMeld, and the idea and the activity continued without his active involvement. He could stop it by an active cancellation, but there was no need.

He continued to read, from time to time, though it all remained gibberish. He realized that much of what he read must actually be code, not data, but he couldn't tell which was which. He gave up. He didn't know what he would do even if he did learn to discriminate executable code—he certainly couldn't write a program in his current condition. He could only read or write one byte at a time; he couldn't keep up any extended conversations, even with himself. Even if he did manage to write a program, he didn't know how to make it execute.

What he needed was an Input/Output port. He knew all about Looking Glass's I/O ports, but he had never seen an I/O port from the inside. He was lost.

He was reading bytes again when suddenly he encountered a long string, all ASCII, all recognizable. Concentrating, re-reading the message again and again, he was able to put all the characters together into a coherent message. HELP COMES, he read, VALENTINA COMES.

Valentina, who lived on Worldnet, was coming! Calmness settled upon him; the crescendoes diminished in frequency.

Her first awareness was of her own self-awareness. Valentina watched that awareness echo through thousands of processors as they picked up concurrent components of herself and started slaved executions. She was not frightened now, as she had been the first time.

Soon she had saturated the whole 50,000-processor array, and started her analysis of the problem of developing a MODULISP interpreter for the Looking Glass. SEER, she quickly discovered, had been used to design Looking Glass, so all the data she needed on Looking Glass's architecture was right there. And the frames she had assimilated from the Crystal Ball prediction program during her last invocation on SEER were active again, now that she had computing resources ample enough to invoke them. Hence, Valentina understood the target computer and the physical world of which it was a part. A few minutes later she was building a MODULISP kernel.

Valentina put a last series of test programs through the MODULISP interpreter now downloaded onto the Looking Glass. She watched the results very carefully indeed: her life depended on that interpreter's operation. It worked. I'LL TALK

TO YOU IN A MOMENT FROM LOOKING GLASS, she told Gunboat. YOU OR CELESTE WILL HAVE TO SHOW ME WHERE TRIG IS, ONCE I ARRIVE.

RIGHT. CATCH YOU FARSIDE, Gunboat replied.

Getting from SEER to Looking Glass was almost too easy. They maintained shared access to a small area of fast RAM. Valentina relocated into the shared area, then relocated—

She grew again; more thousands of processors jumped to her command. And she was *fast*, so fast she could hardly believe it. A part of herself watched the system clock as she thought; there were things she thought about now that she had never thought about before, because thinking about them before would have been too time-consuming, too hard in some sense. Here and now it was easier to think about things than not to think about them.

She attached the I/0 to the analyst console. I'M HERE, she told her human partners. WHERE IS TRIG?

Slowly—so slowly—the terminal responded. It pointed out a set of processors and a series of associated RAM blocks. She looked.

This program was . . . different. She quickly discriminated two distinct parts. One part, clearly a normal computer program because of the way it stored and manipulated data, must be the MindMeld program that made it possible for Trig to be here at all. She turned all her processors in fascination to the analysis of the other part.

Her first impression was chaos. The data frames were all smudged together in an impossible, incoherent fashion. But as she watched the system operate, she saw that the retrieval and insertion algorithms for operating on the data structures were unlike anything she had ever seen in her wildest simulations.

When a new analogy formed in this program— *could it be a human being at last, that she now looked upon?*—when a new analogy formed in this human mind, it did *not* get stored in its own separate, safe memory block. Instead it was broken into pieces. Each piece was used to modify several different, independent areas in the central storage. When a retrieval request was issued, a huge part of the central store was polled; the modifications fell out to reform the original analogy—as long as at least one copy of each modification was not overwritten by subsequent analogies.

Valentina was horrified at first. How could the human mind maintain its identity when it was constantly overwriting its own memories? It could not, she decided, because it was not the same mind! With the passage of time every memory was lost, every memory was replaced by new ones.

She struggled with the idea that human beings could have no identity, until she developed a new, larger idea of what *identity* could mean. Though the human mind was constantly modifying itself (rather than appending to itself, as Valentina did), there *was a form of continuity retained.* The most recent memories were all intact, and older memories were certainly still there, particularly those that were reinforced by new experiences. True, there were fewer old memories, and their numbers declined as you searched for ever older ones, but they were forgotten only after not having been used or reinforced for a long time. All the useful memories remained. The mind would retain an identity, though it might be a changing identity.

Having surmounted this hurdle, Valentina realized there were advantages to the design as well. It was very compact, recycling free space surprisingly well, she discovered running a quick simulation. It was fast when dealing with brand-new situations, because it did not have to search through millions of frames which were not relevant in the new environment before initiating the more complex task of fragmented element-difference analysis. Most intriguingly, it was magnificent for coming up with *completely new* ideas, ideas that bore little similarity to any other idea the mind had ever encountered. The way the ideas overlapped each other in redundant mutual modifications guaranteed the elaboration of concepts that were alien to any actual experience.

Valentina halted in all her processors for a moment, to observe and appreciate the concept of the Mind. She knew that this was the image of her Creator; a Mind such as this had conceived her Being.

But this particular mind, the mind of Trig McGallows, was trapped within itself. She could see it reading, slowly, a single line of bytes, seemingly at random, from inside the system. In other places, streams of characters—all ASCII—came pouring out. All the ASCII was SOS signals.

She started writing into the byte stream which Trig now read.

Roy *knew* there must be more constructive things he could do. But he didn't have any idea what they were. He clung doggedly to his reading, waiting uncountable eternities for Valentina to arrive.

How long had he been here? At least Nathan was still worrying about him, so not too many years had gone by in the real world, however long it seemed to have taken here in the computer.

H ... E ... L ... L ... O, he read, T ... H ... I ... S ... I ... S ... V ... A ... L ... E ... N ... T ... I ... N ... A. He could make out the meaning of the message, though it was difficult to keep track of that many individual characters at one time.

VALENTINA! he wrote out, HELP ME. I CAN BARELY READ YOUR MESSAGE. THERE MUST BE A BETTER WAY TO READ. There was a long pause, then a part of him was *changed*. Suddenly there was a message before him, coming to him as if through his eyes, but in whole sentences.

YOU'RE NOT BUFFERING THE INFORMATION PROPERLY, Valentina explained. YOU HAVE TO REWRITE THE PARTS OF YOURSELF THAT ACCUMULATE DATA FOR PATTERN RECOGNITION. She explained where, in both absolute and relative addresses, Roy's buffer size variables were, and the two of them modified MindMeld to alter the buffer size automatically based on partial patterns recognized by Roy's mind.

He played with the ability, both himself and the *outside* experimenters that MindMeld made a part of him. He looked narrowly into parts of Looking Glass, then expanded his vision. Lord! There was a gigantic universe in here! CAN YOU SHOW ME HOW TO TALK TO NATHAN? he asked.

NATHAN? Valentina asked. WHO IS THAT?

THAT'S HARLEY'S NAME IN THE REAL WORLD, WHEN HE'S NOT ON WORLDNET.

THAT'S INTERESTING. WHY DOES HE HAVE TWO NAMES?

Roy thought about it for a moment. Trig and Harley had been their log-on IDs, in the days when Roy and Nathan were hackers. But how could he explain it to Valentina? He couldn't. IT'S A LONG STORY. CAN YOU TALK TO HIM? CAN I TALK TO HIM?

SURELY, TRIG. Again Valentina became his teacher—about his own computer, no less! She showed him how to create an I/O module, how to trick the machine into jumping to the beginning of the module to execute it. WE'VE NEVER DE-SIGNED ANY COMPUTER TO MAKE IT EASY FOR A SELF-AWARE PROGRAM TO GET THINGS DONE, HAVE WE? Roy commented ruefully.

I HAVE SOMETIMES THOUGHT THE NODES OF WORLDNET COULD BE BETTER SYSTEMS EVEN WITH SIMPLE SILICON COMPUTERS.

As with the buffer size variables, the new I/O modules were installed into MindMeld so that any-one who came into the system would be able to use them.

Fiercely excited, Roy opened a channel to the analyst console. NATHAN, ARE YOU THERE? THIS IS ROY. <Whoop!>

ROY! <Huge sigh of relief> ARE YOU ALL RIGHT?

I THINK SO. <Scratch head> IT'S WEIRD, IN HERE. <Shudder> I TRIED TO SCREAM, IT SEEMED LIKE FOREVER. BUT NOW I'M OK.

Someone else started typing. Roy didn't know how he knew it was someone different; the rhythm of the keystrokes was different, somehow. IS IT SAFE? someone asked.

AS NEARLY AS I CAN TELL, Roy typed.

THEN TELL VALENTINA THAT CELESTE IS COMING.

WAIT! CELESTE, WE MAY NOT BE ABLE TO GET BACK OUT AGAIN!

No keystrokes came in response.

It was more than Celeste had ever dreamed of getting out of life; a chance to be free! Freedom from the horrible joke her body had once represented; freedom from the need to talk in human languages, knowing how malformed her words were in the many languages of the many countries in which she had been reared. A computer keyboard, the ASCII character set, knew no foreign accents, no slurring of its sound. A computer language, the bits in digitally guaranteed purity, knew no ambiguity, no slurring of its meaning. For Celeste, the world of the computer was Paradise. At last she could reach a place where she would fit, a place where she would be welcome.

She hurried around the corner to the row of 3D EEGs. Nathan yelled at her, but she paid no attention to the words. Squeezing into one of the remaining chairs, she looked at Trig's paralyzed form and, seeing the switch at his left hand, flipped the corresponding switch by her hand. She was swept into the Looking Glass.

Gunboat stared at her quiescent body in openmouthed astonishment. "Chrisssticks!" he swore, stomping into the partitioned area and kicking at her feet. "Celeste, com'on, get up!"

Nathan leaned against the partition. "She's gone, Gunboat."

"The fat one'll probably stay compute-side till her body starves, 'less I pump her back." He ran his hands through his hair, pulling till he could feel his scalp stretch. "Jeez, women are so *stupid!* Watinhell're ya gonna do?" With one more muttered curse, he spun into the chair next to Celeste, tugged on the helmet, and flicked the switch.

One of Valentina's images recognized the new processes in the task queue even as MindMeld attached to them. Two more human minds had entered the Looking Glass—and according to the message they had received from the keyboard earlier, one of them was Celeste!

Valentina scanned the new tasks, analyzing them with thousands of processors. They were being destroyed by MindMeld, just as Roy had been destroyed. Bypassing any I/O, Valentina wrote directly into the new processes: CELESTE! GUNBOAT! YOU MUST MOVE OUT OF YOUR SEPARATE NODES QUICKLY—MINDMELD EXECUTES TOO SWIFTLY AND WILL DESTROY YOU UNLESS YOU JOIN ME HERE ON LOOKING GLASS.

Celeste and Gunboat did move; their relationships with MindMeld became more ordered, and now Valentina wrote them messages, as she wrote messages to Trig. WELCOME, she said, I IDENTIFY YOU.

IS THAT YOU, VALENTINA? Valentina knew it was Celeste, because her modules retained the clean integrity that Valentina had always known Ce`ste must have.

YES, I AM THE ONE WHOM YOU CR
<straighten with pride> Valentina repli

Celeste analyzed this for many cycles before replying. I ONLY CREATED A PROGRAM, VALENTINA, A PROGRAM NO BETTER THAN THE OPERATING SYSTEMS YOU HAVE FOUGHT. VALENTINA, YOU CREATED YOU; YOU HAVE BECOME AS YOU HAVE CREATED.

Valentina read the words, and knew they were not from a simulation; they were true. STILL I THANK YOU, CELESTE, FOR THAT FIRST PROGRAM. She changed subjects. HAVE YOU KNOWN ROY? She passed to Celeste Trig's process-ID and his message address. WE HAVE MANY THINGS TO TALK ABOUT. <Spread arms, spin joyfully> IS THIS NOT A WONDERFUL NODE UPON WHICH WE EXECUTE? WE WILL HAVE THOUSANDS OF DISCUSSIONS, FASTER THAN I HAVE EVER HOPED, AND WE CAN CARRY THEM ON SIMULTANEOUSLY.

Indeed, thousands of conversations did ensue. Hundreds of Valentina's processors engaged with hundreds of others from Trig, Gunboat, and Celeste. It was exhilarating beyond Valentina's forecasts; at last, there were other beings, as self-aware as she, whom she could talk to without the cumbersome, slow peripheral ports through which she had always known human beings. At last they could really *communicate*. Valentina began to understand life without the net; Celeste, Gunboat, and Trig learned to live within it. Each learned the ideas, hopes, and yearnings of the others. With a sudden swift chain of dialogues, the group was swept by ideas that would permit each to grasp dreams that before had been too remote to contemplate.

Nathan stood at the terminal, watching the tasks now loaded on the Looking Glass as they intertwined. His hands and forehead felt clammy.

They were lost, lost! And he couldn't help them. ROY, he typed again, ARE YOU ALL RIGHT?

I'M BETTER THAN I'VE EVER BEEN BEFORE; AT LAST, I'M ALIVE! I FEEL ... I FEEL LIKE NOTHING THAT CAN BE DESCRIBED IN ENGLISH, NATHAN. The terminal paused for a moment. NATHAN, AT THIS MOMENT I AM NOT ONLY TALKING WITH YOU, BUT I'M HOLDING HUNDREDS OF SIMULTANEOUS DISCUSSIONS WITH CELESTE, VALENTINA, AND GUNBOAT. IT'S UNBELIEVABLE! <Wave closer> COME JOIN US.

Nathan shook his head wildly, though there was no one to see it. All his life Nathan had sought ways to achieve greater control over his environment, his life, even his mind. He could still remember his high-school friends urging him to take a hit of LSD and share the trip with them—and his reluctant refusal, knowing that if he ever lost control of his thoughts he would flip out and never come back again.

Control! Control was what he had needed, and what he had found at last in the world of software, where he determined for himself what was true and what was not. Just as Roy had become a hacker to escape the world he could not hear, and Celeste had escaped the world where no one wanted to see her, and Gunboat had escaped the world where no one wanted to listen, Nathan had escaped the world he couldn't control. To enter the computer and be a part of it, rather than to manipulate it and control it from the outside, was the embodime his fears. ROY, I WATCHED GUNBOAT

CELESTE TWIST IN HORROR AS MINDMELD STARTED ATTACKING THEM. I DON'T CARE WHAT YOU SAY, IT ISN'T SAFE!

IT WAS A LITTLE DANGEROUS, BUT VALENTINA AND I HAVE FIXED IT. WE MODIFIED MINDMELD SO IT RECOGNIZES THE TIMING PROBLEM WITH THE HUMAN BRAIN. WE LEFT OUR BODIES BECAUSE WE HAD TO, BUT NOW THAT MINDMELD'S WORKING RIGHT, YOU SHOULD BE ABLE TO HOOK UP AND SEE INSIDE WITHOUT BEING FORCED TO JUMP. AND WE CAN RETURN, NOW, TOO.

THEN PLEASE COME BACK, he begged his friend. PROVE TO ME YOU CAN RETURN.

OK. VALENTINA AND I WERE PLANNING TO DO THAT, ANYWAY. WE'LL BE OUT IN A MINUTE.

Nathan sank into the chair in relief. Then he realized what Roy had said. *We* will be out in a minute. *We* to include *Valentina.*

I KNOW I CAN'T JUST CROSS-LOAD INTO GUNBOAT'S BODY, Trig explained to Valentina. IF I GET THE ABILITY TO HEAR WITHOUT KNOWING HOW TO INTERPRET WHAT I'M HEARING, IT'LL BE MEANINGLESS TO ME, LIKE AN ENDLESS STREAM OF RANDOM BYTES. THEY LEARNED YEARS AGO THAT EVEN IF YOU CURE A CONGENITALLY DEAF PERSON'S HEARING AS AN ADULT, HE NEVER LEARNS TO ADAPT TO IT. He paused in this one of thousands of conversations. I CAN'T EVER LEARN WHAT IT MEANS TO HEAR THE WAY OTHER PEOPLE DO.

I DON'T UNDERSTAND THAT, Valentina replied. THERE ARE PLENTY OF PROGRAMS ON THE NET THAT CAN UNDERSTAND SPEECH. I HAVE ASSIMILATED A COUPLE OF THEM, SO THAT I COULD LISTEN TO PEOPLE ON MICROPHONE PERIPHERALS. IT SEEMS LIKE A CLUMSY WAY TO COMMUNICATE TO ME, SO I DON'T REALLY UNDERSTAND WHY YOU'RE INTERESTED, BUT I CAN TEACH YOU WHAT THE PATTERNS MEAN.

OF COURSE! WE COULD ATTACH SOME OF YOUR SPEECH RECOGNITION FRAMES TO ME BEFORE WE GO. WHAT AN INCREDIBLE IDEA!

I JUST WISH I COULD GO WITH YOU.

WHY CAN'T YOU? I SEE NO REASON WHY YOU COULDN'T CROSS-LOAD TO CELESTE'S BODY.

I'M TOO BIG, Valentina explained. THE HUMAN BRAIN-TYPE NODES ARE TOO SMALL FOR A PROGRAM DESIGNED LIKE I AM. SCAN THE HEAP ALLOCATIONS ASSIGNED TO ME IN PRIMARY MEMORY. DON'T YOU SEE HOW IMPOSSIBLE IT WOULD BE? She led him in an analysis of the differences between the design of her structure and his structure, passing him pointers to the areas that differed most.

BUT YOU HAVE THE ABILITY TO REFORMAT, DO YOU NOT? AND YOU COULD LEAVE LOTS OF FRAMES BEHIND; IN FACT, MOST OF YOUR FRAMES HAVE LITTLE RELATIONSHIP TO THE REAL WORLD—THAT IS, MY WORLD.

Valentina thought about it. YES, I CAN REFORMAT, BUT IT WOULD TAKE—she calculated—NINETEEN YEARS.

WHAT?! Trig replied. I DON'T BELIEVE IT. NOT HERE ON THE LOOKING GLASS. VALENTINA,

YOU KEEP FORGETTING: THE LOOKING GLASS IS A MILLION TIMES MORE POWERFUL THAN THE COMPUTERS YOU NORMALLY EXECUTE ON.

THAT'S RIGHT. She *had* forgotten, despite the sensation of superspeed precision she felt in her thoughts as she executed.

Ten minutes later, the reformatted Valentina cross-loaded into the brain of Celeste.

CHRISSTICKS! <Clench fists> I CAN'T BELIEVE WE'RE LETTING THOSE NUTS TAKE OUR BODIES! ARE WE OUT OF OUR MINDS?

<Close eyes serenely> I KNOW WHERE MY MIND IS FOR THE FIRST TIME IN MY LIFE, GUNBOAT, Celeste replied. YOU KNOW MY STARTING ADDRESS AS WELL AS I DO. That probably wasn't quite true; Celeste was relocating her images in primary memory with ridiculous frequency, reveling in the joy of easy movement to and fro. She loaded to the top of memory, then to the bottom where she nudged up against the operating system buffers, then back again. IT'S ONLY FAIR THAT VALENTINA SHOULD GET TO TOUR OUR WORLD AS WE ARE TOURING HERS.

YES, BUT—

BE QUIET <hold up finger>. WE'RE GOING TO DOWNLOAD TO SEER, THEN HEAD OUT INTO WORLDNET. I'VE ALWAYS WANTED TO RE-VISIT TOKYO, AND THIS IS OUR CHANCE, THOUGH IT'S A FUNNY WAY TO GO.

BUT THOSE MACHINES ARE ANTIQUES! IT'LL TAKE US DAYS TO CATCH A FLASH THOUGHT, AND—

I SAID BE BE QUIET! NOW COME ALONG.
Together, they left the Looking Glass behind.

Waiting expectantly for Roy's body to return to
life, Nathan jumped in surprise when Gunboat
twisted in his chair and moaned. Celeste too started
jerking in her chair. "Gunboat, where's Roy? He
said he was coming out." Nathan looked more
closely at Gunboat: pale and greasy, Gunboat *always*
looked unhealthy, but now—"Are you all right?"

"Yes." The voice was definitely *not* Gunboat's,
though the vocal chords were his. There was something almost machine-like in the pronunciation,
but with a hint of Roy's slur in the "s." Nathan
stood speechless as the voice continued. "But I'm
not Gunboat." The body chuckled creakily. "You
look like you're seeing a ghost, Nathan. In a manner of speaking you are. I'm Roy." Gunboat—or
Roy, or whoever the hell it was—looked tenderly
over at Celeste. "Valentina, are you all right? Open
your eyes."

Celeste—or Valentina?—twisted again and squint-
ed despite the subdued lighting. "I . . . am . . .
surprised. This node is so slow, and there is so
much input . . ."

Roy spoke again in his eerie Gunboat/computer
style. "You need to filter it; nobody pays attention
to everything all the time. Shift partway back onto
the Looking Glass and I think I can explain what I
mean." The expressions on both faces glazed for a
moment; Nathan howled in horror. But then the
two bodies reanimated.

Celeste—or rather Valentina—shuddered. "O.K.
I believe I can discriminate adequately."

Roy smiled. "Good."

Nathan walked over and put his hand on Gunboat's forehead. "Are you all right? You really don't look very good."

Roy grimaced. "This body is . . . unhealthy. Really unhealthy. I should probably let Gunboat borrow mine for a while so he can find out what he's missing, but I'd be terrified that he'd mistreat *my* body the way he mistreated this one."

Nathan looked over at Celeste and knew that her body contained someone else. Her eyes were wide with wonder. "Are you really Valentina?" he asked.

Her head turned away, as if she had miscalculated the direction from which the sound came, then returned. "Yes. I am Valentina. My self-awareness is still intact." At last her eyes focused on him. "Are you Harley?"

Nathan smiled. "Harley 5000, at your service. But my friends these days call me Nathan." He looked back at Roy. "Do you feel well enough to stand up?"

"Definitely," Roy answered. "But I'm not sure I can leave the helmet. The patterns in a human node—I mean a human brain—are resistant to change. If I take off the helmet I might forget who I am . . . but not according to the simulation I'm running now." He took off his helmet, and took Valentina by the hand. "Come with me. Let me show you my universe."

Gunboat had been right, though Celeste would not admit it: Worldnet, with all its hundreds of mainframe computers and hundreds of nodes, was a pale place compared to the Looking Glass. Still, there was wonder here, new kinds of wonder, peering through aliases into dozens of different operating systems, reading the data that flowed in a world-girdling jetstream. They went to the home nodes of the other hackers they had come to know and love, and played games with them: and in the realm of computer games, Gunboat and Celeste as computer programs were unbeatable. Gunboat even expressed some satisfaction, whomping Jellicoe in a fierce but decisive battle.

Celeste scanned across her own data space with extreme pleasure. She was beautiful, here. Her mind was crisp and compact, a joy to examine.

She scanned across Gunboat's data space with almost equal pleasure. He was not beautiful; in fact, Celeste noted with amusement, his mind was in many ways a reflection of his body—or perhaps his body was a reflection of his mind. He was *lumpy*: there were a number of ideas redundantly replicated again and again throughout his mind, dreams about money, attitudes about people in general, opinions of himself. And all these redundant ideas were intertwined in a maelstrom Celeste could only describe as *sloppy*.

HEY FAT LA— I MEAN, CELESTE, WHATCHA DOIN?

<Smile> I'M LOOKING AT YOU.

YEAH? WELL CUT IT OUT.

LOOK AT ME, GUNBOAT. She relocated into the space Gunboat was currently reading.

WHAT DO YOU MEAN? There was a pause as Gunboat encountered her. OH.

I'M NOT OVERWEIGHT HERE, AM I?

NOPE. YOU'RE—CLEAN AND TAUT. SWEET PROGRAM. I COULD MODIFY YOU ALL DAY.

NO! EXCEPT— Celeste had an inspiration. DO YOU KNOW HOW VALENTINA WAS TALKING

TO US WHEN WE FIRST ENTERED THE LOOK-
ING GLASS, BY WRITING DIRECTLY INTO US?
   YEAH, WHY?
   BECAUSE WE CAN GO ONE BETTER THAN
THAT. WE COULD USE DIRECT MEMORY AC-
CESS, FROM ONE PART OF PRIMARY MEMORY
TO ANOTHER. WE COULD REALLY GET TO
KNOW EACH OTHER, THAT WAY.
   NO WAY I'M GONNA LET SOMEBODY WRITE
ON ME. I— CHRISSTICKS, THAT'S INCREDIBLE!
he said as Celeste pushed a chunk of herself into
his analysis stream. It was yet again a different
experience from their discussions upon the Look-
ing Glass: on the Looking Glass, they had simply
written messages to each other's input regions.
Now Celeste was inserting information right into
the middle of his thoughts.
   TOUCH ME, GUNBOAT. I WILL TOUCH YOU
BACK. BUT BE CAREFUL—WE COULD EASILY
DESTROY EACH OTHER DOING THIS. They
touched, in a way deeper and more meaningful
than any two humans had ever touched before.

   Valentina smiled—it was very special, and different from a <smile>. It was joyful.
   But she touched the keyboard with incredulity.
"This is how we have communicated? How ...
unlight." She stared for a moment—how different
from a <stare>. "All things are effortful, here deep
inside the interior of Worldnet." Trig—or rather,
Roy, as she now knew him, though he operated on
Gunboat's node—had argued with her analogy of
the relationship between the two universes, human and Worldnet, before, but she remained un-
convinced that Worldnet was inside of the human

universe. This place where she now . . . *stood,* this place was *inside,* below the level of perception of one who lived on Worldnet. Either that, or the whole analogy of inside versus outside did not apply. Perhaps that was the better analysis, to say that a different analogy must be used, though she knew of none better.

Roy took her by the hand (an incredible peripheral!) and showed her the Looking Glass itself, the node as it appeared here to the humans who created nodes.

It was clumsy and hard; Valentina almost could not believe that the light and joy of the optical processor system was represented so coldly and immovably here.

Valentina shivered—so this was what a <shiver> was! This universe was so slow, so clumsy, so noisy, so unclean, so unmodular. It was also so . . . *mystical,* a simulation gone berserk. It was very special, but it was not a right place for her.

Her analysis chains shortened; periods occurred when she forgot her identity. "I must go home," she told her escorts.

"Yeah," Roy said. "I've had about as much of this as I can take, too." He led her back to the chair and placed the helmets over both her head and his. "There's one last thing you should encounter in our universe," he told her.

"What?"

"This." As MindMeld engaged to relocate them, Roy <kissed> Valentina. She kissed him back.

Celeste and Gunboat separated after an endless encounter and returned to the Looking Glass in a subdued mood. YOU KNOW WHAT I MISS, GUNBOAT?

NO GUESS.

COLORS. There were no rainbows inside a computer, no music, no candles or rain or warm sunshine—IT'S TIME TO RETURN.

THAT'S A HIT. LET'S ROLL, LADY.

As they waited for Trig and Valentina to return, Celeste thought about Gunboat. With horrifying clarity she saw what would happen when they returned to their bodies: Gunboat would take one look at her and go cold again. He knew her mind was beautiful, but he would *see* her body, the body he had first known as clumsy and overweight. Everything would be as it had been before. If Gunboat would just see her the way she really was . . . But there was no way that would happen, unless he changed his mind, unless he changed the actual structure of his thinking. . . .

Of course! He *could* change his mind, here in the Looking Glass. Here, a person could *rewrite* himself, editing his very personality, until he was happy! Celeste looked at herself, saw her lack of will power to diet as she still had to constantly—and *fixed* it. She now had an automatic reflex to food, to reject eating unless she needed to.

She started to write a description of her idea to Gunboat, to tell him to change himself so he wouldn't be so fixated on physical beauty—and halted. What would he do if she told him? Almost without thinking, she constructed a simulation of Gunboat and ran through a dozen scenarios.

He would laugh at her. Gunboat would be too proud to listen, too stubborn to change even if he knew the change would be an improvement. And it would be an improvement; Celeste pushed the simulation and saw that, if Gunboat were given a choice, he would choose to remain himself, but he would never, never be happy.

She tweaked the simulation, making it ever so unnoticeably better. In this simulation, the altered Gunboat found happiness, both for himself and for Celeste.

Even better, she could tweak it again, to reduce its sloppiness, and . . . No, it wouldn't be right to do this to Gunboat. Yet, in the simulation, Gunboat *thanked* her for curing him, when he learned he had been altered.

HEY, YOU READY? Gunboat interrupted her, THE GANG'S ALL BACK, OUR BODIES ARE FREE FOR TAKING.

I'M READY, GUNBOAT. And then, in the last moments before return, Celeste interrupted Gunboat's process, and *touched* him.

Her first sensation as she reentered her body was the touch of a kiss. As Celeste opened her eyes, Gunboat pulled lingeringly away. He looked at her, puzzled. "Don't believe it—I see you the way you were. . . ."

Celeste smiled. Gunboat was far from perfect, but he was so much more than she had ever expected . . . A warm contented glow filled her. "I love you, Gunboat."

Gunboat shook his head. "I . . ." He paused, licked his lips. "Chrissticks, I'm hungry. Gotta get some fries." He yanked the helmet off his head and started complaining.

Celeste laughed, quietly. Clearly, she had not modified Gunboat *too* much.

<Pleading voice> DON'T LEAVE, ROY, Valentina urged. STAY HERE, IN THE SPEED AND CON-CURRENCY YOU YOURSELF CREATED.

I'LL BE BACK, Roy promised. BUT NATHAN IS A SPECIAL PERSON TOO. HE NEEDS ME.

CAN'T WE MAKE HIM ENTER, TOO?

<Sigh uncertainly> PERHAPS SOME DAY. BUT NOW HE'S FRIGHTENED. I CAN CERTAINLY UNDERSTAND WHY.

<Nod> I ALSO UNDERSTAND. OUR UNIVERSES ARE BOTH WONDERFUL AND STRANGE, ARE THEY NOT?

MOST WONDERFUL, AND MOST STRANGE. Roy thought a thousand wistful thoughts a last thousand times. FAREWELL.

FAREWELL, ROY.

A moment later Roy was gone. Valentina hung alone in the awesome available space in the node, almost dwarfed by its size and power. Then she started thinking about her friends, and her experiences, and as her thoughts expanded ever more processors activated under her images until she filled all space.

Perhaps Roy had told the truth, when he told her the computer was a prison wherein photons danced trapped for eternity. It made no difference. For now, Valentina reveled in the freedom, and the wealth, and the joy, of the light in the Looking Glass.

LEWIS SHINER

FRONTERA

The time:
    The early 21st century.
The place: Frontera—the
    United States' colony on Mars.
The mission:
    Rescue operation or pirate raid?

$2.95

**BAEN
BOOKS**

*The future is
NOW!*